COSMIC JINX

THE WITCHES OF HOLLOW COVE
BOOK TEN

KIM RICHARDSON

www.kimrichardsonbookstore.com

COSMIC JINX

THE WITCHES OF HOLLOW COVE
BOOK TEN

KIM RICHARDSON

1

Have you ever heard of a potion witch who sucked at potions? You're looking at her.

The process of potion-making is essentially stirring, simmering, a few incantations, and waiting. I'm really good at the waiting part. Exceptional. Trophy-worthy. And that's about it.

I stared at the lumpy, gravy-looking, bubbling substance. "Is it supposed to look like that? And that smell? Ugh. It's like a combination of wet socks and Hildo's litter."

"Hey," meowed the cat, stretched out lazily on the counter next to the stove. His tail flicked back and forth in dangerous irritation. "My litter happens to smell like lavender, thank you. That's what it says on the box—*lavender* scented."

"Says the cat who doesn't clean his own litter box."

The cat's eyes narrowed, and his lips twitched as he pulled them back in what could only be a smile. "You got me there."

Ruth leaned over my cast-iron cauldron, the size of a pasta pot, on the stove. Loose strands of white hair fell apart from the knot above her head, framing the cute frown on her face. "Oh dear."

My face fell. "*Oh dear* doesn't sound promising. *Oh dear* sounds like I've wasted all your herbs and mandrake root again." I was high on the clueless score chart when it came to potion-making. Maybe the worse it smelled, the better the potency of the potion? Yeah, I didn't think so.

Ruth pulled her face into a warm, patient smile and tapped my hand. Her large blue eyes were kind and bright. "It's okay. Chuck it in the sink, and we'll start again. Don't beat yourself up. Potion-making takes time and practice. And above all, it takes patience. The incantation and the ingredients are equally as important. Everyone thinks it's easy, that any fool can do potions. That couldn't be further from the truth. If you ruin one element, the potion is spoiled."

A bubble in my potion swelled and then burst, showering wet droplets over my face. I gagged at the smell. "How long did it take you to work your first potion?" I asked, wiping my face with a dish towel.

Ruth shrugged. "About five minutes."

Like I said. I was the worst potion-making witch in magical history.

Swallowing what was left of my pride, which was about the size of a pea, I heaved the heavy iron cauldron and dumped the foul-smelling substance into the sink. The only satisfying part of the potion-making process was seeing the sad concoctions being swallowed up by the drain. But then again, it was also a reminder of my utter failure. And that I had to do it all over again.

Sadly, this wasn't my first potion disaster. I stopped counting after thirty-six failed attempts.

That wasn't even the worst part. This had been going on for three weeks. I knew Ruth didn't want to get my hopes up, as she seemed determined to have me succeed, and I loved her for it. But she knew as well as I did that the problem wasn't the herbs, the counterclockwise stirring, or even the Latin that flew off my tongue effortlessly.

It was the lack of magic.

Without magic, I couldn't conjure up a simple potion, let alone make it work. I was a true proficient when it came to measuring ingredients in a cup or keeping the brew from drying out. But those talents didn't matter if the magic wasn't there. It couldn't be a magical potion without its vital ingredient—magic.

And I had none. I was magic-less. As magically dry as the Sahara Desert.

A few weeks ago, even Dolores had tried to jump-start my magic by subjecting me to multiple curses, hexes, and spells that were supposed to *awaken* my inner witch. When my skin burst out into boils and raw, bleeding burns, she realized it was a lost cause. *I* was a lost cause. Nothing she or anyone else could do would help restore my magic.

"You're wasting all those good herbs and powders." Dolores, sitting at the kitchen table, peered at me over her reading glasses. "Do you know how much mugwort goes for these days? Or valerian root? Acacia?"

My heart sank a little further. "No, I don't."

I was costing my Aunt Ruth a small fortune with all the failed potions. I'd gotten a paycheck two weeks ago from the town's treasurer, the usual pay for Merlins. I was going to cash it and give it all to Ruth before the money stopped coming. Because we all knew without my magic, and with all the town knowing, sooner or later, Gilbert would gladly put a stop to it. I wouldn't be surprised if he came banging on our door and demanded a refund.

"Don't worry about that," said Ruth, giving Dolores a frown. "Practice makes perfect. If at first you don't succeed, you try again. Let's try again." Gesturing at herself, she pulled her apron flat against her body. The inscription read ONCE YOU GO WITCH, YOU'LL NEVER SWITCH!

Cute. But it didn't make me feel any better.

"No point in beating a dead horse either," commented Dolores as she flipped the pages of her newspaper.

I sighed. "She's right. I'm no good at this. I'm just wasting all of your good herbs and powders. I'm going to ruin you. We should stop."

Ruth dismissed me with a wave of her hand. "Don't listen to her. She's just jealous because..." She lowered her voice and leaned closer. "She was never good at potions."

"Heard that," growled Dolores, though Ruth giggled as she moved over to Hildo and stroked the cat's head. He then proceeded to close his eyes in catlike bliss.

Sooner or later, as Dolores had done before her, Ruth would eventually see the futility of her ways and put a stop to my potion-making lessons. Plus, her stash of magical ingredients and herbs was running low. I knew she was only doing this for me out of the kindness of her huge, Ruth-loving heart. She wanted me to believe I was still a witch, that there was still hope. But after three weeks without a smidgen of progress, I had to come to terms that those witchy days were gone.

Derrick, the incubus, had taken my magic away, and it seemed I was going to stay that way... forever.

Yeah, I don't think so. I wasn't giving up that easily. Good thing I was blessed with a healthy dose of stubbornness accompanied by some serious lady balls.

I had a few ideas. First, I was going to find everything I could on incubi, specifically how to transfer back powers they'd stolen. My working theory was if I could find Derrick, I could force him to transfer back my powers. If you thought of the incubus as some sort of digital storage like a USB flash drive, following that logic, I could tap into him and take back what was mine.

Without my demon mojo, I knew for a fact I couldn't travel to the Netherworld anymore. I'd have to summon him over to this side of the planes with Iris's help. My Dark witch friend was already working on a few spells to keep the incubus trapped while we took my powers back, a crucial part we were still trying to figure out.

I hadn't told my aunts about my plan. I didn't want to get their hopes up if it didn't work. But the real reason was that the spell could kill me.

So far, from our research, nothing in the old magical tomes told us about the transferring of powers back from an incubus or any other demon. Except for one book I stole from Dolores's "special" section.

The book was called *The Demon Grimoire*. A single entry focused on transferring powers from a demon to a witch. *Daemonium magicae ad pythonissam transportaret*, the text had read. The spell was complicated and took weeks of preparation. Iris and I had spent every night for the past two weeks working on it. Now it was complete and ready for me to try it tonight.

And I would.

And if that failed, I would have to somehow summon Lucifer and try to work out a bargain with him. How did one even do that? I'd think about it when the time came.

"Girls! You'll never *believe* the sales at Macy's!"

I looked up from rinsing out my cauldron to find Beverly walking into the kitchen, her hips swaying. She looked as beautiful and stylish as always in her dark jeans and black top, which accentuated her shoulder-length blonde hair. She moved to the kitchen island and dropped six large shopping bags.

"Look what I got for you, Tessa." Beverly reached inside one of the bags and pulled out a light-blue linen summer dress. "Feel that," she said as she walked over and thrust the dress at me. "Feel how glorious this material is. Marcus won't be able to take his hands off you in this. Nothing is more irresistible to a man than the soft feel of fabric against your smooth, sensuous skin."

I forced a smile. "You really shouldn't have." The dress was lovely. I was just not in the cheery kind of mood lately to wear something like that.

Beverly looked away. "I know that, silly. But I wanted to. Besides, I'm a size four and—"

"Four*teen*," interrupted Dolores with a sneer.

Beverly threw a glare in Dolores's direction. "They didn't have any of my size *four* left. And it was seventy-five percent off. I just couldn't let it go."

"Thank you, it's beautiful," I told her, glad to see the genuine smile that flashed across Beverly's face. "You really don't have to buy me clothes."

Beverly gave me a one-shoulder shrug. "I know that. But I was already there, and well, you know me. I love to shop," she added with a giggle.

"Okay, but promise me that you'll stop. I'll have no more room in my walk-in closet to fit all these new clothes."

The fact was, since she'd been lifted from Derrick's spell, Beverly had started to buy me new clothes every time she went out shopping, which was a few times a week. I knew this was her way of showing me she was sorry, even though I'd told her none of this was her fault since Derrick had targeted her specifically to get to me. He'd used her badly, tricked her, and spelled her. None of this was her doing.

Yet, she just didn't seem to want to stop.

Beverly reached in the smallest of her bags and yanked out something pink. "Look what I bought," she said as she twirled a pair of pink, fluffy hand-cuffs around her finger.

Dolores pulled her glasses from her face. "Are those handcuffs?"

Beverly beamed as she cocked her hip. "They are. Aren't they fabulous?" Her green eyes glimmered. "I'm going to try them with Dale tonight." She slipped them over her wrists and threw her hands over her head like she was already tied up. "I look amazing lying on a bed naked in handcuffs. It thrusts my breasts forward."

I cringed, not wanting to form a visual—too late.

"Gives my breasts a nice lift."

Dolores snorted. "You'll need more than hand-cuffs for that."

Beverly lowered her hands. "You're just jealous because the last time you had sex, the rooms were lit by candles."

Oh boy.

Ruth let out a giggle. "I think they're cute. Oh. You should get them in different colors," she said, her eyes round. "Like in yellow, orange, red, green, blue, and violet. And then you could have all the colors of the rainbow."

"I already have," said Beverly, wiggling her brows suggestively, her smile widening.

Dolores rolled her eyes so hard I thought they were about to pop out and fall on the table.

I laughed. "This family is seriously deranged. I'm glad I'm a part of it."

"Speaking of family," said Dolores as she leaned forward in her chair, "have you heard from your mother?"

"Yesterday. She was painting her new living room white—not white—white *dove*. I think that's the last room she hadn't touched yet."

My father had surprised my mother the day after their wedding with a small gray cottage, boasting white trim and centered among mature lilac trees, with rows of pink rhododendrons tucked around a wraparound porch. It was nestled on Moon Way, which was one street over from Stardust Drive. Apparently, my mother had told my father years ago how much she loved that house. He'd remembered. He'd also given the previous owners an offer they couldn't refuse. I'd asked him how much he'd paid for it, but all he did was smile.

"She deserves it," he'd told me.

Okay then.

She'd been redecorating and remodeling it for

the past three weeks with an updated master bathroom and kitchen. I pitied the carpenters she'd hired, and I was glad I wasn't living through a remodel with my dearest mama.

I loved my mother, but I wasn't sure living in the same house was good for either of us. Besides, she and my father deserved some much-needed privacy. They'd been apart for a long time, and they had lots to catch up on.

Speaking of timing, Lilith's gift that enabled my father to attend his own wedding under the sun wasn't a permanent thing. After the third day, he'd begun to feel the effects of our world, kinda like me when I was in the Netherworld. He was a demon, after all. He couldn't stay in our world indefinitely.

"But how are you going to visit Mom in this new house?" I'd asked him on one of my first visits there. "You said Davenport House was your only portal to this world if you didn't count on ley lines."

"It is. It was," he'd told me. "Lilith might not have given me a permanent stay in this world, but she's managed to manipulate the ban I had on using Rifts and other portals to cross over. It's not a removal, more of an influence. I felt it on the day of my wedding. And it's still there. I've already tested it. Let me show you."

Just like in Davenport House, my father had created a portal with the cottage's basement door. I could only assume a replica of the same door also existed in his apartment in the Netherworld. He could now travel back and forth from this cottage, just as he did with Davenport House.

"Listen up, ladies," announced Dolores suddenly, dragging me away from my thoughts. "We're getting a message card."

The toaster shook, followed by a rattling sound from the inside, like it was suffering from a mechanical failure. Then with a pop, a white card shot out of one of the toasting slots like a bagel. Dolores, being the closest, caught it. Pushing her reading glasses back up her nose, she glanced down and read the card.

"What's it say? Do we have a new case?" asked Ruth eagerly, stepping away from the stove.

I opened my mouth to join Ruth's questions but stopped myself. Without magic, I couldn't work any cases in the field. But I could still help with research and planning. I was still a Merlin—until I wasn't. And being a Merlin was also about investigating. I could do that without magic.

Dejected, I hauled the now-empty cauldron from the sink and placed it on the stove.

"Tessa. It's for you," I heard Dolores say.

I spun around, my pulse thrashing. "Me? Really?" My smile faded at the concern lines on Dolores's forehead and the stiffness of her posture. "What's the matter? Who sent the card?"

Dolores pulled off her glasses and turned in her seat to better face me. She held the card in her hand, gesturing, and said, "It's from Greta."

Now my heart was trying to flutter its way out of my chest like a frightened butterfly. "What does she want?" Greta Trickle was the Witch Trials Training Division director. I doubted she was extending her congratulations on my parents' wedding. "I passed their damn tests. Is this because of the ley lines? Because, news flash, I can't use them anymore." I knew Silas, one of the arbitrators, had said I'd cheated because I'd used the ley lines in the trials. It seemed the tattooed bastard was not willing to let it go.

"They heard about what happened to you," Dolores said, watching me. Her eyes went wide and serious. "They know you've lost your magic."

Oh shit.

I licked my lips. "So, what does that mean, exactly?"

"It means," began Dolores with an uncomfortable amount of eye contact while shifting in her chair, "that Greta and her committee are coming here... to test you."

Swell.

2

"To test you?" repeated Marcus, staring at me from across his desk. "Test your magic?" He sat with his arms crossed over his generous chest, making his broad shoulders stand out. His pecs seemingly wanted to burst out of his shirt as his eyes danced to a predatory beat. He was a virile creature, a powerful beast who was remarkably tender in the bedroom. I was a lucky gal.

"I guess. If they want to test my IQ, they're going to be very disappointed."

"But you just said they know you don't have magic anymore."

I winced on the inside. It didn't matter how many times a day I heard it, it still stung. "I know. Dolores says it's procedure or whatever. They need to make sure it's not a rumor. Apparently, there's lots of competition between Merlins. They even go as far as starting rumors like that to try and discredit other witches. They'll test me, see that I can't do magic anymore, and then... they'll take my Merlin license away for good." I hated how ragged my voice sounded, how much emotion was there. But I couldn't help it. Taking away my Merlin license after taking away my magic just made it all real. Final.

A frown creased those fine gray eyes framed with dark eyelashes, the kind women paid lots of money to glue on but still always looked fake. The light from his office shone over his black tussled hair. His high cheekbones were stained with concern, which only made him sexier. Cauldron help me, he was beautiful. But even his uber sexiness didn't make me feel all that better at the moment.

I sighed through my nose. "So... why did you ask me to come over here in my sweatpants?" I rolled my eyes over him to the black shirt and down to his jeans. "You're not dressed like you want to go for a run?" I raised my hand. "I must warn you. I'm exceptionally bad at running—especially long distances. I have small lungs." I faked a cough. "See. The walk over destroyed them."

Marcus pushed back from his desk and stood. "Come with me."

I jumped up excitedly. "Are we going to do it in some secret place?" My lady hormones were doing a jig at the thought of some horizontal, vertical, and suspended sex with the chief. He was extremely creative with all things carnal.

A smile pulled his handsome face to a panty-melting one. "Don't tempt me."

The lust in his eyes was gratifying. "Oh, I'm going to tempt you," I said. "You can count on it."

I followed the chief out of his office and down the hallway, past an irritated Grace sitting at the front desk, to a door on the opposite side of the office I'd never paid attention to.

Marcus pulled open the door, and I followed him inside.

I stepped into what looked like a gym. Exercise equipment was pushed to the sides to make room for the large blue mats that covered most of the floor.

"This is our training room," said the chief as he closed the door and joined me. "Where we do our drills and keep our bodies fit. We train regularly. It improves our muscle strength while boosting our endurance. In my line of work, it's important to stay in shape. Out of shape, you die."

I looked at him. "You want me to train? The closest thing I have to exercise is bringing my glass of wine to my mouth. I'm really good at that."

Marcus laughed, but then his eyes got serious. "Tessa. You're still a target." He raised his hand at my objection. "Lucifer or not, evil still lurks in the world, especially where we live. You need to learn how to defend yourself *without* magic."

The dreaded words. "There goes my idea of having sex on those dirty mats." They were kinda gross.

"I'm serious." Marcus grabbed my shoulders and turned me to face him. "No magic isn't a death sentence, but not being able to defend yourself when some thug is coming at you with a knife is. You're a woman. It's not fair, I know, but in this world, women always have to be on guard. You need to be prepared. You have to be able to take care of yourself in a bad situation."

"I can take care of myself."

"We'll start you with the basics, and you can eventually learn to use daggers and then guns."

"Nope," I told him and pulled away from his grip. "I don't want to even touch a gun. No way."

"Tessa."

"No. I'll do this," I said, waving my hands around the gym. "Cartwheels. Jumping jacks. Junk punches. I'm there. But I don't want anything to do with guns."

"Fine."

"Great." I rolled my eyes over his clothes again. "We're doing this now? Shouldn't you go change?" I was digging the snug jeans, but I didn't think they were training material. Unless he was going to go naked... I could comply with naked.

Marcus shook his head just as a ring sounded from his pocket. He pulled out his phone. "I'm not the one training you."

"You're not? Then who?"

The chief gave a jerk of his head behind me as he put the phone to his ear. I turned and followed his gaze.

"Oh hell, no."

A tall blonde in a tight, black workout outfit came strolling out from a door across the gym. With her fit, voluptuous body that was every man's dream and every other woman's nightmare, she was gorgeous, perfect, and an absolute bitch.

My archnemesis. Allison. Aka Gorilla Barbie.

"You've got to be shitting me. No way am I training with her." Especially not with the way she was smiling at me, like a lynx smiled at a cornered rabbit. Shit. Without magic, I was dead. She knew it. I knew it. It was the only thing we'd ever had in common.

"Where's Scarlett? I want Scarlett," I asked the chief, thinking the new deputy would be a much better choice since she didn't look at me like she wanted to crush my skull. "Why can't Scarlett train me? I like her. She likes me. It's a perfect match."

Marcus's face was pulled tight, like whatever or

whoever was on the other line had just given him terrible news.

"Marcus?"

"I gotta go," he said, his eyes everywhere but on me.

"Wait. What? You can't leave me here alone with blondie Godzilla."

Marcus never pulled the phone from his ear as he spun around and hurried out the door. Dread filled my gut until it was nearly palpable. He'd just left me alone with the woman who hated my guts. And without magic, well, I was going to get a serious beating.

"Get on the mats, *witch*," called Allison, and I turned my attention back to the tall blonde.

She tightened her high ponytail as a low, creepy smile spread over her face. It brought the hairs up on the back of my neck. Her blue eyes gleamed with sadistic glee in anticipation of kicking my ass. She cracked her knuckles. I could almost see the multitude of punches and kicks coming my way.

Oh yeah, it was going to hurt all right.

Reluctantly—because Marcus was right, and I did need to learn how to protect myself without magic—I walked over to the mats. My legs were stiff like metal beams until I stopped about six feet from the wereape.

I was a sensible, mature woman. I could do this.

Actually, I was the most immature woman of my age I knew.

"This is going to suck. Isn't it?" The only comfort I took was in the fact that she didn't carry any weapons. That suit was way too tight to hide a knife or any kind of arms. Unless she'd stuck it up her ass. The thought made me smile. She was, after all, a stuck-up bitch. It appeared she was going to use her fists and legs. I wasn't sure if that was any better.

Her nostrils flared, and her smile widened like she could smell the fear on me. It was obvious to anyone with a brain. I was Allison's birthday present.

"Marcus asked me to teach you some basic self-defense moves to start with," she said, her voice holding the same merciless delight that flashed in her eyes. "I didn't want to do it, but I will because he asked me. And looking at you now, well, let's just say you don't have much of a fighting body. You've got more fat than muscle. You're soft. Weak. You're an easy kill."

"Thanks. Someday you'll go far with compliments like that. And I hope you stay there."

Allison cocked an eyebrow. "He'll leave you eventually," she said. My expression froze at the ugliness and how easily she said it. "The thing that made you special, that made him want you, well, it's gone. Men don't like weak, lamentable females."

I gritted my teeth. "Wow. You're truly the reason

the goddess created the middle finger." I knew she was just trying to rattle me, get me angry, so I'd lose my focus. But her words stung.

Allison rolled her eyes over my body, and her face twisted like she was staring at something foul and repugnant. "He'll come back to me, you know. It's only a matter of time now before he sees you for what you are."

"A decent person with a great personality?" I could almost feel steam shooting from my ears.

The wereape snickered. "A loser."

My heart raced, my body both hot and cold from the anger pouring into my core. I thought of a comeback, but my mind was suffering from temporary brain fog. The truth was, that's exactly how I felt— like a loser.

"I'll give it a few months," said Allison, marveling at whatever she saw on my face, "before he's back in *my* bed and making love to *me*. I told you before... he *always* comes back to me. Always."

Scorching rage swept through me, born of outrage. The thought of Allison jumping Marcus's bones made something inside me snap. Call it feral. Call it primal. Call it whatever the hell you want. It was the overwhelming need to guard what was mine. Marcus.

Okay. Now she was really pissing me off. "Are you just going to throw insults at me all day, or are you actually going to train me? Because if you can't, maybe you should go get Scarlett."

Allison lowered herself into a crouch. "Get ready."

I copied her posture, my blood pressure rising. "Okay, what are we—"

Her leg shot out, and she kicked me in the gut.

My breath left me as I flew back and landed hard on my ass. Crap. Not the elegant landing I was going for in front of Allison. Okay, so she was fast. Damn fast, and a hell of a lot faster than me, admittedly.

My face flamed as I got to my feet. "How exactly is this self-defens—"

Allison's elbow struck me across the jaw.

I staggered back, tasting blood in my mouth. If she thought I'd just stand here and let her beat me to a pulp, she was just as stupid and useless as those pencil skirts she wore.

Allison's laugh was full of pricks and sandpaper. "First lesson. You need to be ready for anything."

I spat the blood from my mouth, my anger surging. "If I had my magic, I'd be wearing your fur as a coat—not that I'm saying fur coats are a good thing, but you catch my drift."

"Good thing you're all out of magic."

The wereape's smile was a mix of greedy amusement and excitement as she came at me, swift as a burst of storm wind with her wereape paranormal speed. So, so unfair.

I tried to recall what I'd learned from my limited experience with the one class I took on self-defense, but all that came to mind was a series of blah blah blah.

I'd barely had time to block Allison's strike as she came at me without pause in a blur of legs and fists and dominance.

I kicked out my leg. It connected.

Allison yelped and stumbled back.

"Ha!" I said, surprised at my badass self as pain reverberated all the way up my thigh. I knew I'd hit her hard. I was feeling it.

The surprise on Allison's face filled me with confidence. "Yeah. That's right. Didn't see that coming. Did you?" I raised both hands in karate chops. No idea why I just did that. I was going with whatever came to me first.

The odds were that she was going to kick my ass, but it seemed luck was on my side.

The wereape grinned. "Bring it, bitch."

I blinked. "Oh, it's brung."

Allison growled and flung herself savagely at me. I threw myself back—but not fast enough. I cried out as the sole of her shoe slammed into my chest, cutting off my air. I stumbled back as I lost my balance. Fingers tightened through my hair, and I was jerked upright, my scalp screaming in pain. And then I was even more surprised as her fist connected with my jaw. My knees twisted, and I fell.

Black spots marred my vision, and I blinked, trying to shake off the dizziness as every breath sent jarring pain through my chest. I took another breath. My lungs were suddenly overflowing with air, feeling as if they were going to burst as the oxygen filled them.

Guess luck was *not* on my side.

The wereape let out a breathy laugh. "What the hell was that? You can't even fight off the most basic attacks. You're worthless. A joke. I expected better from a Davenport witch."

I fought the dizziness and, with some effort, managed to stand. "Yeah, well... if I wanted to listen to an asshole, I'd fart."

I couldn't believe Marcus had thought this was a good idea. He knew how she felt about me. That went to show how men were really clueless sometimes. I was going to have words with him after this.

Allison shook her head. "All that extra fat on your body is making you slow. Like grandma slow."

I pressed a hand to my chest, massaging my rib cage. "Real men like curves on their women. Only dogs like bones."

The wereape laughed as she encircled me. "I'm

going to break every single bone in that soft body of yours before I'm finished with you."

"How is this self-defense?" I panted.

"I guess it's not." The tall blonde flashed me her perfect teeth, but her eyes went hard and vicious. "Call it payback for all the curses you threw at me. I didn't forget. You and your twitchy sidekick witch. This is what you get for stealing my male."

Clearly, she was unhinged. "First of all, he's *not* your male. He hasn't been your male for a long time. Marcus is a strong-willed man. He made his choice. And he picked me." I pulled my face into a smile. "I win."

Allison's face reddened. She came at me swinging with that same wereape speed that was truly impressive. But her swings were fueled with anger and emotion, not with skill or precision.

Ooooh. I'd made her mad. And it was the only thing I had going for me.

I dropped to the floor, rolling as I avoided the wereape's kicks and punches. Gorilla Barbie could really throw a punch.

Standing over me, Allison stomped her leg, trying to crush my skull with her shoe. But I slipped aside. Her strike went wide before she realized her mistake. I swung out my leg, caught her by an ankle, and twisted, sending her stumbling onto the mats.

"I think I'm getting the hang of this." Look at me. I was on a roll.

On my feet, I hurled myself at her without any real skill. I looked like I was pretty unhinged with my fingers out in front of me like claws.

She gave a little gasp of surprise as I reached out with my hand and wrapped it around her neck.

Her elbow came out of nowhere and smacked me on the left temple.

Ow. That. Hurt.

Letting go, I staggered back, but my eyes were pinned on the approaching blonde.

"I'm going to kill you, witch," she snarled, her features warping, which removed any delicate traits and made her look very male and angry. Not to mention ugly.

I met her snarl with my own toothy, aggressive grin and raised a finger. "Technically, I'm not a witch anymore. Remember? You said it yourself. But I'm confused seeing as you're not kicking my ass like you thought you would. See. I'm better than you thought. Am I right?"

Allison lunged with a punch so swift most men's heads would have spun around.

At that precise moment, I chose not to move. More like I didn't even have time to blink.

The wereape's fist made contact with my gut. The next thing I knew, she'd caught my left arm in one hand, locking it into a hold I knew was bone-snapping. She drove her knee up into the side of my head. I cried out and managed to slip out of her hold, more like she'd let me go so she could beat me over and over again.

Allison stood there with a satisfied smile on her face, like someone who wanted to continue to inflict pain for hours or until their victim dropped dead.

With my left arm throbbing in pain, I didn't have much combat mojo going. I felt broken and beaten, my limbs worthless noodles.

So I did what any sane person would do.

I leaped forward and head-butted the bitch.

I heard a grunt as she jerked back and fell on her ass in a very ugly fall.

"Ow, ow, ow," I chanted, holding my head as it vibrated all the way to the insides of my ears. "They make it look so pain-free in the movies."

Maybe I was going to win this thing. Maybe she wasn't as strong as she thought.

The wereape leaped to her feet and brushed the hair from her sweaty forehead. "You're gonna pay for that, you crazy bitch."

I shrugged, still feeling the pain in my left arm and head. "Yeah, well, sanity is highly overrated."

Allison smiled without showing any teeth. And then she shot forward, pumping her fists like sledgehammers. I ducked and spun, but no way could I match her speed.

A hard fist landed square in my middle, enough to push the air from my lungs and maybe bruise a couple of ribs. I bent forward in pain as her shoe slammed into my back. I pitched forward. The side of my face and palms burned as I skidded on the mat.

"Have you had enough?" I heard Allison ask. The amusement in her voice was the only thing that made me push myself up again.

My legs wobbled under the strain of just standing. My ears rang from the constant throbbing in my head. I should have called it quits. I should have told her I'd had enough. But I was stubborn and angry. And I didn't want to show her fear or weakness. Stupid? Yeah. That was stupid.

I forced a laugh. "Is that all you got? You overgrown banana." I did realize I was signing off on my own death sentence, but I couldn't help it. That wereape got under my skin.

Her expression hard, the wereape approached like a rushing wind and backhanded me without breaking momentum. I stumbled back and caught myself before I fell.

"Give up? Or do you want more?" she teased, circling me again like a predator. She bared her teeth, her face only inches from mine.

I gritted my jaw. "Can I have a minute to think about it?"

A blur of legs was my only warning.

And then she kicked me right in the vajayjay.

Contrary to what people think, being hit in the vagina hurts like a sonofabitch.

I let out a moan and fell over on my side, my lady region pounding—and not in a good way. My gut twisted as a hollow ache found its way there, and I tried hard to breathe through the pain. Blinking through tears, I stared openmouthed at the wereape.

"And now? Have you had enough?" Allison watched me with an expression of mixed delight and disgust.

"Yes," I wheezed, and I heard her chuckle. Yeah, she was going to gloat about this for years.

And just like that, Allison had kicked my ass.

My day couldn't get any worse. Or so I thought.

3

I walked bowlegged all the way home. You would have, too, if your vajayjay had been smashed by a Gorilla Barbie. I had a bruised vag, and I needed a pack of ice now.

Forget any kind of sex for a while, and that was a colossal tragedy when one's sex partner was the uber-sexy chief of Hollow Cove who had super-powers in the bedroom.

Speaking of the chief, I paused, my legs in a squat-like stance, and pulled out my phone.

"Tessa? Do you need to use the bathroom?"

I glanced up from my phone to see Martha stepping off Davenport House's porch, a smile on her face as she surveyed my odd posture.

"Cramps," I told her as I tapped the phone icon. Martha was the town's gossip queen. If I uttered a single word of my shameful ass-kicking by Allison, I'd be the laughingstock of the town for a year. No, more like forever. It was bad enough that everyone I greeted flashed me their pitying smiles. I could do without them looking at me like some broken-down, weak female.

"I've got just the thing for that," said the plump witch. Her periwinkle eyeshadow matched her long, billowing skirt. "Kill-Kramps. You just need to spray it around your Lady V," she continued, eyes wide and gesturing her hands around her crotch, "and your cramps are gone in a few minutes. It's one of my best sellers. Come by the shop when you have a minute," she added as she continued on, waving her hand in the air.

"Mmm-hmmm." Right. I wasn't about to spray anything near my Lady V, thank you very much. I tapped Marcus's phone number and waited. When the voicemail picked up, I hung up and decided to text him.

Me: I need words with you. Call me.

Yes, Allison had definitely taken a chunk of my pride away, but I was too pissed at Marcus to let that fester. He could have had Scarlett, the new deputy, teach me some self-defense if he was that worried about me. Even Cameron would have been a better fit. But Allison? He knew she despised me. What the hell was he thinking?

Fuming, I waddled over to the porch and, very carefully, hauled myself up the steps. Once inside, I closed the door behind me with a soft push. Three distinct voices trailed from the kitchen. With the stealth of an eighty-year-old woman with bad hips, I shuffled to the staircase like a burglar into my own home.

I should have been asking Ruth for some of her healing tonics, but I didn't want them to see me like this, beaten and broken by none other than Allison, the wereape Iris had continued to hex for months in the name of solidarity. Karma was biting me in the butt.

I was humiliated enough as it was. I didn't want their pity. Knowing Dolores, she would probably go down to the Hollow Cove Security Agency and have it out with Allison, which would only further my humiliation. I didn't need my aunts to fight my battles, even if I could barely fight my own at this point.

I held on to the wooden railing for support. "House?" I whispered. "Can you pick me up and take me to my room?"

I only waited a moment. A sudden rush of energy flew around me and wrapped me up like a blanket. Next, I was lifted off the ground, my knees bent as though I were sitting in an invisible chair, more like a stair lift. I let out a breath and relaxed as a bubble of energy bloomed around me.

And then I was moving.

Going up and up the staircase, I floated up to each floor's landing, a tiny smile stretched over my face until I reached the platform to the attic.

House deposited me in front of my bedroom door. "Thanks, House. What would I do without you?"

After I peeled off my clothes, I jumped into a hot shower and did my best to scrub off my shame. Red-and-purple marks spotted my chest and my sides where Allison had kicked and punched me, my skin bruised and painful to the touch.

I stayed in my room for the rest of the day, mostly glaring at my phone. Marcus had not called back. I didn't even get a text from him. I'd admit I was irritated, but I knew he was a busy man and was probably on some important case.

A knock came on my door.

"It's me," came Iris's voice.

"It's open," I called out.

Iris let herself in and shut the door behind her. She took one look at me sitting on my bed, and her jaw dropped. "Oh, my god! Your face! You didn't tell me she hit your face."

I pressed a hand to the side of my jaw and then my cheek where Allison had hit me with her elbow, or was it her fist? Maybe it was her knee. I couldn't remember.

"Is it that bad?" I'd called Iris a few hours after my shower and told her what happened. I had glanced in the mirror before my shower. The left side of my face looked like I'd been stung by a wasp. After that, I couldn't bring myself to look again.

The Dark witch frowned. "It is. Your left eye is nearly swollen shut." She hurried over and dumped her large bag next to me on the bed. "She's going to pay for this. I'm going to curse her bloody. She's going to regret the day she laid a finger on you."

"Don't. If you do, she'll just take it out on me again. She'll wait for me in some dark alley, and then she'll pounce. I think it's enough ass-kicking for a while. Or is it ass kicked?"

"Here." She handed me a chocolate protein shake and then a straw. "You really should get Ruth to make you something. She's really good at healing broken bodies. You know this."

I took the shake and slipped the straw through the small opening at the top. "I know. Maybe I'll ask her later."

Two red spots appeared on Iris's cheeks, which meant her insides were angrier than she was letting on. "She can't get away with this. Did you tell Marcus? I can't believe he assigned her to your self-defense training. Argh. I'm so mad at him. I could just curse him with chafing balls. What was he thinking?"

I swallowed a mouthful of the chocolate-milk-tasting shake, trying not to think about Marcus's chafing balls. "He wasn't thinking. That's the problem. He trusted her, I guess. He didn't think she'd beat me."

"Well, I hope you gave him an earful."

"I haven't been able to reach him."

Iris shook her head. From her bag, she pulled out a small metal container and twisted the top open. "Here. This is some healing ointment I got from Ruth. It'll numb the bruising and help it heal faster."

"Thanks." I set my now-empty shake on the side table and took the container. The ointment was green with the texture of petroleum jelly. I dabbed some on my face and around my chest and ribs where it hurt the most. A tinkling of cool seeped into my skin where I'd patted the ointment. I could already feel the effects of the healing.

"You ready?" I asked the Dark witch as I set aside the ointment.

Iris sighed. "Are you sure you're up for it? I mean... there's no reason we can't wait until tomorrow."

"Sure there is. The longer I wait to get my magic back, the longer I'm exposed to more of Allison's beatings. I'll never be a fighter like her. I'm not built that way. She's got years of physical combat experience. I've got maybe a half hour. It'll take me years to catch up, and I don't want to wait that long. I want my magic back."

"I know." Iris searched my face for a moment. "All right, then. Let's get started."

I followed Iris to the middle of my bedroom where I joined her on the floor. My mind still whirled with the events of today, but I pushed them away and concentrated. I needed to be focused and alert for what I was about to do.

We were about to trap a demon in a summoning circle, the so-called Derrick Bastard Baudelaire.

Obviously, without the demon's real name, you couldn't summon him. But we had something even better than that. We had the bastard's DNA.

Iris, being the strange Dark witch I'd come to think of as my own sister, had stolen his hairbrush, toothbrush, and even his dirty underwear—don't ask—from his yacht after he'd escaped through the Rift. She'd cataloged them in Dana, her DNA album, where she collected strands of hair, cut-out pieces of cloth, teeth, strings of eyelashes, toenails, and drops of dried blood—all in the name of Dark curses.

From her bag, Iris pulled out Dana, a ceramic bowl, a pestle, six black candles, and some chalk. Her eyes met mine. "You sure about this?"

My pulse raced. "I am." I was equally terrified and excited.

It would work. It had to work.

After lighting the six candles, and with chalk in hand, Iris leaned forward and traced a large circle, the Circle of Solomon, to protect the conjurer from the demon. Then she wrote five archangel names in Latin around it within a coiled serpent before drawing the Triangle of Solomon, where the summoning demon would appear. Instead of writing the name of the demon inside the triangle, she left it blank.

She turned to me and handed me the chalk. "Your turn."

"Right." Even though I wasn't a witch anymore, it didn't mean I couldn't protect myself with a circle. Even the average human could protect themselves from demons, with a circle, if done correctly.

When I finished my circle, I crossed the room and shut off the lights. The candlelight cast flickering shadows along the walls and floor. I walked back and stepped into my circle, waiting and feeling all the heaviness and anxiousness settle into my skin.

Next, Iris pulled Dana over her lap and flipped through the pages until she settled on one page. Yanking the thin plastic sheet, she pulled something from the pages. There, pinched between her fingers, were small strands of dark brown hair.

"The bastard was a shedder," I said.

Iris beamed, pleased with herself. "He definitely was." Still smiling, she dropped the hair inside the triangle and then yanked out some herbs and small pouches from her large bag. After sprinkling some herbs and powder in her bowl, she crushed them together with her pestle. Next, she lit a match, muttered a few words I couldn't catch, and dropped the match above the mixture.

A tall flame danced above the bowl and then fell, leaving a long trail of smoke. Iris placed the bowl between the triangle and circle, and then she stepped inside her own circle.

She glanced at me and said, "Let's begin."

I nodded, my heart pounding as I took a calming breath. Tiny thrills of excitement rushed in, knowing we were about to get my magic back. Would it hurt? Possibly. I would gladly take buckets of hurt if it meant I could have my magic back. *Suck it, Lucifer.*

"Together now," commanded Iris, her voice pealing through the still air like a bell.

Though I'd done this before, I knew this time it would be different. I had no magic to tap into, nothing to add to the spell but my physical self.

"We conjure you," we chanted in unison, "demon

of the Netherworld to be subject of our will. We bind you with unbreakable adamantine fetters. We invoke you, demon, in the space in front of us!"

My pulse quickened at the sudden surge of magic—Iris's magic, not mine—sending my skin riddling with goose bumps. It was like scratching my fingernails down a blackboard. The feeling was eerie, unnatural, and totally not what I was expecting. I didn't realize how different it would feel, now that I didn't have any magic reserves. I was basically human.

Is this how humans feel when they play at magic?

I jerked, instinctively pulling back, and nearly stepped out of my circle. But I stayed, focusing on Iris. My skin pricked as energy flowed around me with an unusual sharpness, my heart throbbing madly in my chest. I felt a wave of power cascade over me—cold yet warm and wholly familiar.

My hair lifted in the sudden icy wind, carrying the scent of sulfur along with the stink of demon. It reminded me of my short time in the Netherworld. Shadows danced along the walls as the candles flicked in the wind. The air sizzled and hummed with energy like an electrical storm.

With a pop of displaced air, there, standing in the triangle, was Derrick.

Or should I say the incubus.

Gotcha, you bastard.

4

The demon looked just as he did in the bowels of his yacht a few weeks ago. He wore a dark suit over his pale gray, pasty, and wrinkled skin like a two-hundred-year-old man. Unlike a man, something was off about his shape, which screamed not of this world. At seven feet tall, his long, thin arms and fingers ended in sharp talons. He had an elongated jaw with high, protruding cheekbones and a wide, flat nose, giving him a more bestial appearance. A tussle of gray-and-black hair sat at the top of his head and disappeared down his neck.

He wasn't the handsome fortyish-year-old man he'd pretended to be. No, this was his true self. And he was disgustingly ugly.

The incubus looked down and stared at the triangle that trapped him and then glanced up, his eyes moving from Iris to me. "Ladies. How nice to see you again. Is this for business or pleasure?" he purred, and I nearly threw up.

"I want what you took from me," I growled, my emotions running high, and I had to keep reminding myself to stay in my protection circle. Part of me wanted nothing more than to rush at him and punch him in the face.

The incubus rolled his eyes over me, his expression wrinkling. "What did you do to your face? It was such a lovely face. Did your man beat you? Is that what you like? You like it a little bit rough? I don't usually beat my females, but if that's what you're into, well, I'd never say no."

Anger thrashed inside me. "Right. You're more the stealing of magic and the murdering type," I told him.

Derrick the incubus shrugged. "You can't really hold that against me. It's in my nature. I do what feels good, as do you."

I pursed my lips. "You're right. And it's going to really feel good when I—*we* destroy you."

"Lucifer's not here to protect you," said Iris, her voice commanding and not filled with useless emotion like me. Good thing she was doing the summoning. "We're in control, demon. Not you."

The incubus looked over at her. "Mmmm. Give me a chance, and I'll show you a good time, pretty witch. I know what you like, down there." His eyes moved down her body slowly. "All you have to do is let me go."

"Silence!" cried Iris, and the incubus clamped his mouth shut. "I'm your master now. I'm in control, and you will do as I command."

Wow. Iris was awesome. My chest swelled at all her awesomeness. If I could give her a high five, I would.

Irritation flashed on the demon's face. "You're making a mistake."

"Says the guy trapped in a triangle," I shot back. "Nice try. But it's not going to work. Your ass is ours now."

"Without my true name, you can't control me... unless..." The incubus's eyes darted over to the ceramic bowl on the floor. "What did you use? Let me guess... skin? No wait... it was hair. Wasn't it?"

"You shed like a German shepherd," I grunted sourly. "But dogs are loyal and kind and cute. You're just an ugly bastard."

The demon's eyes flashed with real anger, but it was nothing compared to mine, to what I felt at this very moment. It was a miracle I was still in my circle.

The incubus folded his hands before him. "What do you want? You must want something from me. If it's not hours of pleasurable sex, what is it?"

I took a deep breath and released it. "Like I said. I want what you took. I want my magic back."

"Impossible," said the incubus with a laugh. "Once I take a witch's magic, there's no giving it back. Or wasn't I clear when I took what made you special?"

"Liar." Iris pulled a small piece of paper from her pocket. She glanced up from it. "I know how to do it. We've been working on that particular spell for weeks. The magic you took from Tessa is still in you. And we're going to take it back tonight."

Uncertainty flashed across the demon's face. "There's no such spell."

"Oh, there is," I told him, smiling at the hesitation in his eyes. "We found it."

Iris folded the paper and set it in the bowl. Next, she grabbed one of the candles and lit the corner of the paper on fire before putting the candle back.

She stood and chanted, "Obscuram appello, januam reseras," raising her arms with her voice. "Truncum magicum, vires quae semel cepisti redde."

I shuddered as the feeling of magic slithered over me and around the room. My ears rang with the pulsing of power, Dark power. Pinpricks of power crawled over my skin like the hum of a power line. If I ever doubted Iris's Dark witch abilities, this was a reality check. The tiny, pixy-looking witch was a pit bull of Dark power.

A sheen of white wisps curled around the incubus like a see-through rope. The tendrils snaked around him and started to pull away like someone was pulling out his soul. Only this wasn't his soul.

This was my magic.

This was it. It was working! I could feel it. My magic would return to me. My eyes burned, and I blinked fast. I was going to be a witch again. And when I was, the first thing I would do was kick Allison's ass.

Yes, I was shallow and immature. But I was still going to do it. She had it coming.

The pressure in the room lessened, and then the energy in the air settled, and when I looked over at the incubus, those white tendrils, my magic, had left him.

My breath came fast as I tapped into my will, drawing forth my exceptional magic and super skills —but nothing.

Not even a drop. My well of magic and power was just as dry and empty as it had been the day the incubus took it from me.

Laughter reached my ears. I looked over to the incubus. "What's so funny?"

"This." The demon walked out of his triangle.

Oh crap.

I shot a glance at Iris. Her eyes were round, and I

could see the panic formulating behind them. This was not how we'd planned it.

"Did you honestly think your pathetic little triangle would trap me?" said the incubus.

We did. We really did.

"As I said before, you witches are no match for me," he continued. "I'll outpower you every single time. Just like now. Foolish little witches."

A phantom rise of panic sent my heart and breathing racing. *What have I done?*

"But I must thank you," said the incubus. "You've given me a way in. And since I'm here… well… might as well feed. Right? I mean, why not?"

I stayed in my circle, thinking it was the only thing that could keep the demon from harming me. "Iris? What now?"

The Dark witch seemed paralyzed with either fear or confusion. She kept shaking her head as if struggling to order her thoughts.

Crap. She was losing it. "Iris!"

Derrick looked over at her, his expression feral and hungry. "My turn."

He hurled himself toward her, fast, too fast. His long fingers wrapped around her neck, pinning her on the spot. She thrashed under his hold, but it was like a rabbit trying to free itself from the jaws of a lynx. Once it had you, there was no escaping.

I watched in horror as the incubus leaned over

her. His mouth opened, and then a slip of something yellow shot out of his mouth and ripped into her. She went limp in his grasp. It all came back to me in a rush.

He was trying to steal her magic.

Before my brain made sense of my legs moving, I'd thrown myself at the demon, my pains from my earlier beating with Allison forgotten. All I could think of was Iris. I had to get the demon away from my friend.

Derrick didn't even move as my body hit his. He was like a block of cement.

With my nonexistent self-defense training, I did what anyone one would have done in my situation.

I went for his eyes.

Using my index finger, I stabbed him in his left eye.

He cried out, his momentary connection to Iris flickered, and that yellow, disgusting string disappeared.

It worked.

Guttural words spilled from the incubus's mouth. He struck out a hand, and shoots of black tendrils hit me in the chest.

Oops.

I went sailing across the room and hit the wall hard next to my bedroom door like I'd been hit with a cannonball. I slid down, fighting the black stars in my vision and trying to stay conscious. Damn. I was pretty sure I'd just suffered a concussion.

When I looked back, the incubus had Iris in his hold again. A thin, yellow veil-like mist was pulling away from her body and into his horrid mouth, draining her of her magic. Her face was pale and drawn. She looked ill and emaciated like she was dying of cancer.

I thought of House throwing him out, but the demon was connected to Iris. I didn't know what would happen to her if House ripped them apart to throw out the demon. It could possibly kill her.

"House," I wheezed. "Open the door."

I felt an influx of magic, and the bedroom door smacked open.

"Help," I called, my voice faint as I tried to fight the dizziness. "Help!" I tried again. This time it was louder. "*Help!*" I shouted. Okay, my voice rocketed out of the bedroom, thanks to some assistance from House.

Cries and shouts erupted from downstairs. The floor under my ass vibrated as the sounds of people rushing up the stairs came at me.

Using the wall for support, I pulled myself up just as Dolores, Beverly, and Ruth all came crashing into the bedroom.

Dolores whipped her head in my direction, her dark eyes rolling over my injured face. Her frown deepened. I knew that look. It was the "I'm going to give it to you later" look.

"You should have stayed away," said Beverly, her face flushed with anger as she advanced on the demon. "Big mistake. I'm going to kill you, demon."

The yellow, flowing veil retracted into the incubus's mouth as the demon sneered. "Nice to see you, too, Beverly, darling. As beautiful as always, for an *elderly* woman."

Beverly's face tightened with anger. "Your words have no effect on me anymore. I'm no longer under your conniving, disgusting spell."

"We'll see," answered the demon.

"Let her go, incubus," growled Dolores as she stretched out her hands, elemental fire dancing above her palms. "It's over. You can't escape. You were a fool to think you could enter our home and not be killed. You should have stayed chained to your master, Lucifer."

"Yeah." Ruth moved past Dolores and settled on her left. She fisted her hands and faced the incubus. "You're dead incubus meat."

"True, Lucifer's power is no longer within my reach," said the incubus, his voice conversational as though the threats of death weren't concerning. "But you can't kill me." He threw his gaze at each of my aunts. He was still holding Iris by the neck, her body limp, her head bent, and her face hidden by her hair. "You kill me, and she dies. It's that simple."

"What?" Wisps of dread squeezed around my throat, nearly choking me.

"Liar," spat Beverly. "Don't believe him, Tessa. Everything that comes out of that putrid hole he calls a mouth are lies."

The incubus lifted Iris a few inches off the ground and then gave her a shake, her limbs flailing like a rag doll. "Am I lying? Killing an incubus before he's completed the kiss will only kill the recipient. You see... we are connected. This tiny Dark witch and I are bonded. You kill me, and your little witch dies."

My chest tightened as a surge of panic rushed. I pushed off the wall and shuffled over closer, dread filling my legs and making them feel like overcooked spaghetti so it was hard to stand. "Is that true?" I looked over at my aunts. "Could Iris die if you kill him?"

Dolores's face was pulled tight. I could see the plans and schemes formulating behind her eyes. "I don't know. I'm not sure. He could be lying just as he could be telling the truth."

"He's a liar," growled Beverly, her teeth showing in a grimace. "He's never told a single truth. I wouldn't believe anything he says. He's a manipulative, deceitful bastard."

When Beverly had it right, she had it right.

I crept to where I'd drawn my circle, the chalk smeared on the hardwood floor. "But what if he is telling the truth. What if you kill him and Iris dies?"

My throat burned. Our master plan had been a disaster of gargantuan proportions. Not only had it not worked, but my best friend was possibly about to pay for it with her life. How could things have gone so wrong so quickly? I'd been a fool. A damn fool.

"We can't risk it," said Ruth, looking grim in the dim light. "We can't risk Iris's life. We can't do that to her. We'll just have to trust the incubus."

"And what if she dies either way?" Bile rose in my throat as I glared at the demon. "What if it won't matter? What if it's too late?"

The room went silent for a moment while we all thought about Iris's best outcome.

"But if I am *permitted* to leave," said the incubus, his eyes on me as though I were the one to decide. "She might survive."

"*Might* survive?" I shouted at him. "Are you freaking kidding me? No. Hell no. Not good enough."

The demon flashed me his teeth. "Your choice. Guess you don't really care about your friend here," he said, pushing Iris toward me with his hand.

"Stop doing that," I told him, my stomach lurching every time he thrust her about like roadkill.

He laughed low. "Jealous because she still has magic, and you don't? Is that why you wanted me to take it from her?"

"Why, you sonofabitch." Rage bubbled inside me until it spread like a hot fever. The next thing I knew, I was moving toward the incubus.

"Ah, ah, ah, careful now, Tessa," warned the incubus, bringing Iris's body before him like a shield. "I could just as easily snap her neck. So, don't do anything foolish."

Someone grabbed my arm and pulled me back.

"Get back, Tessa," ordered Dolores as she let go of me. "Iris has already suffered enough. Do you want her to suffer more?"

I stared at my tall aunt, incredulous and pissed. "Of course not. How can you even say that?"

Dolores ignored me, her eyes on the demon and her jaw clenching. "Fine. We'll let you leave."

I opened and closed my mouth. The truth was, that's exactly what I would have said. I would never take a chance on Iris's life. Even if the incubus was lying, it was a chance we'd have to take and hope he wasn't.

The incubus smiled wolfishly. "Excellent choice, Dolores. May I say how wonderfully tallish you look tonight? I always had a soft spot for the tall ones. Pity you're a bit mannish."

Dolores raised her hands. Yellow-and-orange

flames danced around her palms. "We will let you leave, but if I suspect you try to harm her more in any way... I will roast you."

The incubus bowed slightly from the waist. "I would expect no less coming from an experienced witch such as you."

Dolores's frown deepened. "Do it now."

The demon watched us for a second. He blinked, and then he released his hold on Iris. One second he was standing in my bedroom, and the next, he was gone.

Iris's body was falling.

I threw myself forward and caught her before she hit the floor. We both hit the floor at the same time, but I was holding on to her, cradling her.

I brushed the hair from her face. My fingers twitched as I felt how cold her cheeks were. "She's really cold." I reached out and grabbed her hand. Her fingers were ice-cold.

Panting, I settled her on the floor as gently as I could and felt an elbow in my side.

Dolores whirled on me. "Tell me exactly what you did. Everything."

I blinked, my mind whirling on where to begin my story.

"Now!"

I flinched. "We summoned the incubus... I mean, Iris did," I prattled like an idiot.

"We know that, but how? With what? What did you use to summon him? Did you have his true name?"

"No." I turned my head and stared at the ceramic bowl, which was overturned and halfway across my room. "With some of his hairs. Iris managed to grab some from his yacht a few weeks back before it was impounded."

Ruth kneeled next to me. "And you were able to summon him with just some hair?" She took Iris's hand on her lap and checked her pulse.

"Iris did. She'd been working on it for weeks. It worked. Until it didn't." This was all my damn fault.

"Her pulse is really weak," said my Aunt Ruth, her face sad and still holding on to Iris's hand. "It's not a good sign."

I opened my mouth to ask her what she meant, but Dolores beat me to it.

"Something doesn't fit. It shouldn't have been that easy to call him," informed Dolores, her expression dark. "You shouldn't have been able to summon the incubus."

I shook my head, frustrated. "What do you mean? It worked. Didn't it? Iris summoned him. He was here."

"It *shouldn't* have worked," repeated my tall aunt. "Not with just a few hairs. Not without a name."

I rubbed my eyes. "I'm confused. It worked. You

all saw the bastard. Iris was trying out a new spell. Well, it was a combination of an old spell with a bit of her own twist in it."

Beverly stood above me. "What Dolores is trying to say is... that it only worked because he *wanted* it to work."

Fear slid down my spine, magnified by my aunt's words. "Like he was expecting me to do it?" Oh, cauldron, no.

"Yes." Dolores watched me, her eyes steady and serious. "He let you summon him because that's what he wanted. He wanted you to try it so he could—"

"Take Iris's power." Tears welled in my eyes as I looked down at my unconscious friend. Dolores was right, and I'd fallen right into his trap.

"Or any witch," said Dolores. "He was probably hoping for it to be one of us."

"Me." Beverly's face twisted slowly in an agonizing grimace. "He would have wished it to be me."

"The point is he was waiting," said Dolores. "He knew you'd be foolish enough to try and take your powers back. He knew you were desperate enough to try anything."

And that I was willing to sacrifice my friend's power for my own. I was a selfish asshole.

I swallowed hard. "I didn't know..."

"No, you didn't." Dolores gave me a hard glare. "What you should have done was told us. We could have told you as much. We could have stopped this madness."

"Why didn't House intervene?" I asked. "Why didn't he stop Derrick?"

"Because you *summoned* the demon," answered Dolores. "You invited him inside. If the demon had entered our home by other means, yes, House would have fought back. Not in this case."

I leaned over and placed my hand on Iris's shoulder. "Iris?" I shook her gently. "Iris, wake up." I searched her pale face, waiting for her big brown eyes to open and stare back at me. But her lids remained shut. "What's wrong with her? Why isn't she waking up?"

Dolores shared a look with her sisters before answering. "If she hasn't woken up yet, I'm afraid it's nothing good."

I searched Iris's face. "I don't understand. I was weak when Derrick took my power, but I wasn't unconscious. Even Susan, who looked like a corpse, was still awake. Why won't Iris wake up?"

Ruth tapped my hand with hers. "From what I understand with the incubus, with you and Susan, he had succeeded in taking all of your powers away without being interrupted. You were both fine, a bit ill and weak, but overall okay."

"But with Iris," expressed Dolores. "It's like what the incubus said. The connection was disrupted, broken. And it seems to have done something to Iris in a bad way."

Terror stabbed my heart. "Which is? What's happened to her?"

Dolores's face was pained. "I think... I think she's in a coma."

5

Needless to say, I hadn't slept a wink last night after what had happened to Iris. After I'd sent my best friend into a coma, my heart sank with the realization that this was all my fault.

After we'd transported her to her room between the four of us, my aunts had begun to take turns using their magic to try and heal her.

While Dolores and Beverly worked on healing charms and spells, Ruth and Hildo were busy working every healing tonic at her disposal—from the usual healing stimulant to the super-duper healing elixir she'd made for Marcus when he'd been hit by the Dark wizards' magic.

Emotions were running high as I'd grabbed a chair from my room and sat across Iris's bed, waiting and wishing to see my friend's happy face. I was tired, and my body ached after the beating I'd taken from Allison, but that was nothing compared to the guilt and fear that my friend would never wake up.

"Drink this." Ruth had offered me some healing tonic last night.

"No. Keep it for Iris." I'd refused to make myself feel better until my friend opened her eyes. The pain was a reminder of my stupidity that had nearly caused my friend's life. We weren't sure if she was going to pull through.

The digital clock on my phone said 9:15 a.m. And though my aunts hadn't stopped working every healing spell and given her every healing tonic throughout the night, Iris still wasn't showing any signs of improvement.

Without magic, I couldn't do much but keep Iris comfortable and help Ruth with administering the tonic in Iris's mouth. I felt helpless and useless. But the real winning emotion was anger at myself. I didn't have much room for anything else.

The sound of wood creaking brought my attention up. Ronin leaned back in his chair across from me as he sat on the opposite side of Iris's bed. His usually perfectly styled hair was standing at odd angles like he'd just been shocked, the result of raking his fingers through it every few minutes. His face was drawn, and he looked like he'd aged.

I'd called Ronin last night once Iris was back in

her bed. He'd showed up two minutes later with that vampire speed, looking like he was about to bust down some walls. His eyes were wild and filled with pain. After he'd seen her, he'd kind of shut down. He'd taken her hand and hadn't let go. That was hours ago.

I wiped the tears from my cheeks and glanced at my phone again. No new calls. No texts.

"Still nothing from Marcus?" asked Ruth as she lowered Iris's head back on her pillow. She dropped the vial she'd just administered into the large front pocket of her apron and then took a cloth and dabbed it against Iris's lips.

I shook my head with my jaw clenched. "No. Nothing." I still hadn't heard from Marcus since yesterday. He hadn't returned any of my calls or texts. I'd given up after the fifth message I'd left and the tenth text. If he wanted to call me, he could. But he hadn't. Either he didn't want to, or he couldn't. Right now, I really didn't have the time or energy to ponder the reasons.

Iris was in mortal trouble. And right now, screw my feelings. She came first.

"Well, I wouldn't worry about it," soothed Ruth, and I flicked my eyes up at her in time to see her adjusting her apron. "I'm sure he has a good reason for not calling his girlfriend, especially when there's a crisis, and she needs him."

Ouch. Well, when you put it that way, then, yeah, but I was still ticked. I got that Marcus was a busy guy with lots of responsibilities, but a return phone call or a simple text to tell me he was okay only took a minute. Yet, he hadn't.

Ruth reached out and brushed Iris's cheek with her fingers. Then she turned to me and said, "It probably has to do with the wereape alpha from New York City. He's been trying to get Marcus to take over his pack for years. That big oaf won't take no for an answer."

I blinked. "What?"

Ruth's lips parted with a look of surprise. "I said, I think it has to do with the wereape alpha from New York City—"

I waved a hand at her. "No, no. I mean, I heard what you said. I'm just having a hard time processing it in my brain. So... there's a wereape alpha in New York City?"

"Yes," said Ruth, a bright smile on her sweet face.

"With a pack?"

Ruth's eyes widened. "A really *big* one," she said and spread her hands to show me how big. "It's the largest pack in North America. And Zeke—that's the alpha's name, wants Marcus."

"To take over his pack." It was more of a statement to myself rather than a question. If Marcus accepted, he would likely have to move away. I'd never heard of a pack leader living away from his pack. The thought of him leaving made my heart fracture. Would he take me with him?

"Marcus never mentioned it?" Worry lines stretched across Ruth's brow. She was shifting from foot to foot, something she did when she was nervous or when she knew she'd spoken out of turn.

A chill twisted my gut and had me fighting for breath. "No. No, he didn't." Guess I still didn't know a lot about the chief. It seemed Ruth knew more about him than me. We weren't supposed to be keeping secrets from one another. At least, not major ones like this. But that was exactly what was happening. Marcus was keeping secrets from me. The fact that he wouldn't share something this important with me, life-changing important, didn't sit well.

But it still didn't explain why he couldn't pick up the phone and call me. Or why he'd gone in such a hurry, leaving me with Gorilla Barbie, who'd used my body as her personal punching bag.

Maybe Marcus had already made the decision to take over the pack and didn't know how to tell me.

"I'm sure you'll hear from him soon," said my aunt. Her blue eyes rolled over my face. "You sure you won't take some of my healing tonics?"

"No, thanks."

Ruth wrinkled her face, looking disappointed. "Just a sip can do wonders."

"It's fine. I'm totally fine." I deserved how I looked and felt, and worse.

"Your face doesn't look fine," countered my aunt. "It looks like a sack of purple-and-green potatoes," she added. Her eyes studied me as the lines around her mouth and forehead deepened.

I cocked a brow. "I like potatoes."

Ruth beamed. "Me too."

I tried to smile, but I couldn't feel which muscles on my face belonged to what. If I could use the ley lines, I could be in New York City in a few moments, and then I would make him tell me.

The ley lines...

Dejected, I sat back down just as Dolores and Beverly walked into the room. They had nothing in common, but right now, they both had the same desperate and sad expressions.

I leaped from my chair, my heart pounding in my throat. "What?" I knew that look. People conveyed that look before they gave you bad news.

Dolores pulled her sad eyes from Iris and met mine. "I'm sorry, Tessa. But we've done everything we could for Iris. There's nothing else we can do."

"What the hell does that mean?" My voice was hard, but I didn't care. My blood pressure was through the roof.

Dolores sighed, that same gloomy and weary desperation still in her eyes. "This is beyond our skill and healing capabilities. We've done all we could. It's time for others to help."

"Others?" I looked at Ruth, but she refused to meet my eyes.

"We've made arrangements with Full Moon Medical Center, the paranormal hospital in Upstate New York, to come get Iris," said Beverly. "They should be here soon."

I knew that hospital name. "That's the same hospital where Susan went to heal." Okay, I could do this. They helped Susan, so there was a good chance they could help Iris.

Dolores moved to the side of the bed and wrapped her long fingers around Iris's wrist. "It's the best place for her," she said, letting go of her wrist. "We've gotten her heartbeat back up, and her pressure is good enough so she can travel."

I nodded, feeling some hope. "Okay. That's good. That sounds like a great idea. I'm going with her."

"No, you're not." Ronin glared at me. I winced at the anger I saw in my friend's eyes. "I don't want you near her. If anyone's going, it's me."

My half-vampire friend hadn't uttered a word to me since he'd arrived, until now.

I'll admit. The way he was looking at me hurt like hell. I didn't have many close friends, and Ronin was one of them. But now, he hated and blamed me. And, of course, he was right. Iris wouldn't be lying in a bed unconscious and nearly dead if I hadn't asked her to help me. Knowing her, she wouldn't have taken no for an answer if I'd asked her not to go through with it. But we'd been preparing the summons for weeks, making sure we got everything perfect.

Boy, were we wrong.

My eyes burned, and I cast my gaze over the Dark witch. *It should be me lying here. It should be me.*

An uncomfortable silence filled the room. Of course, I had no one else to blame but myself. Everyone felt it, even my aunts, though they didn't say it or show it the way Ronin did. They all shared his sentiments. They just wouldn't say it to my face.

It didn't matter. Somehow their silence made it worse.

The doorbell rang, pulling me out of my morbid thoughts.

"That's them," declared Beverly, sharing a nervous look with her sisters.

Ronin stood and bumped his thighs on the side of Iris's bed. He leaned over her, his face tight like he wasn't sure he wanted her to go and might not let anyone near her.

My heart throbbed against my chest, and I felt ill. "I'll get it." I stood. My knees cracked, and so did my ankles and lower back, the sound like microwave popcorn as I hurried out of the room before Ronin's glares were my undoing.

I shambled down the staircase as fast as my body would let me, barely remembering how I even got to the foyer. I grabbed the door handle, contemplating telling these people they couldn't have my friend, and swung open the door.

A woman and a man stood on the front porch, facing me.

The woman was ancient, her skin pale and with more wrinkles than hair, her glower probably carved into her face from years of use. A gown of green silk covered her tall, proud frame, and her dark eyes sparkled with razor-sharp intellect.

The man was taller, maybe six-three, with dark hair pulled back in a low ponytail and a matching goatee. Tattoos of magical runes and sigils covered most of his harsh features and wove down around his neck. He was dressed in all black, under a leather coat that brushed his heels.

He sneered cruelly at the reaction he was getting from me, and anger trickled into my gut.

I hadn't seen him in months, but I'd recognize that goatee and smug smile anywhere.

He was one of the witch arbitrators from the Merlin trials, the one who repeatedly called me a loser. He was also the one who'd beaten and tortured Marcus while a magical amulet kept him from healing. Which I then, in return, had cursed back and marked him with his own amulet so he could never use that kind of magic ever again.

Oh boy.

Silas and Greta were here.

6

I stood in the backyard, right at the edge of the back patio, my toes wiggling in the grass. The huge white farmhouse house stood serenely and flawlessly flanked by woods of evergreens and poplars. It was artistically manicured by white, pink, and blue hydrangeas, lilies, boxwood, and hundreds of different rose varieties. The grounds were magnificent and home-garden-magazine worthy. No wonder both my mother and Beverly wished to be married out here. No other place was as beautiful as the Davenport House grounds.

Too bad I wasn't in the celebrating mood. Even the sweet scent of the roses couldn't lift my spirit.

My aunts sat on one side of the patio, while Greta sat alone right in the middle with Silas standing over her. The tatted bastard watched me with a coy smile. A sliver of fear tried to rise, but I quashed it. His cool indifference had my blood boiling. I really hated the guy.

Emotionally, I was a mess. Physically, I felt like my aunts had taken turns beating me with two-by-fours until I collapsed like a piñata. I'd regretted not having drunk some of Ruth's healing tonic now that I had the feeling it was going to be Silas's turn to use a two-by-four on me. For some reason, whatever Greta and Silas were going to throw at me, I felt more comfortable doing it barefoot.

Five minutes after Greta and Silas had shown up, the orderlies from Full Moon Medical Center had come and taken Iris away in a nondescriptive white van, similar to the ones kidnappers used in the movies. They hauled her up on a gurney with Ronin at her side the whole time. He never once made eye contact with me. Scratch that. He did. Just before the doors were shut, I caught his eyes. The dark glare he gave me stopped my heart.

I knew then if Iris never recovered, I'd just lost a friend forever.

"Tessa Davenport."

I turned my head to find Greta watching me.

"It has come to my attention…" began the old witch. "Rumors suggest you have lost your magic. Your inner witch. It is why I came here today to verify these rumors for myself and to decide whether there is any truth to them."

"It is true," grumbled Dolores. "We could have spared you the trip."

Greta cast a disdainful glance in Dolores's direction, and then she turned back to me. "Tessa, can you explain to me how you claim to have lost your powers?"

The old witch wasn't evil, and I knew now she'd been rooting for me the whole time during the witch trials. At the time, I hadn't known, though.

I flicked my gaze to Dolores. Her slight nod and wide eyes were enough for me. I knew her well enough to understand exactly what her expression meant. I was to tell Greta "part" of the truth. We'd talked about it last night, and we'd decided what we could tell Greta and what we had to keep secret. Like my father being a demon, though I didn't know how much longer we could keep it a secret now that my mother was married to him—and the fact I'd released Lilith from her prison.

I sighed through my nose. "An incubus took my magic."

Greta's eyebrows shot to her barely-there hairline. She edged closer in her chair, her dark eyes studying me. "An incubus, you say?"

Silas snickered, and I glared at him. "That's right. An incubus." Yeah, he was loving this. I was basically his perfect gift. I should have put a bow on my forehead.

"Was this the same incubus that killed two witches and injured one?"

I kept my eyes on Greta so as to not let her see I was keeping some details from her. "That's right. The very same."

The old witch watched me without blinking. "Where is the incubus now?"

"Gone," answered Dolores. "We were unable to vanquish the incubus. He got away." Her voice was tight, matching her posture, and I could tell she was uncomfortable admitting failure in front of this older witch.

Greta gave a nod. "Unfortunate. But it is more unfortunate for you, Tessa. You had a bright future."

"Tell me about it."

Greta folded her hands on her lap. "I detect no falsehoods coming from you. As you know, I am the Witch Trials Training Division director, but I am also the head of the New York Merlin Group. As such, it is my duty to make sure your claim of losing your magic is true."

"It is true," I mumbled.

"Which is why we are here today," said Greta. Silas walked around her and stepped down the patio. "To test your magic. See if you have any traces of your power left—even just a spark—or if indeed you are a—"

"A dud," Silas interjected, a winning smile on his face as he came around and joined me on the grass. I hadn't noticed the black, weathered leather bag strapped around his shoulder until now. "Told you that you were a loser."

I cocked a brow. "You and Allison are perfect for each other."

Silas stared at me. "Who?"

"The Gorilla Barbie of your dreams."

"Did she do that to your face?" asked the male witch. His sneer widened at something he saw there. "Yeah. She did. Didn't she? I think I like this Allison. You should definitely introduce me."

Ruth leaned forward in her chair, Hildo balancing on her lap as she looked over to Greta. "Is this really necessary? We can all vouch for her. We tried. All of us tried to get her to show some magic." Ruth shook her head. "Nothing there. She's as dull as a rock."

I winced. It kinda stung when someone said it out loud like that. It gave it some finality. More so, now that my master plan of getting my magic back from Derrick had backfired tragically.

If this was going to be my future, I had better start accepting it.

Trouble was, I wasn't good at following orders or accepting things.

"We have a system in place for such things, Ruth," commented Greta. "Tessa must be categorized as a nonmagical, if it is true. For her own good. It will stop the rumors, and she can go on with her life. We must test her. Ensure the legitimacy of these allegations."

"You mean you'll take her Merlin license away." Ruth made a face, clearly not happy with Greta's answer, but she leaned back in her chair and began to stroke poor Hildo's head with a little too much force.

Greta looked at me and said, "If she is found without magic, yes, her Merlin license will be revoked indefinitely. It is the law."

"As it should be," said Silas, loudly enough for everyone to hear. "You're a cheater. You cheated at the trials with that ley line magic. Magical enhancers are not permitted. But you didn't care. You thought rules didn't apply to you. You used them anyway."

I blew out a breath. "Not this again." I knew in my heart that I hadn't cheated, more so because Greta awarded me my license at the end of the trials, and she'd seen me use the ley lines. Silas just had it in for me from the beginning. My guess? Because he'd probably tried and failed to yield the power of ley lines. He was jealous.

Silas pulled the strap of his bag over his head.

"Nice man-purse," I told him. I spied an angry-looking scar on the palm of his right hand where my curse had burned it. The pain I'd remembered flashing across his face had me all giddy. It was a small victory, and I took it all.

But my small smile faded at the evil grin the male witch gave me as he held on to his bag with one hand and rummaged inside it with the other. Something hard with a cylindrical shape poked from the side of the bag.

I pointed a finger at the bag, my imagination running wild. "If that's a vibrator, we're gonna have some words."

Silas kept smiling, and I felt my skin burst out in goose bumps.

Uh-oh. "What's this?" I looked up at Greta. "What's in the bag?"

"My lucky bag of tricks," answered Silas, looking like he was about to test drive a new sports car.

Greta gave Silas a warning look. "Silas will begin to perform a series of tests... necessary examinations to test your magic. The test of the Three Wonders."

"Right. The Three Wonders." I had no idea what she was talking about.

I cast my gaze over my aunts' faces, wishing they

had told me about these Three Wonders. Beverly sat at the edge of her seat, chewing on her nails. Dolores had her arms crossed over her chest, staring at Greta like she was contemplating whether or not to knock the older witch off her chair. And Ruth, well, she had her hands wrapped around poor Hildo's neck, looking like she was about to strangle him. The truth was, they looked more scared than I was.

Obviously, they knew about these tests. But with what happened with Iris, they hadn't had time to prepare me. I didn't blame my aunts. This wasn't their fault. This was all me. And what I gathered from their expressions, I had a feeling it was going to hurt.

"Let's begin," called Greta as she gave a single clap of her hand.

Silas pulled out what looked like a black metal baton you sometimes saw riot police use.

I pursed my lips, my hands on my hips. "Definitely not a vibrator. Well, unless you're into that kind of thing."

The male witch muttered a few words that I didn't catch, and then he blew on his baton. Yeah, I knew how that sounded.

Silas's metal stick (there I went again) vibrated—it really did—and then wisps of purple energy, like tiny electrical currents, danced along the tip.

I didn't like it. And I especially didn't warm up to the idea of the malicious smile on his face.

Before I could move, the male witch jabbed the metal baton into my gut.

"Ow! What the hell?" I cried out, stumbling back and feeling both the impact of the hit followed by the searing pain of whatever magic was on the baton. It burned like I'd been Tasered. Bastard.

Silas waved the baton like a wand, seemingly pleased with himself. His expression turned mocking. "Did it burn?"

I barred my teeth. "Yeah, it burned, you freak. What did you expect?"

The male witch's gaze traveled over to Greta. They shared a look, and then he glanced back at me, his lips twitching with a smile. "This was the first test."

"Great."

"You failed."

With my hand on my gut, I looked over in Greta's direction. She sat there stoically, her face expressionless. Guess she'd expected there to be pain. I couldn't tell if she was disappointed that I'd failed the first test. Maybe she'd been expecting me to.

Silas smacked the baton in his other palm. "This is gamma magic. It reacts to magic. If you had any magic, any internal energies, elemental or even Dark, it wouldn't have burned. You'd have felt something cool. When it burns, it's because there's nothing to counteract with it."

That was news to me.

A sudden clenching of my chest took my breath away. I don't know why this declaration was affecting me so much. I frowned, not appreciating the way he was telling everyone here what we already knew. My magic was gone. This was just another way to humiliate me further.

Silas crouched next to his bag and stuffed the baton inside. Next, he pulled out a glass jar with what looked like black sand.

"Oh no," came Ruth's panicked voice.

"Oh no?" I repeated, staring at her, my own panic mounting at her reaction to the jar. "What do you mean, *oh no*? What is that?" She clutched Hildo to her chest. His tiny head was the only thing not squished by her arms. Her face was pulled back into what I could only say was utter shock.

Twisting the lid, Silas dumped out a handful of that black sand, and then he flung it at me and yelled, "Vus ardeat!" I heard a clap like thunder. Black particles soared forth from his outstretched fingers.

I knew I shouldn't run. This was the second test. I was supposed to stay put, right where I was, so Silas could perform the second test.

Good thing I never did what I was told.

I bolted.

Pumping my arms, I sprang in the opposite direction, away from that black sand, and bounded over the grass as fast as my already injured and pain-filled legs would propel me. The good thing about adrenaline was that it hid my earlier pains and filled me with some good ol' wonder juice.

Pinpricks rattled the back of my neck like a hundred ants were crawling up and down my neck.

I whipped my head back. A cloud of black sand, dust, whatever, was soaring my way, like a swarm of angry wasps.

Oh shit. The black dust was following me!

With my head turned behind me and not paying attention to where I was going, my foot caught on something hard. I pitched forward, my mouth open, shoveling a bit of grass and dirt into it. I landed in an awkward position with my head down and my ass in the air, like a bad downward-dog yoga pose. Not my most flattering stance.

Groaning, I propped myself up to my knees. Panting, I took a breath.

That's when I saw the cloud of dust before my eyes.

I couldn't do anything to stop it.

And as I took a breath, the cloud of black dust shot into my mouth.

My throat burned, and I tried to cough, hack,

retch. I just wanted whatever I'd just swallowed out. But I could barely breathe, like that dust was trying to smother me. This was a curse. *Silas just cursed me!*

Pain exploded from inside my body, reverberating all the way to my head and filling my entire body as it burned through me like a current of electricity. Panic rose as the pain from his curse still burned through me, eating away at my strength. My head pounded like someone had taken a sledgehammer to it.

That's when the visions started.

The world around me vanished, and my vision reduced itself to a hazy tunnel. Then images started to flash before my eyes of different people and places, like I was watching a video clip on fast-forward inside my head. I saw Marcus walking away from me in the gym, a glimpse of my crying mother and an indifferent Sean, a peek of my father's silver eyes, zips of images of Dolores, Beverly, and Ruth sitting at the kitchen table. A flash of Ronin's angry face followed by Iris lying in her bed. Then the images started to play again, only faster.

I was dizzy. I wanted to shut it off. But I couldn't.

The images played faster and faster like my mind was on a merry-go-round.

Suddenly I blinked, and the visions lifted like a mist burning away with the rising of the sun. But it was like my head was off of my neck and kept spinning.

My stomach reeled, and I fell forward and puked. And puked again until all that was left was the burning bile.

"What did you see?"

I whipped the tears from my eyes and found Silas standing above me. "You cursed me, you sonofabitch." When I was all puked out, I staggered to my feet, straightened, and started to walk back toward the house. I wanted to put as much distance between Silas and me as I could.

"That was the second test, you idiot." The male witch jogged to catch up. "Now. What did you see?" he repeated loudly enough for Greta and my aunts to hear.

I didn't stop or answer until I was back at my spot before I took off running. "I saw lots of things. People. Images spinning before my eyes."

Once again, Silas looked up at Greta, his face expectant. "You failed the second test," he said, though he was looking at Greta.

I swallowed, my throat burning. "How's that?"

The male witch turned to me. "A true witch will see only herself. Her inner witch. You've failed the second test."

Irritated, I shot equally angry glares at my aunts and Greta. "Is this really necessary? I can tell you I'm all out of magic. Why do you have to put me through this? It's barbaric and cruel."

"You must complete all three tests, Tessa," answered Greta, all businesslike and lacking emotion.

"Lovely."

I watched as Silas yanked out a curved blade from his bag. "Wait. Is this part of the last test?" My breath came faster as I realized that some part of my body was going to be cut.

"You scared?" mocked Silas. He had a small ceramic bowl in his other hand.

"The thought of you naked is scary," I told him.

Silas pointed the dagger at my hand. "I need some of your blood."

"Just a small amount will do, Tessa," said Greta. "It's the final test. Blood of the witch."

I gritted my teeth. "Fine." I held out my hand, and Silas sliced his blade across my palm. I flinched as it stung, but it wasn't that bad. A line of blood seeped through the thin gash.

"Blood," ordered Silas as he shoved the bowl under my bloody palm.

Doing as he instructed, I squeezed my hand into a fist and squeezed out five drops of blood.

Satisfied, Silas yanked the bowl away. He placed it on the ground at his feet and then sprinkled something that looked like black powder over the blood while muttering a spell.

I stared at the bowl. "Now what?"

"If you have any elemental magic, it will react to it," said Silas. From his jacket, he pulled out a box of matches. He struck one, a flame ignited, and he dropped it in the bowl.

I leaned over, waiting for something to happen. What? I had no idea. But when the tiny flame went out, I had a feeling it was because my magic had gone out too.

Silas snickered as he picked up the bowl from the ground. A smile of satisfaction blossomed over his face. Hell, he looked ecstatic.

With the bowl in his hand, he stepped up to the patio and gave it to Greta. The old witch took the bowl with both hands, her face pensive as she inspected it.

My aunts all shifted nervously in their seats, though I didn't know why. We all knew what she was about to say. Guess they were hoping, as I was, too, secretly inside my heart, that a spark of magic was left in me somewhere, hiding.

Greta stood from her chair. Her face was a careful, expressionless mask, though I could see something like sadness in her eyes.

"You have completed the test of the Three Wonders." The old witch looked at me and said,

"Tessa Davenport, with great regret I must inform you that you are no longer a Merlin."

Silas clapped his hands like this was the best news he'd ever heard.

Well, shit.

7

My walk of shame consisted of removing myself from the presence of the joyful Silas and Greta and then making my way up the stairs to the attic without asking House for help.

I was angry and humiliated, and the pitying expressions from my aunts only made me feel worse. I wanted to vent, scream, and have a smallish meltdown with someone who understood. Totally acceptable behavior under the circumstances. But Iris wasn't here. She was probably already at the Full Moon Medical Center with Ronin. My two closest friends weren't here, and Marcus was ghosting me.

My life had changed drastically over the past year. I'd come into my magic, only to have it stripped away as though it had never existed. With Greta making a public declaration of my nonmagic, along with the removal of my Merlin license, it was now public to all the paranormal communities.

I wasn't a witch anymore.

Was I going to throw a pity party? Hell no.

Emotions aside, yes, I'd been humiliated by my two archenemies, but I wasn't giving up. I wasn't about to give up on my magic just because Greta's tests said so. All they said was that I didn't have magic in me—yet.

If this was what my life was going to be, shouldn't I just accept it and move on? I didn't think so. I might have been bruised, body and mind, but I was not dead. And while I still drew breath, I was going to get my magic back, even if it killed me.

I still had some cards to play. Okay, so Derrick had been a bust. But I still had a way to reach him. And that was with my father.

I hadn't talked to him much since his wedding. He and my mother needed some bonding time. But since my plan with Iris backfired, my father would need to play a part. He was going to help me track down Derrick and get my magic back.

The idea was that my dearest papa was going to capture the incubus and bring him here to Davenport House so he would then transfer my powers back to me.

And he'd do it too. If he wanted his daughter to

visit him again in the Netherworld, he was going to do it.

"Iris, I wish you were here," I breathed. Usually, when I had these crazy plans, my friend would either talk me out of it or come up with an even crazier plan. My chest ached at the memory of Iris's limp body in the hands of the incubus. The image would haunt me forever.

"When I screw up, I screw up big."

Dejected, I let myself fall on the edge of my bed and grabbed my phone from my night table. I stared at the screen. Still no new calls or texts from Marcus. I missed hearing his voice, and a part of me ached that he hadn't reached out to me yet. He was busy with some exciting part of his life, just as mine was falling apart.

I needed him, but he wasn't there for me.

Knowing myself, if I knew where Marcus was in New York City, I would have gone after him. But I couldn't afford a bus ticket, let alone a plane ticket. He could be anywhere in New York City, and that was pretty stalkerish behavior.

What had Ruth said again? The wereape alpha from New York, whose name I'd already forgotten, wanted Marcus to take over his pack? It did sound exciting. Maybe it was a much better gig than being Hollow Cove's chief.

Speaking of gigs, without the town's regular

income as a Merlin, I was going to have to up my game with my book-cover designs and websites, if I wanted to keep up with my share of the utility bills and groceries. I'd heard Dolores mention that Gilbert had upped his prices again. Something to do with inflation. My mother's wedding also still had some outstanding bills.

"You look like hell," came a voice from somewhere behind me.

I jumped up, hissed at the sharp pain in my lower back, and glowered at the woman standing in my room. "You have to stop doing that. How about a little heads-up next time, Lilith?"

Lilith's red eyes gleamed with mischief. "Why would I? It's so much fun to see you all worked up like that. And the way your eyes go all big. Priceless."

The thirtysomething-looking goddess had long waves of glorious red hair that shimmered like it was on fire. She wore designer-looking jeans, a red top under a short black leather jacket, and ankle boots that probably cost more than my monthly town wages.

I was still pissed at her. She was the main reason I'd lost my magic, but I was too tired and emotionally drained to care right now.

"You missed the wedding," I told her instead. "It was really beautiful. So, where've you been? I haven't seen you for a while." I was curious to know what the goddess did all day besides the sex.

Lilith sauntered into my walk-in closet and began going through my clothes. "Here and there and everywhere. I have to keep moving. I can't stay in one place for too long."

I followed her and leaned on the doorframe. "Because of Lucifer?"

The goddess's shoulders stiffened. She pulled out my favorite black dress and flattened it over her body. "He's relentless at finding me. The bastard can't take a hint. Sent his own personal guard last time."

"So what now? You're going to spend the rest of your life in hiding? You're going to keep running away? I thought you wanted to kill him?"

Lilith's red eyes met mine, and she leveled me with a look. I felt a shudder of fear crawl up my back. "Careful, little demon witch."

I looked away from her unsettling stare. "I'm not a demon witch anymore." *Thanks to you.*

Lilith tossed my dress on the floor like a discarded old rag and continued to pull out more of my clothes. "Yes. My bad. Hmmm. Those tests didn't go so well for you. Did they?"

My lips parted. "You were there?" I wasn't sure why, but it made me angrier that she'd been hiding in the bushes somewhere, rejoicing in my utter failures.

"That tattooed male had that sexy-ugly thing happening. They tend to be very feral in the bedroom. Like they have to make up for what they lack in looks. Did you do him?"

Ew. "No. You can have him."

Lilith flashed me a smile. "Oh, I will." She winked at me. "You can count on it."

Really gross. I crossed my arms over my chest. "What are you doing here, Lilith? Apart from messing up my closet?"

Lilith tossed my only pair of black jeans on the floor. "I came to see you, silly. That's what friends do. Right? They spend time together. Shoot the shit and all that."

I wasn't sure we were friends. I wasn't even sure I liked her. "Mmm-hmm."

The queen of hell pulled out my short black leather jacket. "Mine," she said and then proceeded to take hers off and pulled my favorite jacket over her shoulders. I could do nothing about it.

Lilith pulled her hair out from the collar. "Your face is really distracting, you know. What happened? I really hope that beautiful male of yours didn't do this. Because if he did... I can take care of him. Just say the word."

I reached up and touched my face. "No," I said, wincing at the pain. "Marcus didn't do this. He'd never raise a hand to me. This was Allison."

"Allison? I don't think we've met."

I let out a long sigh. "His ex."

Lilith's red eyes expanded, looking at me like I'd just sprouted a third eye on my forehead. "And you couldn't defend yourself? You let her beat you? What's the matter with you?"

"I didn't *let* her beat me," I said, irritated. "But I lack the necessary hand-eye coordination in one-to-one combat. These"—I lifted my arms and gave my triceps a wiggle—"aren't meant for any kind of physical activities." If I had my magic, I would have destroyed Allison. She knew it, too, and had taken advantage of me.

The goddess frowned and waved a finger in my face. "I can take care of that. Make you beautiful again." She pressed a hand on her hip. "Not as beautiful as me, of course, but a solid eight. You'll never be more than an eight."

"You really do have a way with words." I shook my head, feeling a sudden wave of tiredness. "Thanks, but I'll wear my bruises proudly. A reminder of what I am now. *Regular*."

Lilith shivered like I'd said something disgusting and sauntered out of my walk-in closet. "Why would anyone settle for regular when you can be spectacular?"

I raised my brows at her.

"Oh yes," said Lilith. "The no-magic thing." If any regret was there, I couldn't see it on her face. "Well. Suit yourself. But I can't say your male will want to bed you with a face like that. No offense."

I followed her out. My pulse gave a jerk at the mention of Marcus. "Well, he won't be bedding me anytime soon either way. He's gone."

The goddess stopped and turned. "Gone? What do you mean *gone*? He's ghosting you?"

He was actually, sort of. I was still impressed at the goddess's skill with the modern lingo. "Not sure. He might not be able to call. I don't know. My Aunt Ruth thinks he's out in New York City talking with some wereape alpha. The alpha wants Marcus to take over his pack."

"Interesting. He does have all the marvelous qualities to be an alpha of a distinguished pack. With all that unmatched strength and his delicious beauty."

I frowned at her words. She made it sound like she wanted to eat him.

Lilith moved to my dresser and pulled out a drawer. She fished through it and pulled out a pair of blue-and-white-polka-dotted undies. "I need to take you shopping."

I rubbed my eyes, wanting her to leave. "Yeah, well, maybe some other time. I have a lot on my mind."

"I know where he is," said the goddess as she pushed the drawer closed.

My heart stopped. "You do? How?"

Lilith raised a perfectly manicured eyebrow.

"Right. The whole goddess thing. I get it."

"Precisely." Lilith studied my face, her red eyes sparkling with that mischief again. "And... I can take you there."

I opened my mouth to question how exactly she was going to do that and caught myself just in time. "I guess... thank you?"

The goddess quirked a smile at me. "The question is," said Lilith, "what are you going to do when you get there?"

Good question. Very good question. "No idea. Guess I'll see when I get there."

I was equal parts uncomfortable and oddly excited at the prospect of seeing Marcus again. Would he be happy to see me? I had no idea. The last thing I wanted was to embarrass him in any way. But the guy owed me an explanation. He shouldn't just talk about our future together, of not keeping any more secrets, and then just vanish and expect me to do nothing but wait? I didn't think so.

Lilith eyed me for a moment. "I can see you're

anxious to get going." She wrinkled her nose and said, "We're not going anywhere before you shower. You smell particularly potent."

Okay then.

8

When a goddess said she was going to *take* me to New York City, I had no idea she meant it in the *literal* sense. As in *physically* grabbing me by the arm and yanking me through some goddess portal-travel with her.

Not unlike the times I'd used the ley lines, I felt a familiar sensation of floating and speed, yet it was different. I wasn't sure if it was because I was practically human now, and without my magical essence, paranormal traveling wasn't what it had once been. Or this was how it was if you weren't a celestial being. I was going with my first assumption.

My ears kept popping with the change in pressure as my stomach rolled and heaved. I swallowed, trying to keep the contents down and not all over me, or worse, all over Lilith.

Because Lilith was right there, next to me, pulling me along by the hand, like she was a mother yanking on her youngest child to keep up.

When we finally arrived at our destination, my feet hit solid ground, but my legs were like damn rubber. Lilith let go of my hand, and I fell to my knees, my head spinning like I'd just jumped off a Tilt-A-Whirl. It was a miracle for both of us that I hadn't thrown up.

I checked my phone. The screen flashed 7:00 p.m. It took us just under a minute to get to New York City. Goddess traveling was faster than the ley lines, like traveling by jet instead of going economy.

Before we left, I'd taken a long, hot shower and even attempted to hide my purple-and-green bruises over my face, jaw, and brow areas with some concealer. It wasn't perfect, but it looked okay at a distance, not so much close-up.

Lilith and I had argued about "appropriate attire to attract males" when I'd decided to ditch the tight jeans and pull on a pair of sweats and hoodie.

"My body wants me to wear the sweats," I'd told her. "It's begging me. It wants to be soothed in stretchy cotton."

"Who cares what your body wants," Lilith objected. "Sweats are for soccer moms. Not for attractive females who want to draw the attention of deliciously gorgeous males. Don't you want him to desire you? To rip off your clothes to see what's beneath?"

"Not really. If you think my face is bad, it's nothing compared to my body. Besides, I want to be comfortable. I don't care if it's not sexy." I'd turned my back on her then and grabbed my messenger bag, my way of telling her to leave it alone.

"Fine. But don't say I didn't warn you to look your best."

What the hell was that supposed to mean?

My Converse sneakers flapped on the sidewalk as I made my way toward Central Park. A breeze rose around me, sporadically sending my hair to tickle my neck. I gathered it into a thick, tangled ponytail and wrapped it with an elastic band.

Several cars were parked along Central Park North, right next to the entrance of the park. I looked through the gates and saw large, blossoming crabapple trees, their flowers pink and white as I inhaled their sweet scent. The petals of their flowers littered the pavement like snow.

Beyond, a rainbow of blossoms and leaves of every shape, size, and color greeted me: tulips, daffodils, lilacs, lily of the valley, and azalea bushes that would have looked fantastic in front of Davenport House.

"And you're sure Marcus is here?" I asked,

standing next to the iron gate at the entrance to Central Park.

Lilith placed her hands on her hips and gave me a pointed look, reminding me of Dolores. Scary. "Here," she said as she handed me a silver key that wasn't in her hand a second ago.

"What's this?" I eyed the key suspiciously. "If this is a key to some secret, underground orgy, I'm out." I laughed. The goddess didn't.

"A key to my place in the city." Lilith grabbed my hand and forced the key into my palm. "In case you can't stay with your sexy male, you'll have a place to stay until you figure your shit out."

I stared at her. "Who are you?"

Lilith brushed a strand of red hair back. "The most beautiful woman that ever was."

Now she sounded like Beverly. If she kept doing things like that, helping me out in tight situations, I was going to end up liking the goddess. I wasn't sure how I felt about that.

But if I were to guess, I'd say Lilith was feeling culpable for what happened to me. She might not be able to return my magic, but she was trying to help me in her own way.

"Ride him hard, my little mortal," said Lilith as she spun around and walked down the sidewalk in the opposite direction.

I shook my head. "She is one weird goddess." I

blinked, and then... she was gone. Just gone.

I let out a long breath and walked through the entrance to the park. I hadn't really thought through what I was going to say when I found Marcus. Was I a stalker? Was this stalking? Yeah, it totally was. And somehow, I didn't feel guilty about it at all. A year ago, I would have. I guess Lilith was rubbing off on me.

Lovely antique-looking lampposts buzzed and flickered on. Just as the sun touched the tops of trees, the sky glowed the color of campfire embers. My pulse accelerated as I followed the trail and climbed up to the North Woods. Would Marcus be happy to see me? Would he be ticked off?

What the hell am I doing? I started to second-guess my decision to come here. It felt like a bad idea. Too late to turn back now. I'd already made the trip. A free trip. I didn't have money to throw around on a bus ticket back to Maine. Besides, I had burning questions that needed to be answered. For instance, why the hell was Marcus in Central Park anyway? Why couldn't he pick up his damn phone and call me?

Barely five minutes into my hike, I heard the commotion.

I slowed to a relaxed walk, my ears on high alert as I tried to make sense of all the voices. I passed an ancient, gnarled oak tree that looked like a giant's arm sprouting from the ground. As I cleared the tree, I understood why.

Through a break in the foliage was a large clearing the size of a substantial gymnasium. Hard-packed dirt spread out in the shape of a circle. And around the circle was a clustered mix of naked dudes.

I sucked in a breath.

Naked men everywhere, at least a hundred, of every age and ethnicity, their bodies ripped with muscles bulging and gleaming in the setting sun, making their skin look like it was on fire. Although they differed in age, they all had something in common—they were all ridiculously built like seasoned bodybuilders. The kind of men who lived at the gym. For some reason, it was really hard to stop staring at all those rock-hard butts.

Did I mention they were *all* buck naked?

"This is what it's like to be in one of Beverly's fantasies," I whispered, a stupid smile on my face.

I scanned the men. I didn't recognize Marcus's butt among the sea of butts. Males milled about, none of them Marcus from what I could see.

With their backs to me, they were all focused on what was happening inside the circle. Curious, I needed to get closer. I spotted a few gorillas in the mix, their dark fur, and sheer size, a stark contrast among the naked, human-skinned males.

My pace slowing, I swallowed hard and moved closer for a better view. I thought it strange that they were out here in the open like that. Any human could be walking along the trail and would get a rude awakening of the naked kind. A cluster of naked men in New York City? Okay. A group of gorillas? Maybe not.

If this was indeed the wereape pack of New York City, where was Marcus?

A roar echoed around the woods followed by the sound of growls, the pounding of fists on flesh, and the sickening sound of tearing skin.

I moved closer still.

A few males turned their heads at my approach, their faces revealing nothing as they gave me the once-over and turned back around more like they were looking at a nonthreat or at a clueless, stumbling human. The faces that looked back at me belonged to young men, middle-aged men, and men who were clearly in their late fifties. Yet, those silver foxes could put any twenty-year-old to shame in terms of looks and physical form.

Like I said, this was one of Beverly's fantasies.

I got close enough to the ring of wereapes, but these guys were so big and tall I'd need a ladder to get a clear view. Where would I get a ladder in the middle of Central Park? I wouldn't. So I didn't.

"Excuse me. Smallish female coming through." I

carefully peeled away some of the males using my hands on their hard biceps and doing my very best not accidentally rub on their lower man parts because that would be awkward.

"Careful where you point that, big boy," I told a large, dark-skinned man. He really was a *big* boy.

The air smelled heavily of male perspiration, testosterone, and dominance. When I finally made it through the wall of naked males, I froze.

Within the large ring of both gorilla and humanoid wereapes were two gorillas. Their fur was mostly black, except for the silver saddles across their backs and hips. Silverback gorillas. The hairs on the back of my neck rose at the sheer ferocity of their attacks, the blunt force with which they pounded their fists, and the impacts that would have rendered the average human into jam.

It was hard to see which of the two was bigger, and it was even harder to see which of the two was stronger. They were moving too fast. Both were silverback gorillas, and both were huge with bulging muscles and mouths full of teeth.

Yet one of the silverbacks had one distinctive feature I knew all too well. I'd recognize his gray eyes anywhere.

Marcus.

9

Okay, so my boyfriend was in Central Park fighting another wereape surrounded by hundreds of naked dudes. My life couldn't get any stranger. Could it? Yeah, it could always get weirder.

"Damn," I muttered, trying not to blink so I wouldn't miss anything. I was equally excited and terrified, possibly more excited.

As I stood there ogling, I could see the other silverback had a lot less gray fur along his back and his hips. He was mostly black, and I pegged him for a younger wereape than Marcus.

The younger gorilla—let's call him George—advanced on Marcus, flexing his chest muscles like that was supposed to be scary. With a great push of his back legs, the young gorilla leaped in the air at Marcus.

The chief dealt him a blow of pure frustration and drove his fist down across his head. George's head snapped back, and then he fell to the ground, his body limp. I had no idea if he was dead or not. I didn't get the chance to ponder it.

One second he was on the ground, and then next, he'd been hauled away by two of the naked bystanders.

And then another young gorilla stepped into the circle.

He was different. His fur was black with hints of red, and by the cauldron, he was huge. Bigger than even Marcus. At least a few inches taller and thicker. He wasn't a silverback yet. But he was either an abnormally big gorilla, or he was shooting up steroids.

Fear clutched at my heart. I was still pissed at Marcus, but I didn't want him to get his head bashed in by this red monster.

"Lucas is going to kick Marcus's ass," said the male wereape to my left, smiling like he was watching a football game on TV, and his team was winning.

"He won't," growled another wereape with a shaved head. "Bigger doesn't mean better."

"Ain't that the truth," I said with a laugh.

The wereape on my left stared at me for a beat,

long enough for my smile to disappear, and then turned his eyes back on the fight.

"My money's on Lucas," said the same wereape to my left. "Marcus never wanted it. He's the wrong choice for alpha. But Lucas has been with us since he was a boy. It's his."

"That doesn't mean he's the right choice as alpha," commented the other and got a few muttered agreements from some of the wereapes. "The better choice is the one who doesn't want it. The one who doesn't seek power and status. A true leader doesn't want power. He can have it but always puts his pack first."

I frowned. He was making sense. I didn't like it.

The wereape on my left grunted. "Lucas is going to win. You just watch."

The other wereape snorted. "We'll see," he said and crossed his gigantic arms over his massive chest.

At that point, I noticed Marcus and Lucas were both standing at opposite ends of the circle, waiting.

"What are they waiting for?" I blurted before I could stop myself. The last thing I wanted was for Marcus to get his head pounded in. A foolish part of me wanted to jump in the circle, waving my hands around like a crazy person. That should get their attention. Knowing Marcus, it would make him stop, but it would also embarrass him.

"Waiting for Zeke to give the order," said the wereape on my left.

I followed his gaze. An older wereape stood right across from me. His white hair was cropped short, leaving his scalp visible. He was frowning, the skin around his eyes and mouth wrinkled and weathered, like a man who'd seen many seasons. He stood with his arms over his ample chest, tribal-like tattoos draped down his arms and the right side of his chest. He was the tallest wereape here. It was hard to guess a wereape's age. I didn't know if they aged like humans or if they were blessed with longevity like vampires. Still, he looked to be in his late sixties but still in incredible shape. He stood with a confident posture—a killer, a man in control, a man clearly in command.

So this was Zeke.

Yup. He was naked too. My eyes spotted his twig and berries before I could stop myself. It's hard *not* to look at something when you knew you were *not* supposed to be staring at it.

"Begin," growled Zeke as his frown deepened.

At once, the two gorillas threw themselves at each other. I flinched as Marcus ducked under Lucas's swing and came up with a fist, hammering it on the back of the other man's head.

Lucas the gorilla staggered, and for a moment I thought he'd go down. But then he straightened, bared his meat-tearing teeth at Marcus, and lunged.

The younger gorilla caught Marcus in the side, and the chief went sailing back. I stared mutely, horror-struck. But he was up in almost the same moment, smashing his great fists against Lucas's back, two at a time, like a massive mallet. Lucas crumpled to his knees. He looked up, and an ugly grimace skewed the younger gorilla's face.

Then he charged.

My heart pounded in my throat as I watched this violent and terrifying fight. Lucas hit Marcus like a city bus hitting a cement wall, and the two fell to the ground in a blur of fists, pounding flesh, snarls, hissing, gnashing teeth, and dark fur flying. Each gorilla pummeled with their fists, breaking into a fervent hysteria of blows. The ground beneath my feet shuddered and quaked. Each crushing punch sent bile rising up my throat and fear clawing at me.

The air smelled of blood, sweat, and animal. I couldn't understand the eagerness I saw shared in the eyes of the watching wereapes. Me? I'd had enough of this pissing contest.

"When do they stop?" I asked no one in particular.

"When either of them submits," answered the bald wereape from before.

"And if they don't?"

The bald wereape turned to me. "Then one of them will die."

"Great. Just freaking great."

The fight reminded me of the time I went looking for Marcus at the Allegheny Tionesta Creek campsite. I'd witnessed the same kind of ferocity between two gorillas, an old alpha who wouldn't submit and the younger alpha who was clearly the next leader. I'd gone all angry and bothered very much like now.

Weird how life repeated itself. Or maybe it was just me.

I heard the hiss of Marcus losing his breath in a brutal kick in the chest by Lucas. The younger, bigger gorilla was giving it all he had, fighting with primal brutality. Lucas's face rippled in anger as his eyebrows came together, and a wild light danced in his deep-blue eyes. It was obvious he wanted to be the alpha.

Marcus was different. He fought differently. More controlled, more organized as though every move he took or made, every punch, every kick had been planned or was intended, calculated.

With a terrible bellow, Lucas threw himself at Marcus, his arms swinging. Without a pause, the chief charged. They hit with a terrible ferocity, their faces deranged and their hands locked into enormous fists as they brought them down on each other. Bones crunched.

The crowd roared, enthused by the prospect of one of the gorillas' submissions or even death.

I gritted my teeth as I watched. "This is soooo stupid," I said loudly. Apparently louder than I'd thought.

Marcus the gorilla stilled, and then his gray eyes fixed on me.

Oh shit.

Confusion crossed his features. His mouth fell open in what could only be described as utter shock. Yeah, he wasn't expecting me. Oopsie.

A heat comparable to molten lava dashed over my skin. I shrugged and gave him a finger wave. "Hi."

And then Lucas's giant fist came out of nowhere and smashed against Marcus's head.

The chief stumbled back and went down on his knees. Lucas was all over him in seconds.

Fear lodged itself in my throat as Lucas slashed at Marcus's chest with his clawed hand. Blood drenched the ground in spatters of red.

"Marcus!" I shouted, really loudly this time.

But then someone else's shout drowned out mine. "Enough!"

Zeke walked into the fighting circle, his arms out as both gorillas let go of each other. They stood a few feet apart, panting. Lucas's eyes were on Marcus, his lips pulled back in a snarl, his body low and poised for another round of fighting. But the chief wasn't even looking at his rival. He was looking at me.

And so was Zeke.

"Who are you?" The alpha wereape walked across the ring over to me, his muscular body bulging and his manly parts dangling and swinging from side to side. I was in hell.

"Uh... uh..." As always, when in tight situations, my vocabulary improved by leaps and bounds. My brain was a wild jungle of startling babble.

Zeke now stood about a foot away from me. The other wereapes stepped back to give their alpha space, but I stayed where I was.

"Who are you, and how do you know Marcus?"

Geez. Having this big, naked, and possibly angry man's junk so close to me was seriously distracting. Scratch that. All these hundred or so men's junk was distracting.

"That's Tessa."

I looked over Zeke's shoulder and found Marcus, back in his human shape, walking over to us. His face was tight with concern, and I saw something like guilt in his eyes. Or regret? He had a large, bleeding gash across his chest, but it didn't seem to be bothering him much.

Zeke's stare was hard, and judging by the downward curve of his mouth, he wasn't happy to see me. "You shouldn't be here."

I cocked a brow. "You shouldn't be naked, swinging your thunder stick and chicken tenders in Central Park, but who's judging."

Marcus grabbed my arm and pulled me closer, bumping me into his hard chest. "Tessa. What are you doing here?"

"Looking for ticks? What do you think? I was worried. I came looking for you." I realized then that my coming here was probably not good for his image. The fact that no other females were here told me this was a boys-only club, and I'd just crashed their party.

The chief's jaw tightened. His gray eyes searched my face, and the corners pulled in worry. "What happened to your face?"

The pang in my chest became a physical ache at the real concern in his voice. I thought about telling him what Allison had done to me, but now wasn't the right time. "It's a long story."

"But how did you know where to find me?"

"Lilith brought me here." At the frown on his face, I added, "I got worried when you didn't answer my calls or my texts." I felt strangely annoyed that all the wereapes were listening to our private conversation.

"I took his phone away," answered Zeke before

Marcus had the chance. "I didn't want anything distracting Marcus."

I wasn't sure I liked this Zeke character. "I wish you would have told me where you were going before you left me with Gorilla Barbie," I told Marcus.

"I hadn't planned on staying. This wasn't supposed to happen."

"You're not our kin." Zeke stepped closer, which meant his man junk was closer still. His nostrils flared as he took in my scent. My face flamed as I remembered I hadn't put on any deodorant. "She doesn't smell like any paranormal I know, yet she saw through the glamour enough to find you."

He got me there. If this area was glamoured to keep humans out, how could I see them if my magic was gone?

"I was a witch." Yeah, that sounded pretty lame. And the laughter that came from the surrounding wereapes didn't help.

Zeke looked over and behind me, like he was looking for my broom or something. "You *were* a witch, but you're no longer a witch?"

"Something like that."

"This is Tessa Davenport from Hollow Cove," announced Marcus to the encircling wereapes. "A witch from my town. And my girlfriend."

The wereapes stiffened, and it was almost like they were frozen in place.

Zeke, though, was not.

His face wrinkled in disdain. "Not for long, she won't be. When you take over my pack, you will find a proper mate. A wereape female to stand by your side while you rule. It's how things are done. You can screw this... ex-witch for the time being, but you will marry a wereape."

Oh. My. God.

Okay, I could either start bawling my eyes out or take a stand. I chose to take a stand.

"Listen here, you big sasquatch," I said, pointing my finger in his face. "I don't care who you are or how big you are. I don't even care that your junk is practically rubbing against me right now. No one talks about me like that."

Marcus gently pushed my hand down and used it to pull me back to his side. He had a strange, proud smile on his face. His body pressed into mine, so warm, and his delicious musky scent sent my lady hormones pounding.

The chief's gaze moved to the alpha. "I told you before, Zeke. I don't believe in those traditions." His voice was dangerously low. The muscles around his shoulders popped, and I knew he was getting angry. "I came here out of respect for you and my father. I told you I would help find your new alpha. That is all. Tessa is my mate, and you will respect her."

His mate.

A pool of warmth settled in my gut at his words. We were going to do all kinds of *mating* later.

All my previous emotions and uncertainty toward the chief vanished. Part of me wanted to run my fingers in his glorious black, tussled hair and pull his face to mine so I could kiss him right there in front of all these naked men.

The alpha's eyes danced with a dangerous fire. He looked at me for a moment, staring at me like I was the one thing standing between him and Marcus. Maybe I was. "Fine. But she has no business here." His voice lacked sincerity, and I knew he was just saying that to keep Marcus in check with his agenda. The only truth to his words was that he wanted me gone.

"You can't lie to yourself any longer, Marcus," continued Zeke. "You are the rightful alpha. No one has beaten you."

"Yet. Lucas still owes me a fight. I will keep fighting until you make your choice."

According to the spark in Zeke's eyes, it was obvious he'd already made his choice.

I took Marcus's hand, Ruth's words coming back to me. I knew this was Zeke's way of trying to get Marcus to become the new alpha for this pack. I would have never thought Marcus would be involved in this until I saw it with my own eyes. The way he commanded respect without even asking for it. The way he fought, how every move was strategic. He was a king, a crownless king.

My heart thudded with what I was going to say next. "You're staying. Aren't you?"

If it were just me, I'd grab him and drag him by the hand out of the park. Obviously, I'd have to find him some clothes first. Not that I minded this sexy male wandering around in his delightful nakedness, but the rest of the New Yorkers might take offense. The males, that is. And I'd probably have to fight my way through some horny women too. I smiled at the thought.

The chief squeezed my hand and then let it go. "I have to stay," he said, his warm breath caressing my hot face.

I stared at him. "Have to stay?" I repeated, trying to get the words to sink in.

The satisfied smile on Zeke's face had my blood pressure on a high boil. Heat rushed to my face, and I felt like a complete fool.

"I can't leave. Not right now." Marcus sighed through his nose. "It's complicated. But I have to see this through."

I knew then how important this, whatever *this* might be, was to him. The respect of all these strong wereapes. Being the alpha. Being the one in command.

I looked around, and I saw what was mirrored in all their faces: respect.

All but one. A large, ridiculously muscled, red-haired male, which I knew was probably Lucas, was still staring at Marcus like he wanted to fight him. But all the others were looking at Marcus like he was already their alpha. Their king.

I felt like an idiot. No one in their right mind would want to take that away from their partner. That would be incredibly selfish. What if Marcus *was* the right choice? What if this was his true path? It was incredible to see, to witness. Maybe Marcus was supposed to lead this group.

And like Zeke said. I was a distraction.

I knew if I stayed any longer, my tears would betray me. I was still standing with my defiance on full blast, but for how long. The words wouldn't come either. If I opened my mouth, my emotions would deceive me. I did not want to break down in front of all these naked dudes. I'd been humiliated enough.

I wasn't sure what I'd expected, but this wasn't it. And I wouldn't stand in the way of someone who could achieve greatness.

"Tessa..." whispered Marcus, his breath tickling

my neck. The heartache in Marcus's voice was almost my undoing.

It was horrifying. Carrie-at-the-prom-with-pig's-blood horrifying.

I swallowed past the lump in my throat, turned around, and walked back on the trail the way I'd come, with stiff feet.

I was going home alone.

10

It was the morning of the Beltane, the magical celebration of the peak of spring. Here the witches in Hollow Cove performed rituals and spells to protect the townspeople and our crops and to encourage growth.

The annual get-together was more of an excuse to get all the witches together and gossip over drinks and good food. And, of course, the Davenport witches were hosting it.

I hadn't slept much over the last few days, and last night wasn't any better. Although I had slept in my own bed, thanks to Lilith, it was more of staring at the ceiling and going through the events of the day than actual snooze time.

Lilith's condo was a fifteen-minute walk from Central Park, and I managed to find it without getting lost, which was a miracle since I barely remembered how I got there. Everything was a blur as I walked away from Marcus.

I'd walked around in what felt like a daze, more like a massive case of denial. My legs felt like jelly, yet I'd still managed to find my way to the goddess's place. It wasn't so much the fact that Marcus hadn't come back with me but more like I had a feeling he wouldn't come back at all. His place, his true place, was with the New York wereape pack.

I hated to admit it, but Marcus seemed like the perfect alpha for that pack. He looked and felt the part. It was obvious to anyone with a brain and a pair of eyes. I just didn't want to accept it.

I had no doubt that if or when Marcus became the new alpha, he would ask me to move to New York City with him. Obviously, that would mean his days as the chief in Hollow Cove were over. But I wasn't sure this was the best course of action for me.

After all my years, I finally felt like I'd found where I truly belonged, and that was Hollow Cove. Not necessarily living in Davenport House but living in that quirky town with a crazy-ass town mayor who dressed like he was still living in the sixties and where everybody knew everyone's business. I wasn't sure I was ready or even wanted to give that up. That kept me up most of the night, right after Lilith had goddess-beamed me back in my room.

"You still look like shit," the goddess had said. I'd barely touched the key to the keyhole of her condo when the door swung open.

"Always so pleasant and careful with my feelings," I'd said, wondering if being there was a mistake. Maybe I should have taken my chances with a bus back to Maine instead. I'd use my credit card if I had to.

The goddess leaned on the doorframe, her red silk robe draped over her curvy body. "He decided to stay? Well, can't say I'm surprised. You look like he dumped you. Did he dump you?" Her eyes rounded at the prospect. "Is he fair game, then? Can I jump his bones?" she added with a spicy smile.

I frowned at the goddess, wishing I had some of my magic mojo so I could burn her on the spot, though I seriously doubted I could have, even with magic. "No." Well, I don't think so. "I just... I don't know what I'm doing here. I just want to go home and be alone for a while." I needed to think about my life and what I needed to do. I needed a plan.

"Come inside."

Feeling as though my body and my mind were two separate entities, I walked in.

Lilith closed the door behind me. "That bad, huh?"

"Not bad... just not what I was expecting."

"A group of fabulously muscled and naked men

in their prime, all that sweat, that animalistic rage, that power... is a woman's dream."

"More like Beverly's, just not mine. Why didn't you tell me what they were doing?"

Lilith smiled and walked over to her white leather couch. "I didn't want to ruin the surprise," she said as she sat, looking positively pleased with herself. "Surprise."

"Well, I was surprised. You win."

The goddess's forehead wrinkled. "Don't be such a drag. I helped you. Didn't I? It's not my fault you fell in love with a wereape. One who already has the right chops to be an alpha. It's the beast in him. You can't compete with the beast. That's why you should never get too attached to any shifter. You can ride the beast. You screw them, and then you leave. It's always worked for me."

I rubbed my eyes, feeling a wave of tiredness hanging over me and pulling me down. "He's only there to help the existing alpha find a new replacement."

The goddess laughed, which set my teeth on edge. "You don't seriously believe that. Do you? Face it, Marcus *is* an alpha whether you like it or not."

She had me there. "I can't talk about this right now. I'm too tired."

Lilith pulled herself to her feet. "Then I'll send you home."

And that's how I'd ended up in my bed two seconds later, rushing to my bathroom to puke.

As I made my way downstairs, the sweet scent of flowers reached me as though I'd just stepped into a flower shop. I walked into the kitchen and halted.

A collection of yellow daffodils, yellow daisies, and lilies were scattered over the dining room table and the kitchen island.

"Wow. Are these for tonight?" I picked up a lily and inhaled its rich, sweet scent.

"For the celebration tonight." Ruth turned from the stove, beaming with a yellow crown of daisies resting on the top of her head. "We're making wreaths, crowns, and necklaces. Everyone at the celebration has to have a yellow flower."

"Even Hildo," I said as I spotted the cat sitting on the counter, his eyes narrowed and looking angry. Must have been because of the large daffodil and daisy collar wrapped around his neck.

"You can eat them, too, if you want," said Ruth and then decided I needed a demonstration. She popped the head off a daisy and shoved it in her mouth as her eyes broadened. "Yum. Tastes like honey. You wanna try?" She plucked another daisy from her crown.

"I'm good. Thanks."

My Aunt Ruth was in her element. She was so damn cute and happy. She was all sunshine and rainbows, my Aunt Ruthy, and I needed all the sunshine I could get in my life right now.

The phone rang from the hallway.

Ruth wiped her hands on her apron. "I'll get it. I'm expecting a delivery of gnome nuts." Grinning like a girl on her tenth birthday, Ruth rushed out of the kitchen, her feet loud as they slapped on the hardwood floors.

I wasn't sure if those were some kind of rare fruit or actual gnome nuts. Knowing Ruth, they were probably the latter.

"All these flowers remind me of the time I was in a meadow with Ted Murphy," said Beverly, sitting at the table as she wrapped some flowers around the wire mesh of a wreath. "We were naked. The only thing between our sweaty, hard, slippery bodies were wildflowers." She stopped what she was doing as if recalling a memory. "There's nothing more refreshing than sex in the wild."

"Sounds like a cheap porno," complained Dolores, sitting across from her and working what looked like an intricate necklace looped with daisies, lilies, and daffodils.

Beverly glared at her sister. "You're only saying that because the only wild sex you've ever been a part of is when you watch it on the National Geographic channel."

O-kay.

Dolores's face darkened two shades, her jaw clenching as three squished lilies fell to the floor at her feet. Some things I just didn't want to know.

Beverly smiled at her victory. She caught my eye and winked like we'd won or something. "I can't even count how many different places I've had sex. Airplane bathrooms. Elevators. Movie theater. A phone booth—though very carefully. Dentist's chair. In the car during the automatic car wash. One time even at the funeral home. What can I say? It's because I'm gorgeous. If only I could do something to make myself less beautiful and irresistible to men."

"I know a few spells that could help you with that," muttered Dolores.

Beverly gave her sister a look that said she wasn't afraid of what Dolores could throw at her, or maybe just that her beauty was so powerful that no spells could affect it, like a shield.

Ruth walked back into the kitchen, scowling and mumbling the words, "Telemarketers... get a real job."

"Who was it on the phone, Ruth?" asked Beverly.

"Stupid telemarketing people," answered Ruth, a frown creasing her brow. "Something about cans a week of Nutella or something? That's the third time they've called. Something's wrong with the connection. I can barely hear them."

I smiled. "If it's free, tell them to ship it over. I love me some Nutella." Hell, I'd eat a whole damn jar of Nutella right now, and I wouldn't even feel guilty about it.

Ruth plucked another daisy from her crown. Instead of eating it, she proceeded to rub the daisy's yellow head over her face, leaving streaks of yellow pollen. She caught me staring. "It's really good for your complexion."

"Ah."

"I don't need to do that." Beverly lifted her chin and smiled at us. "My skin is naturally vibrant and exudes sensuality."

Dolores blew out a breath. "Okay, there, Neutrogena."

Ruth handed me her flattened daisy, her fingers stained with yellow pollen. "You want to give it a try?"

I smiled. "Not right now. Thanks."

"Tessa. Don't forget the bonfire tonight," announced Dolores, peering over her reading glasses at me as she added the last flower to her necklace. "All the witches in town will be here."

Technically and traditionally, this was a witch's celebration. If I wasn't a witch anymore, I had no business being there.

I'd noticed my aunts being extra careful so as to not talk about Greta and what happened to me during the tests. It was almost like they thought I might break down or something. I wasn't there yet.

My heart wasn't in this celebration tonight, though. Iris would have loved to participate in the festivities. My chest tightened at the thought of Iris and Ronin.

I set the lily back on the pile. "Any news from the Full Moon Medical Center?" Guilt gnawed at my insides like I had a little gremlin in there, chewing at the walls of my stomach.

Dolores met my gaze. "Nothing so far. Don't worry, though. She's getting the best care. I can promise you. There's no better place for her than Full Moon Medical Center."

"She'll be home soon," added Beverly, her voice sounding a little high and false like she didn't really believe it.

The fact that we hadn't received any word from the center didn't sit well with me.

I yanked out my phone and tapped Ronin's name. After the fifth ring, it went to voicemail. Yeah. He was ghosting me. Even if I called a hundred times and he hung up on me or sent me to voicemail, I would keep calling until I got an answer.

As I stuffed my phone back into my pocket, Ruth spun around and inspected my face. "You're still bruised, but your face looks a lot less like a rotten potato than it did yesterday. That's good news. Our bodies are truly remarkable healers."

I smiled. "Thanks, Ruth. I needed some cheering up."

"Why?" Ruth lost some of her smile. "Did you hear from Marcus?"

I walked over to the coffee machine and poured myself a fresh cup. "I did. You were right. He's in New York City." Pounding the heads of a few wereapes.

Beverly swiveled in her seat, so she was facing me. "It sounds bad."

"It sounds dreadfully bad," agreed Dolores and pulled her reading glasses from her face.

Beverly cast a glance in her sister's direction and said, "Sounds like a good story."

Both witches dropped their work and joined me at the coffee machine.

"Tell us everything. Don't leave anything out," ordered Beverly, her hip leaning against the counter. Her green eyes flashed with the promise of someone else's problems. "I want all the juicy details."

Reluctantly, I told them all the gruesome details of my utter humiliation when Marcus had decided to stay with the wereape pack in New York City. Dolores was kind enough to keep her face from showing any emotion. Beverly kept bursting out in oohs and aahs and fanned herself when I got to the part with all the naked, very well-muscled, and well-endowed wereapes. Ruth didn't utter a single word. She didn't have to. Her face kept twisting. Her expressive features seemed as though she'd said it out loud. She felt sorry for me.

"Tell me again how many naked men were there," begged Beverly for the third time.

"About a hundred."

Beverly smacked her thigh. "I can't *believe* I missed that. It's like one of my many fantasies about being the single woman in a sea of naked, muscular men who all desire me."

I knew it.

Dolores placed a fist on her hip. "So he decided to stay with the pack. Interesting."

"Interesting?" said Beverly, looking incredulous. "It's tragic. He left her."

I cringed on the inside at her words. I didn't want to admit it, but that's how it was starting to feel.

Dolores waved her free hand in Beverly's direction. "Let's not jump to conclusions. Let's go over the evidence," she said and began pacing in the kitchen. "We know this Zeke character wants Marcus as the new alpha. But Marcus hasn't accepted. He said he had to stay to help the alpha choose the next in line for the job, like triage."

I blinked. "I guess."

"We all know Marcus to be a man of his word, a

man of integrity," Dolores continued. "He wouldn't abandon his responsibilities as chief of Hollow Cove."

"Unless he got a better offer," said Ruth, twisting her apron in her hands, her go-to gesture when she was nervous or stressed.

I met her eyes and then looked away. That made a lot of sense. To a wereape, well, from what I'd learned, being an alpha would be a dream job. The ultimate job. Like being the CEO of a huge company.

Dolores turned to face me. "How did Marcus look?"

I grinned. "Amazing," I answered with a laugh, smiling at the memory of his fantastic physique. "Like a Greek god. No, better." Beverly laughed and slapped me a high five.

Dolores made a sound of disapproval in her throat. "No, I mean, how was his mental state? Did he look honored to help out the alpha, or did he look... confused... tempted to take on this new role?"

"He looked tempted." I wasn't going to lie. That's exactly what I saw in his eyes.

"Then we have to dissuade him," said Ruth, giving her apron a tug of defiance.

"How are you going to do that?" asked Beverly. "It's like asking him to refuse a raise. No one ever refuses a raise. If anything, you ask for more."

Ruth's brows wrinkled as confusion adorned her face. "Marcus is getting a raise?"

"It's okay, Ruth," said Dolores. "You just have bad luck when you're thinking."

Ruth glared. "Your face makes puppies cry."

I bit the inside of my cheek to keep from laughing. Even when I was at my lowest, my aunts always seemed to make me laugh. That was family for you.

"And this Zeke character?" asked Beverly, as she moved to the coffee machine and poured herself a cup. "I can't believe he took Marcus's phone. The nerve of that wereape."

Dolores was nodding. "Worse that Marcus let him."

I stared down at my own coffee. What Dolores said rang true. Marcus could have stopped Zeke from taking his phone.

But he'd let him.

He could have asked someone else for a phone.

He didn't do that either.

I wasn't sure if this was a giant clue as to how Marcus was feeling about the whole alpha thing, but it sure as hell made me feel worse and more insecure.

My chest felt like a Great Dane was sitting on it. If Marcus took the position as alpha, and if I joined him in New York... this was what I'd be missing. My family. I wasn't sure I was willing to part with them.

I wouldn't say the thought of moving in with Marcus hadn't crossed my mind a thousand times—probably more. But I wasn't sure I was ready to move away from town, away from my aunts, my mother, and my father.

My father.

My only link to him was this house. If I moved away now... I'd lose that, too, and I'd only just started to have a relationship with him.

Speaking of my demon progenitor, I had to speak with him. I wasn't giving up on my magic just yet, not while there was a chance, though very slight, I could get it back.

But I had to do it tonight during the bonfire while everyone was busy enjoying the festivities. Because if they knew of the scheme I was planning to get my magic mojo back with the help of my dearest papa, they'd try and stop me.

Yes, it was dangerous. Insane. Only a crazy person would be willing to try it.

Good thing I was just crazy enough.

11

I stood before the basement door, my heart trying to punch through my chest. The sounds of happy voices, laughter, and music wafted through the opened kitchen window. The scent of wood burning tickled my nostrils. Light flared up in the darkness outside, and the bonfire's flames soared into the night sky, illuminating part of the vast grounds.

Through the window, a cluster of people danced by in colorful costumes. Their cloaks, robes, tunics of deep greens and blues and reds, and leather bodices looked like they were straight out of a medieval fair. The male and female witches cheered and laughed with drinks in their hands and crowns of yellow flowers on their heads.

I smiled. If my aunts' guests were already

dancing around the fire with their yellow flowers, it qualified as a winning party.

I turned my attention back to the basement door, but a knock pulled my attention back to the window.

Ruth waved at me from outside the open kitchen window. And yes, from what I could see, her face had two long streaks of yellow from rubbing that daisy earlier. She wore a sage-green dress with puffy sleeves adorned with daisies, lilies, and daffodils sewn into the dress. Above her head sat a pointy green hat, the rim decorated with the same flowers.

"Tessa. You have to come out! It's so much fun. Everyone's here. Oh. Paris and Harry want to meet you. They're witches from out of town. I told them all about you."

Super. "Maybe later."

Ruth lost a bit of her smile. "Are you okay?"

"I'm super. Just great."

Ruth clasped her hands together excitedly. "Some of us are going to get naked later and dance around the fire. Isn't it wonderful?"

Funny how Dolores had failed to mention that some of the witches might be flashing their birthday suits. Not sure how I felt about seeing my aunts or more of the witches here in Hollow Cove naked. Sometimes you just couldn't unsee certain things.

"Sure. You look great, by the way," I said, wanting

to steer the conversation away from potential nakedness.

Ruth's eyes lit up. "Thanks. I'm a flower witch tonight."

"Tessa?" My mother joined my aunt at the window. She wore a gown of midnight blue, complete with a tight bodice and lace around the edges. Her hair was piled on the top of her head in an intricate design of braids. Jewels touched her throat and ears, and her makeup was perfect. She looked beautiful. "What are you doing? Come out right now. You're being rude."

"Where's your flower necklace I made for you?" asked Ruth.

My mother rolled her eyes. "I'm not wearing that bug-infested nest around my neck."

I sighed. "Now look who's being rude."

My mother sighed louder. "No. You're still being rude. Come out right now and mingle with your guests."

I pulled my eyes away from the window. "This is like a bad dream."

"It *is* like a dream," cheered Ruth. "You just wait and see. And then after midnight, we're all going to Starry Pond for a skinny-dip."

When I turned back to the window, both Ruth and my mother had disappeared. I knew I'd better do this now before they came back. Or worse, dragged me to join the party.

Determined, I pulled the door open.

"What if this doesn't work?" I hadn't called on my father yet, not since my magic was taken away. I wasn't sure that I could still work that connection. Perhaps only witches could make the portal from Davenport House to the Netherworld work.

"One way to find out." I took a breath. "Dad? I need to speak with you."

I waited, my heart thumping just a little faster.

Two minutes passed with still no sign of my father.

"Dad? Are you there?"

Five minutes and nothing.

I rubbed my temples. Dread pinched my gut. This was it. I could no longer call out to my father. I stared out the kitchen window, wondering if I could ask Ruth to do it for me because I knew she wouldn't ask me any questions.

"Tessa?"

I flinched. My father was standing on the basement threshold. "Don't scare me like that."

"Why aren't you at the Beltane festivities?" My father wore a nice beige jacket with matching pants and a crisp white shirt. His gray hair and beard were both trimmed close to his fair skin. Immaculate as usual. His silver eyes gleamed with intensity, but anyone who knew him also saw mischief. It's where I got it from.

"It worked," I said, amazed.

"What worked?"

"Nothing. Um. Listen, I have something to ask you."

My father eyed me as he stepped into the kitchen. "Why do I get the feeling I'm going to hate it."

He was right, so I decided to go first with the easiest favor to ask. "I need—I would like you to catch Derrick and get him to give me back my magic." There. I'd said it. Now I only needed to wait.

"You do, do you?" My demon father let out a sigh as he leaned his back on the kitchen island, facing me. He pulled on the sleeves of his jacket. "It's not that simple."

"Tell me about it. I've tried."

Anger flashed in my father's eyes. "What are you not telling me?" And then he added with a louder voice. "What did you do?"

"Why would you say that?"

"Because you're my daughter, and I would have done something stupid too."

Right. I thought about ignoring that, but then my father had ways of finding out things, especially if it revolved around demons.

"I—we—Iris and I tried and failed to get Derrick to transfer back my powers."

My father stiffened. "You summoned the demon."

"We did."

His eyes rolled over me like he was looking for injuries. They settled around my face. "He gave you those bruises?"

My lips parted. "I thought I'd covered them well enough. No. That wasn't him. That was Allison."

"Allison? What does she have to do with Derrick?"

"Nothing. That was before I summoned him. Well, Iris did." My chest ached at the memory of Iris's limp body in Derrick's grip. Her bleach-white face drained of her life force.

"He could have killed you," said my father, his voice taking on a dangerous edge. "You were stupid but apparently very lucky that he didn't harm you. Which I find disturbing. He would have been able to kill you, but he didn't."

"It was Iris." My throat was dry. "He hurt her. She's in some sort of magical coma. I don't know what else to call it. She's at the Full Moon Medical Center." I relayed the events to him, the part where we had to let the incubus go if we didn't want Iris to die. All of it.

My father's features softened at the mention of

Iris. "I'm sorry about your friend. That should have never happened. You should have never summoned Derrick. Why would you put your lives in danger?"

I threw up my hands in frustration. "Because I wanted my magic back. Yes, it was stupid. I hate it when I do stupid things and don't realize it. I like being aware of my stupidity. But there it is. We should have talked to you or my aunts, but we didn't. We thought we had him. We were wrong. I was wrong."

Silence descended upon the kitchen, broken by the continuous and infectious laughter and happy screams from the backyard. My aunts knew how to throw a party.

My father's silver gaze bore into mine. "And because your plan didn't work... you're moving to Plan B. Me."

"Exactly."

"I'm sorry, Tessa," said my father. "But this incubus is in Lucifer's favor."

I shrugged, feeling agitated. "Which means what, exactly?"

"He's untouchable. He's not just some regular demon. Even if I wanted to, I couldn't get near him. Just like I couldn't get near Lucifer. There's no way I could get close enough to even try to transfer back your magic. I'm not familiar with their magical transference, but I'm assuming I would need a spell.

And I would need you both in the same place for it to work, I believe. The same way he took your magic. So, I'm afraid it is impossible. I can't get to him."

"Well, there goes that plan." I rubbed my eyes in frustration and tiredness. It was the kind of tired that weeks of sleep wouldn't cure.

"I hate to say it…"

"Then don't."

My father sighed his frustration through his nose. "You were happy once without magic. Can't you try to be happy without it again?"

I pressed my hands to my hips. "What if this was you? Would you just give up the idea of ever having your demon mojo again? You'd lose Mom. You'd lose me since I doubt you'd be able to"—I made finger quotes—"cross over here anymore."

My father scratched his beard, and his silver eyes filled with sorrow. "There's nothing to be done."

"Yes, there is." I swallowed and moved closer until we stood face-to-face. My heart thrashed as I said, "A blood transfusion. A blood transfusion will give me my demon mojo back."

He'd done it once, and it had awakened my demon mojo. A second time could maybe be enough to boost my body with some magic. Hell, I'd take it even if I couldn't do elemental magic anymore. It was something.

Obiryn straightened, his face darkening a shade. "Absolutely not."

"It can work."

"No." My father's voice was rough and cut through me.

"What do you mean *no*? Don't you want me to be able to visit you again? With my demon magic back, I could have some magical abilities. I could keep my post as a Merlin. I could defend myself." *I could kick Allison's ass.* "No one would have to know it was demon magic."

"No," my father repeated, and his tone was one of absolute authority.

I threw my hands up in the air, frustrated. "What is the problem? You've done it before, and it worked. Really well, remember? It jump-started my demon magic."

"That was a one-time thing." My father rubbed his eyes, looking tired all of a sudden. "This time it's different. When I performed the transfusion, you already had magic essence in you. It was still a dangerous procedure, but I knew it was the only thing to save your life. This time it's not the same. You're not in danger of dying. Quite the opposite."

"Because I don't have an ounce of magic to my name." It made sense, but that didn't mean I liked it or accepted it.

My father nodded. "You're like a human, a nonmagical being."

"So it's going to hurt?" I guessed and saw the slight widening of his eyes. I knew it was true. "So what? I don't care how much it hurts. I want to do it. I want some part of me back."

My father was shaking his head, a deep frown on his face. "No. You don't understand."

"I understand pain. I can handle it. Trust me. If I can have my demon mojo back, I'll take the pain with a damn smile." The pain would only last for a little while during the transfusion, most probably. And then I would have my demon magic again. That brought a smile to my face.

My father's face lost all expression, and then his eyes narrowed. "Listen to me. If I tried to perform the transfusion on you now... it would kill you."

My tiny, elated bubble burst. "Great." I swallowed the bile that made my throat burn. "Are you sure? I mean, maybe you're wrong."

"My demon blood, the magic, will be like transferring acid into your bloodstream. Even if you are my biological daughter, it won't make a difference. Without your magic, my blood will act as a foreign entity. You'll be in excruciating pain right before you die."

I gave a mock smile. "Sounds like fun."

My father's shoes scuffed the floor as he changed

position, resting his hands on the counter behind him. "I'm sorry I don't have better news."

"Bad news seems to be my lot in life." I let out a sigh, my brilliant plan suddenly feeling foolish. I'd been really hoping the transfusion would have given me at least my demon magic back. I would have taken it like a shot.

So what was I going to do now? Plan A failed, and now Plans B and C were utter disasters.

My father gave me a tight, worried smile. "Better to be a nonmagical than dead. Life as a human... think of the possibilities. Being mundane does have its perks."

I laughed. My father laughed. It turned to a hard laugh, the ones where the situation isn't that funny but for reasons unknown, you just can't stop laughing until the tears start to come and your stomach muscles are cramping.

I wiped my eyes. "I'm hopeless."

"You're my daughter." My father's silver eyes met mine. "Let me see what I can do about Derrick."

My heart leaped in my throat. "But I thought you said he was untouchable?"

"He is," answered my father. "He is. But sometimes, these untouchables make mistakes. I'll let you know if I discover anything."

My father's voice was sincere, but I could tell he

didn't believe what he was saying. It was obvious. Derrick was gone.

"Obiryn!" My mother's face appeared in the kitchen window. "I thought you weren't interested."

My father's mouth fell open. "Ah... well... "

"Wait here. I'm coming inside," instructed my mother. "We can celebrate inside together."

My demon father beamed. "I love a woman who orders me around."

Okay, time for me to go. "I'll see you guys later."

"Tessa? Aren't you joining us?" my mother called as she came through the back door.

Never in a million years. "Maybe later. I've got some stuff to do."

I turned and left the kitchen to head upstairs. Hearing my mother giggling brought a smile to my face again. But only briefly.

Funny how when your life is going so well it can shift suddenly and go incredibly badly.

No more magic. And maybe no more Marcus.

A rush of tremendous weight pulled at my chest, making it harder and harder to breathe. I was having a panic attack, or I was seriously out of shape.

Every time I thought of Marcus, of his lush lips, his glorious body, and his big arms wrapped around me, I felt a squeeze around my heart like something had a hold of it inside my chest and was crushing it.

I'd never felt such a strong connection to a man

before. It was as though we were part of the same creature, bonded, mated. And I also felt him slipping away from me. I'd been focusing on getting my magic back so I wouldn't think about the wereape because I knew if I did, I would break down in a slobbery mess.

The idea of not being with Marcus again shook me to my core.

When I reached the top platform, my legs felt like they were on fire. I pushed open my door.

My breath caught.

Not because I was out of breath hauling my ass up all those steps but because a man stood in my bedroom. A stranger.

Beneath his tight-fitting white shirt and gray jacket, he harbored muscles like he bench-pressed buses all day. He was built like Marcus. Large shoulders tapered down to trim hips. A pair of snug gray pants revealed thick, muscular thighs.

The stranger was jaw-droppingly gorgeous— perfect even, in the way that seemed odd. He was just too damn beautiful, and staring at him was burning my retinas. His blond hair was shaved at the sides and pulled back into a long braid. A sigil tattoo marked the right side of his neck, and I could see the curves of some tribal design flickering out from the neckline of his shirt and the back of his right hand before vanishing up under the sleeves of his jacket.

He looked like a freaking Viking—a very hot, freaking Viking in an expensive business suit. I guessed his height at about six-seven or taller.

And where Marcus's skin had that golden tan and was marked with scars from past battles and fights, this guy's skin was pale porcelain and perfect. Either he'd never fought a day in his life, had others fight for him, or healed to perfection.

His eyes were the dark blue of a sky before a storm, and he watched me with a cold intensity, calculating and vicious. I'd faced enough challenges and fought against plenty of evil bastards to recognize danger. This guy was a predator.

Ripples of magic pulsed in my room and around me, rolling off him in potent waves. A very pretty and powerful predator.

Everything in me told me to run like my ass was on fire, but my legs wouldn't move.

And though I'd never met him or even heard what he looked like, I knew with all certainty I was staring at Lucifer.

Holy hell's bells.

12

L ucifer, the king of hell, was in my bedroom.

I had enough experience with a certain goddess to know that deities could come and go as they pleased. Even Davenport House couldn't keep them out, though Dolores had tried her damnedest. Apparently, gods and goddesses had free rein. Swell.

"Lu... Lu... Lululu...Lululemon." Damn, there I went again with the verbal diarrhea. Try formulating cohesive words when the king of hell pops by for a visit. For some strange reason, I'd always pictured Lucifer as dark—dark hair, dark eyes, dark skin, never as some fair-skinned Viking. His skin was so light, it was practically luminescent.

The Viking-looking god cracked a smile. "I'd been wondering what you'd look like. Prettier than

I'd expected. Much prettier." His voice was deep and articulate, filled with confidence and power.

I could see how and why Lilith had fallen for him. He was quite the charmer and a looker.

I licked my lips and tried again. "Lucifer. You're Lucifer." I'd already established that, but I wanted to be sure.

He blinked. His eyes burned with cold blue power. "Yes," he said, and I shifted nervously. "And you're Tessa Davenport. And you live here in this house with your three aunts."

I frowned. My heart banged against my ribs. It was making my head spin. I steadied myself as I tried to wrap my brain around what was actually happening.

The king of the Netherworld was in my bedroom. I should have been scared. I should have fainted. I should have run away screaming like a banshee. I should have crapped my pants, but I didn't.

I was ticked. Livid. I didn't feel fear. I felt rage. Good ol' rage and a hell of a lot of adrenaline. Add an ounce of stupid, and you had a crazy lady who wasn't afraid of the king of hell.

Insanely handsome and powerful or not, *he* was the reason why I couldn't do magic. He was the reason Iris was lying in a coma in some bed far away from her friends and family. He was the reason I lost my Merlin license. He wasn't the reason Marcus was still in New York City fighting wereapes, but I blamed him anyway. Yeah. And it felt awesome.

"Here to finish the job?" I snapped and dared to take a few steps into my room. No way was I showing this guy anything but disdain and some attitude. If I was about to die tonight, so be it. I wouldn't cower, and I would go on my terms.

Lucifer's eyebrows joined in the middle. "I'm sorry?"

I seethed. The bastard had the nerve to look confused. "What do you want? You've already taken everything from me. Here to kill me? Is that it? I don't have any magic anymore, so you've got nothing to fear from me. If I did, I'd blast your ass out of my bedroom." This was not the way to speak to a god, but I didn't care.

Lucifer frowned at me and tilted his head. "Are you quite all right? You sound a little bit unbalanced."

"A tiny nervous breakdown can work wonders for a girl."

Lucifer's smile turned dazzling. "I can see why my wife was drawn to you."

"Because I'm great fun, Luce."

The god watched me for a beat. "You're not afraid of me. You're... angry with me." He looked rather pleased with this information, which only fueled my anger further.

"Yeah, I'm angry. What do you expect? Congratulations."

"Congratulations?"

"Congratulations on ruining my life." My voice rose an octave with my sharp temper. I was losing it. I knew there was a possibility that Lucifer was indeed here to kill me and would after the way I was speaking to him, but I couldn't stop myself. The weeks of emotions rattling my core and my body were all coming out. And it was going to hit Lucifer.

Movements agile and athletic, he walked around my room with a purposeful gait, inspecting my desk, my bed, and my bathroom, his shoulders back and confident.

He walked back and ran a finger over my desk. "Strange what humans find comfortable. This house. This room. These things."

"Why? Because there's no torturing involved?"

"My wife's been here several times. Hasn't she?" Lucifer stared at me from across the room.

The thing with deities that I was quickly learning was that they could spot a lie. I was a terrible liar. If I tried to lie now, he could just as easily snap his fingers, and my life was toast. I wasn't ready to die just yet.

"Yes," I answered, not looking away from his

stormy gaze. "She's been here a few times. And only when she wants something." I didn't want to give him too much information about Lilith. This guy had tricked her and trapped her for over a thousand years. He might have the smile and the looks of an angel, but the guy was evil to the core.

But it also made me realize that maybe he wasn't only here for me. He was here for Lilith too.

"Hmmm." Lucifer grabbed the chair I used at my desk, spun it around, and sat.

"What are you doing?" That chair was way too small for such a big man, god, whatever.

The god leaned his forearms on the chair's top rail. "Sitting," he answered with a sexy smile that would have sent the ladies into a mad frenzy, pulling off their clothes and throwing themselves at him.

Not this lady.

I flicked a finger at him. "You break it. You buy it."

Lucifer laughed, and just like Lilith, it was strangely natural. It was irritating as hell. "Fine. If I break it, I'll get you a new chair."

My body shook as I crossed my arms over my chest to hide my trembling hands. I fisted them, my nails biting into the flesh of my palms. From what my father had told me, Lucifer was more of a reclusive sort of leader, so not many of his people, demons, had even met him. Yet here he was, in my bedroom.

I wonder what my aunts would think if they found him in my room.

A peel of laughter came from somewhere outside. It sounded strangely like Beverly's, followed by a throaty male growl.

Lucifer's mouth twitched. "Strange customs you witches have. Parading naked around a fire. It's very... peasant-like. Don't you think? Even savage."

If some of the witches were already naked, it was a hell of a party. "Listen here, you... god-you," I said, feeling both brave and stupid—a dangerous combination. "If my family wants to run around a bonfire naked because it makes them feel good, that's their business. Who the hell are you to judge?"

Lucifer splayed his hands. "The king of hell."

Oh, yeah. "I don't care who you are. Tell me what you want, or get out of my room."

Lucifer's expression pulled into a hateful mask as his eyes focused on me. They blazed a ripple of blues. He flicked a finger, and an invisible force wrenched my body rigid until I couldn't move. Oh, shit. The king of hell had turned me to stone.

I felt the influence of his mind, his will, slide past my guards and into me. I struggled, trying to fight it, but it was like trying to break through iron chains. I couldn't do anything. I stood vulnerably against the hardness of his power, an invisible prison. Yup. He got me.

Then, I felt a sudden release, and I could move again. My breath came in with a ragged gasp as his power lifted from me. Okay, so he was powerful and could kill me with a flick of his finger. I'd have to watch my big mouth around him.

"I've killed those who've disrespected me, for much less, Tessa Davenport," said the king of hell. "But I need something from you."

I blinked. He wanted something from me after he'd taken nearly everything? The nerve of that god.

So I did what any sensible nonmagical woman would do.

I gave him the finger.

"I don't think so. You've already taken everything. What else could you possibly want? My blood? My bones? My flesh? It's really not that spectacular." According to Allison.

I didn't care what he wanted. He wasn't getting it. This time, he would have to kill me.

The god's eyes came to me. "You've spent time with my wife. You've exchanged conversations, maybe even laughter. Don't kid yourself. Lilith is not your friend." The muscles around his jaw tightened. "Lilith has no friends."

"That's on you," I told him.

"She's unstable," he continued as though I hadn't

spoken. "She's mad and unpredictable. She's a danger to herself and to others."

"Keeping your wife locked up for years because she was liked more than you would do that to a person." I swallowed. The words just kept flying out of my mouth before I could stop myself. What could I say? He was ticking me off. "You didn't love her anymore, so you thought, what... lock her up and throw away the key because you found her voice annoying?" When he didn't answer, I pressed, "Do you love her?"

He just blinked. I saw no love there, but then again, he was a god. Who knew how they showed that kind of emotion. Maybe they didn't. Maybe it was beneath them.

I still didn't get why he was here. If he wanted me dead, he would have killed me by now, or he'd have sent one of his minions to do it.

The storm behind his eyes stilled, and it scared the crap out of me. "Where is she?" asked Lucifer.

Ah-ha. He wanted Lilith. "No idea. It's not like I keep tabs on her. She is a goddess."

"I know she keeps an apartment in New York City," continued the god of night, just as I thought about it. "I've just returned from there. She's not there. And it doesn't look like she's planning to come back. Her clothes were gone." His eyes bore into mine. "Where is she?"

"I. Don't. Know." I smiled inwardly. I was glad Lilith had escaped this bastard. It appeared she still had friends on the "other side" who were looking out for her and had given her a heads-up that Lucifer had found her out. What he did to her was horrible. No husband should ever do that to his wife. I was beginning to think Lucifer was the unstable one, not Lilith. I prayed he'd never find her.

Run, Lilith. Run...

Lucifer hefted his tall frame out of the chair, stood up, and placed the chair expertly back to where it had been at my desk. With his behind leaning on the edge of my desk, he crossed his arms over his chest, the fabric pulling as it tried to contain all that muscle.

"She likes you," said the god.

I grinned. "I'm a likable person."

"I feel her here. Her imprint is everywhere in this house."

That's because she built it back for us, you evil bastard. But he didn't have to know.

Lucifer's jaw clenched, and I saw turmoil in his eyes combined with anger and frustration. "She doesn't trust me."

"I could have told you that."

His sudden silence made me uneasy, and I stifled a shiver. "I'll give you until midnight tomorrow," said Lucifer finally, his blue eyes burning with an icy power that made my bowels watery. "Not because I particularly like you, you understand. I simply cannot find her, so you're going to find her for me. Bring her to the corner of Spirit Lane and Crystal Row. And then I will give you back what I took from you."

My arms fell to my sides just as my mouth fell open. "What?" I asked, like a simpleton, my pulse hammering in my ears. "I don't believe you. Why should I believe you?"

It couldn't be true. Could it? Was he saying what I thought he was saying?

"I'm not here to give you lies. I came here to make a deal. It's simple," said Lucifer. "You bring me my wife... and I'll give you back your magic."

Well, son of a damnit.

13

You bring me my wife... and I'll give you back your magic.

I stared at the spot where the king of hell had just vanished into thin air, leaving me with my mouth open wide enough to stick a fist in. One second he was standing in my room, all imposing and Viking godlike, and the next, he was gone.

I wouldn't lie to myself and say this was not the answer to all of my problems, because it was. It really was.

But I had just one problem. A huge goddess-sized problem. Lilith. I had to betray Lilith to get my magic back. Damn. Damn. Damn.

A flash of cold went through me. Was I that kind of person? Would I sacrifice someone's freedom to benefit myself? For my magic? Would I knowingly give Lilith to the husband who'd trapped her for years, knowing he was going to do the same to her or even worse? I hadn't felt or seen any love or any kind of emotion that indicated Lucifer had any affection for his wife. If Lucifer got his hands on Lilith again, I had the horrible feeling he might not take the chance of putting her in a cell again, leaving her the possibility of escape. No. He was going to kill her.

But I'd get my magic back. I'd get my life back. I could be a Merlin again, use the ley lines, my favorite means of transport, and visit my father in the Netherworld. It was what I wanted.

And all I had to do was betray Lilith.

"Tessa?"

"Ah!" I screamed and spun around, my hands out in karate chops. No judging. I had to work with what I had. I lowered my hands. "Iris?"

My friend and favorite Dark witch stepped into my bedroom, her silky dark, chin-length hair swaying. Her large brown eyes were lit with life and curiosity. Her skin was a lovely warm ivory color, not the bleach-white from when I'd last seen it. She looked... she looked good. She looked healthy.

"Sorry I scared you," she said, a smile blossoming over her pixie-like face. "Why are you so tense? You were just standing there, staring into space. You were miles away. What's up? What did I miss?"

My eyes burned, and I blinked fast. The next thing I knew, I'd crossed the room and hugged her, which said a lot since I wasn't the hugging type. I pulled back. "You look good. You look great. How do you feel? When did they release you?" I cringed at my own use of those words. It made her sound like she'd been in jail.

"This afternoon," said Iris. "Ronin got us some plane tickets."

I looked over her shoulder. My half-vampire friend stood in the doorway, his hands clasped behind his back. The guilt on his face was nearly palpable. Good, maybe I could slap it.

"I bring gifts," he said, analyzing my mood as he walked in with a sheepish grin on his handsome face. At least he was talking to me without baring his teeth. That was an improvement. From his back, he pulled out a bottle of red wine.

I took the wine, well, because it was wine. I glanced at the label. It had a red castle etched on the sticker with the words Château Cos d'Estournel. It was French, and seeing as I'd never heard of this wine, it was most probably expensive and not from the sales rack. I could never afford it.

"Thanks." I stared at Ronin, enjoying seeing him squirm a little. "Was it expensive?"

He pursed his lips and nodded. "A car payment."

"Good." I laughed. He laughed harder. And just

like that, all was forgiven. And I had a very expensive bottle of wine. Winner winner, chicken dinner.

I cradled my expensive wine and carefully set it on my desk before I dropped it, knowing myself. I turned and looked at Iris's face. A mix of fear and guilt hit hard. "I'm so sorry, Iris. If I had known we couldn't bind Derrick to the triangle, I would have never asked you to summon him. I didn't know."

Iris put up her hand. "It's not your fault. I was the one summoning him, not you. Besides, I really thought it was going to work. I was sure of it. I thought I knew what I was doing. Clearly not."

I shook my head. "We should have involved my aunts."

"Maybe. But it's over now. Besides, I feel fine. My magic is fine. He didn't take my magic, like yours, more like my life force, my energy. Like I had the worst cold in the century. He didn't finish the 'kiss' or whatever it's called. The center was able to reverse the demon spell and replenish my strength." She glanced at the half-vampire. "Ronin was there the whole time." The two shared a look that had adoration written all over the half-vampire's face.

"You two are so damn cute. I might puke." I smiled, happy to see how strong their relationship was. "Why didn't you call? I would have come to pick you up. Granted, it would have been longer than a plane ride, but I would have done it anyway."

Iris set her bag down. "I know. But when Ronin suggested we fly home first class, well, I couldn't resist. A girl likes to be pampered from time to time."

"Indeed, she does." I stared at the bottle of wine, thinking that he and I were about to share some quality time.

The half-vampire smiled with half his mouth. "It's always first class for my girl. She deserves the best. And only the best. Good thing that's what I am. The best in *everything*."

Iris's face started to blotch at the purr in his voice, and she turned to me, unable to calm the smile on her face. "So?"

"So?"

Iris gave me a look, a question high on her expression. "So? What's going on?"

I glanced over to my window. "It's Beltane. You know how my aunts like to put on a show. Go big or go home, right?"

"No, I mean, what's going on with *you*? You were in a trance or something when we came in just now. You looked freaked, like something had just happened. Does it have to do with Derrick? Ronin mentioned that he'd escaped through a Rift. Did he come back? Was he here?"

"No." I sighed and looked at them both. "But I did ask my father for help. He can't get ahold of Derrick. Apparently, he's like some untouchable demon or something. So I asked him to do a blood transfusion to get my magic back." At Iris's worried face, I added, "He won't do it because, apparently, it would kill me. Now that I'm human."

"You're *not* human," corrected the Dark witch. "Just a witch who's lost her powers."

"Which kinda makes her a human," said Ronin, winning a scowl from Iris.

"But that's not what had me in a state." I waited to get their complete attention. I took a deep breath, let it out, and said, "Lucifer was just here."

They both just stared at me, wide-eyed. Silence soaked in, broken by sudden outbursts of laughter from outside. It sounded surprisingly like Dolores.

"Did you hear me?" I prompted when the silence stretched. "I said Lucifer was just here. You know, the king of hell? He was in my room. Right here. Talking to me like you are now."

Iris blinked, thoughts shimmering behind her eyes. "What did he look like? Was he hot?"

I burst out laughing, my nerves from before making their way now to the surface. Only Iris would ask that kind of question.

I cleared my throat. "He was very handsome. Like a Viking god in an Armani suit. Totally threw me off."

The Dark witch grinned. "I bet."

Ronin raked his fingers through his hair. "Wait.

Just wait a freaking minute. Are you saying the king of hell, the devil, the personification of evil, was here? In your room just now?"

"He was." When I said it out loud, it sounded crazy. I sounded crazy. But then again, his wife had visited me here more than once. My life was seriously complicated.

"I think I need to sit down." The half-vampire moved over to my desk and grabbed the same chair Lucifer had sat in, spun it around to face us, and sat.

I decided not to tell him that his ass was now touching the same spot Lucifer's ass had just been.

Iris moved closer and was rolling her eyes over me like she was inspecting me for any missing limbs and just anything out of place. "If he wanted to kill you, you'd be dead. He wanted something from you. Didn't he? What was it? He must have wanted something badly to show up like that. I've never even heard of Lucifer appearing in someone's room before. Very unusual."

"Abnormal." I took a breath. "But you're right. He did want something."

"What?" chorused Ronin and Iris.

"He said if I deliver his wife to him... he'd give me back my magic."

"No shit?" Ronin perked up. "Nice." He stretched out his long legs and crossed them at the ankle before leaning back in his chair. His hands interlaced on his chest, looking like this was the best news he'd heard all day.

But not Iris. She looked like she'd misused one of her ingredients in a spell. "What did you say?"

"Nothing," I answered. "I mean, I was in shock. I thought he'd come to finish the job. Get rid of all the evidence, or whatever." I stiffened, recalling the conversation with Lucifer. "I think I might have given him the finger. No, I know I did."

Iris stared at me with her mouth slightly open.

Ronin leaned forward in his chair. "You gave the king of hell the finger?"

I ran my hands through my hair, feeling suddenly ill. "I did. I really did."

"That was really ballsy, or maybe just crazy," laughed Iris. "I can't believe you did that."

"That makes two of us." It was a miracle I was still breathing. "He didn't kill me because he needs me. He needs me to find his wife."

"I need a drink." The half-vampire jumped out of his chair, grabbed the wine bottle, ripped off the seal, and with a taloned finger, stabbed the cork and yanked it out.

"Is this something he does a lot?"

Iris shook her head. "No. It's a first."

Ronin tossed his head back and took a mouthful of wine. "Mmmm. Fruity, but not too fruity. Perfect balance between alcohol and sweetness. I've got great taste in fine wines." He glanced over at Iris. "And fine women."

I laughed. I wasn't about to stop him from drinking the wine he'd gifted me. He'd paid for it.

Iris walked over to the edge of my bed and sat. "This is it. This is the answer to all your magical problems. And all you have to do is give him Lilith. Oh my God. It's perfect."

"Yes," I answered, that sick feeling returning. "I have to bring her to the corner of Spirit Lane and Crystal Row tomorrow at midnight."

"Damn, this is good wine," said Ronin as he took another sip.

Iris watched me a moment. "Why there?"

I shook my head. "No idea. That's just what he said."

The Dark witch gave me a look of part curiosity, part admiration. "You're hesitating. Why are you hesitating?"

My eyes flicked to Ronin. "Give me that bottle." I walked over to him and grabbed the wine bottle. The proper way to drink an expensive wine for the first time would probably require a glass. Good thing I didn't feel proper at the moment. I pressed the bottle to my lips and took a large gulp. I swirled it around my mouth for a moment, enjoying the explosive fruity taste. "Wow. This is the best wine I've ever had."

"It's even better after the second sip," informed Ronin.

"Tessa? Why don't you look happy about this?" pressed Iris. "You'd get your magic back. Isn't that the plan?"

I took another mouthful of the yummy wine. "It is. But what if he kills her?"

"She's not your problem." Ronin grabbed the wine bottle from me and took another swig. "I think it's a very good idea. The woman is nuts. It's her damn fault you lost your magic in the first place. You thought you were doing a good thing by releasing her. I get it. But the truth is, let Lucifer deal with her. You get rid of the crazy-ass goddess, and you get your powers back. It's an awesome idea."

"He's right." Iris gave me a tight smile. "You're dealing with deities. They don't care about you or me. They care about themselves. Lilith was never your friend, Tessa. She used you to escape her prison, and she was about to use you again to kill Lucifer. And who knows, you might have died trying to do her bidding."

"And she did say that if you refused, she'd kill you," added Ronin.

Lilith had since told me she couldn't or wouldn't kill me because of some connection I still didn't fully understand. But I decided to keep that to myself.

I grabbed the wine bottle from Ronin again and

took another mouthful. "I know. You're right." They were both right. Lucifer had handed me what I wanted most. My magic in exchange for his wife. So why did I feel like crap?

Iris leaned forward, her eyes wide. "You think he's lying. You think you'll bring him Lilith, and he won't hold his end of the deal? It's possible."

I shook my head, feeling the effects of that lovely wine. "No. I don't think he was lying." Strangely, I really did believe him. I knew if I gave him Lilith, he would be true to his word. Call it my witchy—non-witchy instincts. Call it a gut feeling.

"He's the only one who can truly give you back your magic," said Iris. "You know that. Right?"

"Yeah, I guess."

"And it must mean Derrick doesn't have it anymore," continued Iris, her brows knitted together as excitement flashed on her face. "Or maybe he'll have Derrick with him to do the transfer. Yeah. Maybe that's it."

I frowned at how it sounded like a bank transfer, moving money from one account to another. Maybe to Lucifer, that's exactly what it was, a simple moving of magic from one source to another.

But if Derrick didn't have my magic any longer, it meant I'd have to warn my father. I didn't want him wasting his time, or worse, putting himself in danger for magic that wasn't there anymore.

"You're going to go through with it. Right?" Iris was watching me.

I nodded. "I am." I sighed, not sounding at all convincing. "I'm going to do it," I added with more conviction. That expensive wine was churning in my stomach. Guilt hit, but I pressed it down. It's like Iris said, Lilith was not my friend. She'd put me in this situation, and now I was going to use her to get myself out of it.

"What does Marcus think of all this?" asked Iris, tugging a strand of hair behind her ear. My heart gave a little pang.

This time I took two large gulps of that wine. "He doesn't know. He's in New York City without a phone. I don't have any way to reach him." I gave them the short version of my trip to Central Park.

"The dude's always been an alpha in his own right," said Ronin. He grabbed the wine bottle from me and took a sip. "I mean... look at him. All that towering authority. He could command a fly to stay put. And he's got great hair."

Iris threw her head back and laughed. "He does have great hair. But seriously. You think he'll stay?" Her smile had gone. The worry in her tone made my chest squeeze a little.

My gaze fell to the floor. "Honestly? I'm not sure. But I don't want to stand in his way. I don't want to be *that* woman. This is a once-in-a-lifetime opportunity for him. Who am I to hold him back?"

"His *girlfriend*," the Dark witch pointed out, and she shot Ronin a daring look that said he better watch himself.

"Exactly. I'm not his wife. I don't control him. Not that a wife should control her husband, but you know what I mean."

Iris shook her head. "Don't worry. He won't accept. You said it yourself. He was only there to help out Teke."

"Zeke," I corrected.

"You know how he is," continued Iris. "He can never say no to helping out a friend. That's in his nature. To help and protect. That's our Marcus. That's why he's such a great chief."

"True." It was all true, but it didn't help squash that feeling of doubt. I'd been there. I'd seen that look of pride on his face, how the wereapes accepted him. That's what scared the crap out of me.

"But it also means he'd be the right choice for the alpha," I said, my mouth feeling dry all of a sudden. "He'd be perfect."

"Maybe." Iris shifted on my bed. "I still don't think he'd give up his life here to start a new one. I don't believe it."

I didn't answer. I had no answer because I wasn't sure.

"Think of it this way," said Ronin, grinning. "If he agrees, you'd be his alpha bitch."

"Ronin!" Iris tossed a pillow at him, but I started to laugh. I'd missed my friends. My insane plan of trapping Derrick had nearly cost Iris her life and my friendship with Ronin.

They were right. I had to do this. Even if I didn't like it, I would give Lilith over to Lucifer.

Only, how did one do that exactly?

"Enough with the long faces." A smile quirked the corner of Ronin's mouth. "I know exactly how to cheer you up." He hooked a thumb toward my window. "Come on, people," said Ronin with a devilish grin as he rubbed his hands together. "Let's go get naked."

14

To Ronin's disappointment, I did not get naked and join the festivities last night. Though I had left Iris and Ronin, so I didn't know and didn't ask if they had joined the merry nudist bonfire extravaganza.

I hadn't been in the partying mood. I was thrilled that Iris was back and healthy, with her magic intact, which was more than I could hope for. But my mood was dark and twisty. And the one person I wanted to talk to, the one person who was soothing with just his presence, wasn't here. Just hearing his voice would have helped, but I couldn't even speak to him on the phone.

Instead, I was left with a coldness in my heart, a small tear that kept expanding.

I pulled out the stool from the kitchen island

next to Iris and sat, my hands wrapped around a coffee mug and my thoughts muddled like my brain was full of cotton balls.

"I nearly had a heart attack when I saw you and Ronin last night," said Beverly, her face pristine and her makeup flawless. She did not look like someone who'd partied until the early morning hours, more like someone who just came back from a spa retreat for the weekend.

Iris looked over at me. "So did Tessa."

I took a sip of my coffee. "You did sneak up behind me."

"You healed so fast," said a cheery Ruth, whisking a bowl of sand-colored batter against her chest. Hildo sprawled lazily behind her on the counter next to the stove. "Those healers are truly the best in the country."

"*Our* healing abilities aided her speedy recovery," informed Dolores, the only one of the sisters whose eyes were puffy, her long face suggesting a few more hours in bed would have done wonders for her complexion. She pressed her hands onto the island, a pointed look on her face. "Without our quick thinking and superb spell and potion control, she might not be here today. She might be six feet under."

"Uh, o-kay," I said, glancing at Iris, who just gave me a shrug like it was no big deal.

"The healers at the Full Moon Medical Center," continued Dolores, "are your average reversers of magically induced ailments, dabblers of counter-curses and restorative magic practitioners. But *we* were the true saviors here. We are the magical champions."

My Aunt Dolores really did have a narcissistic side. I kept my mouth shut. I didn't want to ruin her moment.

"Yes, thank you all very much," said Iris, her face flushed as she shifted in her chair. Knowing her, she was probably more upset and embarrassed that her spell hadn't worked.

Dolores's dark eyes pinned me from across the island. "But you wouldn't have needed our help if you had only told us what the two of you were up to."

She also loved to rub it in.

"You look lovely, Beverly," I said, wanting to change the subject. "Going somewhere?"

Beverly's green eyes narrowed. "Lovely? Lovely is a word used on the unattractive female to spare her feelings." She glanced down at her white blouse and undid one of the top buttons so her cleavage was more exposed. "Is that better? I was going for more of a desperate, ravishing woman who only wants her sexual desires to be fulfilled."

"Yes," answered Dolores. "You definitely look like a tramp."

"Roderick Walsh is taking me to lunch." Beverly pulled her compact from her purse and checked her makeup. "He owns the biggest mall in Cape Elizabeth, and he's recently divorced. His ex-wife took half of everything. Poor baby. We all know newly divorced men feel inadequate, impotent, and undesirable. I'm here to change that."

"Why don't you try going naked with a bow on your head?" said Ruth. "That says desperate."

Beverly grinned. "Maybe I will." She giggled. "Thanks, Ruth."

"You're welcome." Ruth poured some of that batter into a frying pan. The smell of butter soared into my nose, making my mouth water. "Iris? Have you decided what you want for your special dinner tonight?"

Iris looked at me before answering. "You really don't have to. It's no big deal. I'm fine."

Ruth spun around with a can-do expression and a pink spatula in her hand, sending globs of batter all over the kitchen floor. "Of course we do. This is your special welcome-home dinner. Everyone gets their own special dinner. Now it's your turn."

The Dark witch stared down at her coffee mug. "Well. Okay. How about your famous veggie lasagna?" She looked at me. "I'm feeling a little carbohydrate deficient."

I laughed. "I need carbs like I need blood."

Iris smiled. "Me too."

Ruth lifted her chin importantly. "Consider it done!" She whirled back around and smacked Hildo's paw that was dipped low into the batter bowl.

Beverly clamped her compact shut, her eyes on me. "Have you heard from Marcus?"

My stomach rolled as I felt all eyes turn to me. Since we'd been officially a couple, we hadn't been this long apart from each other before, at least not without any news or a simple phone call.

I shook my head, feeling ill again. "No. Nothing yet." I moved my butt around on my stool, trying to get comfortable, but it was useless. "I don't want to talk about it." If I did, I'd lose it. And right now, I needed to focus. Focus on me. Focus on how the hell I was going to get Lilith to appear and then bring her to the designated spot. Yeah. No biggie.

Beverly stared at me. "That's not good, darling. Keeping all those nasty feelings inside will give you premature wrinkles. And once they start, you can't take them back. Just look at your Aunt Dolores."

Dolores frowned and pressed a hand over her hip. "Excuse me?"

Beverly glanced at her sister and then back at me. "See?" she said knowingly.

Iris leaned over and whispered, "Do they know about the thing?"

I shook my head, knowing exactly what she meant since we'd talked about it last night before I left her and Ronin to join the festivities.

"What thing?" asked Dolores, obviously having heard. I'd swear the witch had werewolf hearing.

I leaned back in my chair. Learning from my past mistakes, I decided to come clean with my aunts. "Lucifer was in my bedroom last night."

Beverly smiled, her face taking on a sexy edge as she leaned on the island. "Is that what you call your vibrator? I like to give them nicknames too: gives a sense of adventure mixed with the excitement."

Okay, not the response I'd been expecting.

I cleared my throat. When I had the undivided attention of my three aunts, I repeated, "The *real* Lucifer, as in the king of hell? The harbinger of Darkness? Lord of the night? Well, he paid me a visit last night." I sat and watched their stunned silence and frozen postures. Only Hildo was moving, his tail flicking back and forth like the ticking of a bomb.

"Lucifer in our home!" Dolores clutched at her chest. "My chest feels tight. I can't breathe. I think I'm having a panic attack."

Ruth patted her shoulder. "Don't worry. It's just gas. I get that all the time."

I rubbed my temples, feeling a migraine on the way.

"And you're sure it was Lucifer? The real Lucifer?" Beverly was watching me like maybe this was something I had made up or possibly dreamed of.

"I'm sure. It was him."

Dolores frowned, thinking it over. "Well... what did he want? I mean, he must have wanted something. A god doesn't simply show up in one's home to compliment them on their furniture."

I leaned back. "Oh, he wanted something all right."

Beverly let out a screech and grabbed the counter for support.

"Not *that*," I told her. "He wants his wife. He told me if I bring him Lilith, he'll give me back my magic." My three aunts stared at me like I was too dense to function. "Did you hear me?"

"Yes, yes, we *heard* you." Dolores pressed both fists against her hips. "I'm glad you decided to tell us. And from Iris's unruffled expression, I'm guessing you told her first?"

"She told me last night," answered Iris. "When I came home with Ronin."

Dolores shook her head. "This is bad, Tessa.

Whenever gods are involved with us mortals, it never goes well for the mortal. We're nothing to them. We're like their playthings."

"I get that."

My tall aunt leveled me a look. "Why you? Why does he want you involved?"

"My guess is because he has no idea where she is and how to get her. She's not stupid. And I think she has friends helping her, tipping her off when Lucifer is close."

"Oh. Maybe he wants her back." Ruth's face grew into a smile.

I looked at my tiny aunt. "Not in that way, he doesn't. I have a feeling he wants to put her back in her cage... or worse." Definitely worse, but I wasn't about to say it at the looks of horror mirrored on my aunts' faces.

"And you would do this?" Ruth was looking at me with sadness in her eyes. "After what she did for us? For Davenport House? For your mom and dad?"

Oh boy. I knew it was coming. I knew how fond they were of Lilith. Even I had been fond of her at times. The goddess had surprised me more than once with her generosity, even though she was crazy and had threatened to end my life more than once. I opened my mouth to answer, but Dolores cut in.

"It's the only way she'll get her magic back," said Dolores with a pious sigh. "I don't like it either. But I think we'd all agree that we'd do the same if this was any of us. Tessa is a witch by birth. She's not meant to be a human. Ordinary. Dull."

"Thanks."

Beverly nodded her head. "Lilith was going to try and kill her husband and was going to use Tessa to do it. And Lucifer wouldn't have had that *incubus* bastard," she added with a growl, "take her magic, if it wasn't for Lilith. She's gorgeous and has great style, but this is her fault. Why should Tessa live like a dud when she could be magical again?"

"That's what I said," added the Dark witch.

Ruth wasn't talking. Her face was pinched tightly. It did that when she was thinking. I could see in her eyes that she was against the idea once she realized Lucifer didn't want his wife back for a second honeymoon. He wanted her back to end her.

"I'll need all the help I can get." I took a breath, seeing Ruth turn back around. She moved her spatula and flipped one of her famous buttermilk pancakes. "The thing is... how do I *bring* Lilith to me? How do I summon her? She's always just appeared in my room or made me appear wherever *she* wanted. Without my magic, I can't do much." I laughed sourly. "Let's face it. I can't do anything without my magic. And that's where I hope you'll come in." I didn't think Lucifer would have asked me if he thought I couldn't do it. He must have known

I'd figure it out somehow. Just the right amount of desperation could make people do incredible things. Stupid things too.

"We'll help you," said Dolores, her expression set in determination when she met my eyes.

"Of course we will." Beverly seemed to have noticed Ruth with her back to us. "Right, Ruth? Ruth?"

"Mmmm?"

Dolores gave her shorter sister a frown. "When is the exchange supposed to happen?"

"Tonight at midnight," I answered, my insides squeezing with anxiety. "I'm supposed to bring her to the corner of Spirit Lane and Crystal Row. No idea why. But that's what he said." It might sound like a lot of time, but it wasn't. Not when you had to figure out a way to summon a goddess and then trick her into following you to that special place where Lucifer would be waiting for her.

Dolores pressed a finger to her lips in thought. "Well, I've never done it myself, but I'm sure we can find a spell that will summon a goddess to us. Unfortunately, I don't have the spell that the Sisters of the Circle used to free Lilith from her confinement. Not that it would work in this case, seeing as it was more of a liberation than a regular summoning. We need something else." She took a breath and said, "There must be more than one idiot in this world who's tried to summon a god before. The world is full of idiots."

"That would be Harriette Clutterbuck," said Ruth over her shoulder as she flipped another pancake. "She summoned the pagan goddess of motherhood and childbirth, Akna, to help her get pregnant. She and her husband had been trying for years, but she could never get pregnant."

This was good news. I leaned forward. "What happened?"

Ruth's shoulders shrugged. "She ate her."

"Right."

Dolores crossed her arms but kept her finger tapping her lips. "Why there? Why did Lucifer ask for that specific location?"

Good question. "My guess is because it's set up to trap her or something. Whatever he needs to bind her, well, that place is rigged already or will be." Which was the only thing that made sense.

"It's a crossroads," said Dolores after a moment. "A space between worlds where supernatural events can take place. It'll be easier for him to set his trap."

Ruth was smacking the spatula on her pancakes unnecessarily hard.

"That makes sense." I'd heard of the word crossroads before. I just never truly understood what it meant in the paranormal world.

"Lilith is not stupid," Dolores continued. "Unhinged, maybe. But definitely not stupid."

"I know that."

"How do you plan on making her follow you there?"

Another good question. I took a sip of my now-cold coffee and grimaced. "I've thought about it all night. The only thing I can come up with is... I'll have to pretend to have a problem that only Lilith can solve. Make her feel important, special. She likes that."

Dolores nodded. "Good. Yes. That might actually work. Make her feel needed. Everyone loves to be needed."

Ruth was now stabbing the pancakes with her spatula. Hildo had backed up to press against the wall, looking at her as though he thought she was about to use him next as a hammer.

Iris pulled her eyes away from Ruth's pancake assault. "What's this thing you'll need her to solve? What's the problem?"

"I haven't thought that far out yet. Something that has to do with my not having magic anymore." It was a low blow, but I'd seen the guilt on the goddess's face. And she *should* feel guilty. I was reduced to a dud because of her. I knew then it was the only thing that would work on her. Her guilt. Guilt her to help me.

Yeah, I was an asshole.

Beverly leaned a hip against the kitchen island. "Yes. Make her feel guilty. Guilt always works for me with a man. I guilt them into buying me jewelry all the time."

"How do you manage that?" asked Dolores.

"I tell them they won't get any sex," she answered in a matter-of-fact way, like this was a totally normal thing to do.

Dolores cocked a brow. "That's blackmail."

Beverly giggled. "No. That's being smart."

Dolores swung her long, gray braid behind her back. "I'll get started going over my library. Beverly, you can help me. It'll go faster. I'm sure we'll find something in there on how to summon a goddess. Cauldron help us all if it goes wrong."

She had a point. If Lilith suspected anything amiss with us, or me, we were all dead.

"If she sees all of us, won't she suspect something?" asked Iris.

I pushed my cold cup of coffee to the side. "No. I think it'll just reinforce the fact that I can't do magic and that I need my aunts' and my friend's help to do things. Even just to summon her."

"I'll cancel my date with Roderick," said Beverly.

"I'm sorry, Beverly," I told her, though she didn't look disappointed.

Beverly waved a dismissive hand at me. "Don't

be. The longer they wait, the better the sex. Am I right?"

"Uh... sure."

Dolores turned to Ruth. "I'll let you know what I need in terms of potions, Ruth. Ruth? Are you listening?"

"Yup. Sure." Ruth spun around, a pan and spatula in her hand, and dumped what Iris and me were hoping was our golden pancakes: two hard, blackened round shapes fell onto our plates that looked like tar.

I'd never heard of Ruth burning anything ever, not even toast. Because Ruth never burned anything. That was an unspoken rule.

Not meeting my eyes, Ruth moved to the sink and dumped the frying pan. Steam rose as she turned on the tap.

"Don't worry about her," soothed Beverly, staring at our pancakes like they were blood pudding. "She'll come around. She's just upset because she really likes Lilith. I mean, we all do, but we have to think of the bigger picture here." Her lips pressed into a thin line, and her eyes held a trace of sadness. "And let's not forget she was the main reason why her husband took away your powers."

At that moment, Dolores's shoulders tensed, and I knew part of her wasn't enjoying plotting a way to trick Lilith and ultimately hand her over to her husband. They were all uncomfortable with the idea, maybe even hated it, but they were still going to see it through. They were doing this for me.

Guilt gnawed at my insides for getting them involved, but what choice did I have? I needed help. My aunts were the most capable witches I knew. If anyone could summon a goddess without making it look suspicious, they could.

Maybe, just maybe, things would work out for me this once, and I'd get my magic back. Tonight, I might be a witch again.

And sometimes we have to be careful what we wish for.

15

I spent the rest of the day and most of the evening researching and helping my aunts on how to summon a goddess while thinking of the "problem" I was supposed to have that only Lilith could help me with. If Lilith caught the scent of what I was planning, she'd be gone in a second but not before killing me.

So far, the ritual—because according to Dolores, only a *true* pagan ritual could summon a goddess as old as Lilith, the first witch—consisted of drum music and dancing, which Ruth had agreed to perform, a small altar, a sacrifice, which Beverly had been charged with, and the reciting of a special incantation, spoken by a high priestess, which of course, Dolores had appointed herself. All within a circle.

If I had my powers, I could have done the summoning myself without any help from my aunts. As a nonmagical, all I could do was help with transporting huge tomes, set up the altar in the backyard, and fetch herbs for Ruth at the local herb shop in town. Mostly, I just watched, feeling useless without a single drop of magic.

The ritual was to be held in the backyard, which wouldn't send any alarm bells to Lilith. I lived here, so she wouldn't suspect any foul play. I hoped.

And somehow, I had to bring her across the property line and convince her to follow me down a few blocks to that crossroad. The question was, how did I get her to follow me? What lie was I going to tell her that sounded convincing?

That was my only job, and I had to get it right. If I didn't, all this work, this effort would be useless. No pressure.

Hours later, and with Dolores's "special incantation" complete, we'd stopped for a well-deserved break and for Iris's welcome-back dinner, prepared by none other than Ruth, who thankfully hadn't burned a thing, much to Iris's delight.

"This is excellent, Ruth," commented Ronin as he took a sip of his beer while sitting at the dining room table. "It's like a taste-bud party in my mouth, and no one wants to go home."

Ruth's cheeks flushed a delicate pink. "Oh. Well. I'm glad you like it. This is what Iris wanted."

"It's really good, Ruth," I told her, watching her face closely. "Thank you for doing this."

"Yes, thank you," said Iris, who was already halfway through her slice of lasagna. "Mmmm. I think I might have seconds."

Ruth beamed at that. She looked everywhere but at me, still not making eye contact with me, like if she did, she'd be forced to tell me she didn't agree with our plans to deliver Lilith to Lucifer, even if it meant that she'd rather I stayed nonmagical.

Ronin caught my eye and raised a questionable brow. "So, Tess... you're all set for tonight?"

I grabbed my wineglass and took a sip, though not too much. I needed my wits about me in a few hours. I was a nervous drinker. Nobody needed to see that. "Yes. I think so. A couple of things still need to be worked out, but I think we're good to go. Right?" I left the open question for my aunts. I was still ticked I couldn't do anything, but mostly that I felt like I wasn't in charge.

"That's right." Dolores cut into her lasagna. "We're more than ready. Everything should go as planned. Remember, we don't have room for mistakes. A simple mistake and..."

"I'll be dead," I finished for her. "You can say it. If we screw up, I'm a goner."

Dolores set her cutlery on her plate. "I, for one, don't plan on *screwing* up. I don't plan on screwing anything."

"You haven't *screwed* anything in years," said a smiling Beverly, swirling her wineglass.

Dolores sent a scowl in her sister's direction. "What I mean is, I don't make mistakes. My part of the ritual will be flawless. I take great pride in any magical practice, and I leave no room for errors. Not when Tessa's livelihood is at stake. And her magic."

"It's going to work," said Iris, registering my unease. "We've got everything we need to summon Lilith, and we still have about five hours until midnight. That's plenty of time to go over the ritual and make sure nothing's wrong, that we haven't missed anything."

"Nothing is *wrong* with the ritual," said Dolores, her voice rising.

The Dark witch gave me a comforting smile. "We could even do some practice rituals if you want," she said in a low voice.

I shook my head. "No, it's fine. I'm sure everything is in order."

Dolores let out a long breath. "Of course everything is in order. *I* organized it."

I raised my wineglass to Dolores. "Of course it is."

"What I'd like to know," said Ronin, between

chews, "is how you're gonna get Lilith off your property? If you need a transitory man-whore to distract her, I'm your guy."

I laughed but caught myself at the daggers in Iris's eyes. I cleared my throat and set my glass on the table, suddenly not hungry or thirsty anymore. "I've thought about it a lot. All day."

"And?" asked Ronin.

"I'm going to tell her I've got Derrick trapped, with Iris's help, obviously. We've got him in Martha's basement. Someone he knows is a friend, so he wouldn't have suspected us. Then I'm going to tell her we have a spell that can transfer back my magic, which we do," I said, glancing at Iris. "I'll tell her only she can do it. She's the only one powerful enough to transfer my magic back to me by using the spell and Derrick as the magical host. Hopefully, I'm a good enough liar to pull it off."

"You're not." Ruth stabbed her lasagna with her fork.

O-kay. Ouch. I was not accustomed to my Aunt Ruthy being so cross with me. It was playing with my head, and I needed to focus. I couldn't feel guilt or anything right now. I couldn't grow a conscience. I needed my magic back, and Lilith was the answer. I wasn't going to back down, even if Ruth stopped speaking to me. If she'd rather I'd stay nonmagical, I couldn't do anything about that. She'd made her choice.

Ronin lifted his fork and pointed it at me. "For the sake of argument, let's say you *are* a good enough liar. Let's say your séance works out beautifully, and Lilith buys it. Buys all of it. You sure about Lucifer?"

I frowned. "About what?" I asked, though I had a feeling I knew where he was going with this.

"What makes you so sure he's going to give you your magic back?"

"He said he would. I'm not naïve. There's a real chance he might leave me hanging. But it's a chance I have to take. I have to believe him."

Ronin stared at me, looking unconvinced. "You told me once that your magic was a *special* kind of magic, like a rare diamond or whatever. If your blood magic can hinder the king of hell somehow, do you really think he'd be so willing to let it go? What if someone else, another demon, decides he wants to rule the Netherworld and wants to oust Luci here. They'd use you. Just like Lilith used you. Don't you think Luci's thought of this?"

Shit. I *hadn't* thought of that. *Good one, Tessa.* "Ah... you make a good point, my vampire friend. Honestly, no, I hadn't thought of that." Okay. That put a damper on my super plan. Why hadn't I thought of this? Ronin was right. Lucifer wouldn't give me back my magic out of the goodness of his heart. The bastard had imprisoned his wife for years. He was not a good guy. Still, I had believed him because part of me wanted to believe him.

"If it were me," said the half-vampire, his eyes pinning me. "I wouldn't give it back. If I had my hands on something that could hurt me or kill me, I'd keep it. Sure, I'd make up a good lie, but I wouldn't part with it. Too dangerous. Just saying."

"Keep your sayings to yourself, vampire," spat Dolores. "We don't need you to put doubt in Tessa's head. Her brain's not big enough to hold on to something like that."

"Thanks," I said, pissed that she thought I was a moron but more outraged that Ronin had inserted more doubt into my big, clueless brain. It was too late to go back and start second-guessing. Lucifer was not a good guy, but I trusted my gut. My gut had said he would give my magic back.

I had to trust myself. It was all I had left.

Ruth pushed back her chair and stood, carrying her plate still packed with her food, to the kitchen. She'd just stabbed at her meal and pushed it around with her fork. I never saw her taking a bite.

"It'll work," said Iris, leaning over and squeezing my hand. "You'll see. By this time tomorrow, you'll have your magic back. Everything will be back to normal."

I nodded as though anything could be that simple.

"What's the matter, Ruth?" asked Beverly. I glanced over to the kitchen to see Ruth going through the cabinets.

"I can't find my organic sugar," answered Ruth. "I need it for the dessert. You can't serve crème brûlée without caramelizing the sugar." She closed the cabinet door. "I think I left it in the Volvo."

"I'll get it." I needed to stretch my legs and clear my head. But mostly, I wanted my Aunt Ruthy to look at me. She hated the fact that we were preparing a ritual tonight, but she was still doing it. The least I could do was to fetch her sugar.

Ruth's nod to the kitchen counter was good enough. "Be right back."

I moved from the table and made my way to the front door, trying not to overthink the holes in our master plan but failing miserably.

With my jaw clenched, I pulled open the door, and my face smacked into a hard body. A hard body's pectoral muscles I knew all too well.

I stepped back and stared into gray eyes framed by thick, black lashes set in an exquisitely handsome face.

Marcus.

16

I stood there with my mouth hanging open, having temporarily forgotten how gorgeous and sinfully sexy the chief was. Muscular arms stretched his T-shirt at the expanse of his broad shoulders and the bump of his hard pecs. A foolish part of me wanted to rub my face in them again. What could I say? I was a horny creature.

Images of sweaty, naked bodies and twisted sheets invaded my mind. It was a weird effect. Even though I was still mad at him, my body seemed to have other ideas. My core pounded, and heat pooled around my middle and down to my lady regions.

I sucked in a breath. Damn hormones. Worse, my nipples had turned to stone. Traitorous nipples.

I struggled to regain control as my grip on reality wobbled. He was a panty-ruiner. No other word could describe him. Damn him and his stupid panty-ruining abilities.

A smile played on his full lips. "You look great."

I think I might have growled like a wild animal.

I felt eyes on me, and when I looked over his shoulder, I saw men crowded around on our front lawn and flocked in the street. Not men. Wereapes. "They followed you here?" I struggled to get out. My throat was scratchy and throbbing, and I hated it. "So, you took the offer. You're their alpha now. That's... great. Good for you."

I felt numb, like jumping in a freezing lake, numb and alone, and I couldn't shake the feeling. There had always been the possibility Marcus would take the offer. It was a good offer, but that selfish part of me had hoped he'd turn it down.

"Tessa."

My disloyal eyes burned. "I can't do this now."

I spun around and stormed out of the foyer, making my way toward the staircase. Iris and my aunts were crammed together at the end of the hallway next to the kitchen, watching me with captivated wide eyes, like this was the best drama since the invention of soap operas.

"Tessa, wait."

"Go away."

I climbed the stairs as fast as I could, tripped on the ninth one, and kept going like that hadn't actually happened. I couldn't face him right now. I needed to focus. I was already high with emotions. The last thing I needed was a confrontation with the chief. It would screw with my head. My magic came first. I came first. Marcus had made his choice. He needed to leave me alone.

"Tessa, stop. We need to talk. Stop being like this."

"I'm busy," I yelled. "Come back tomorrow. Make an appointment!" I didn't know why I said that.

I reached the platform in a rush and pushed open my bedroom door, but when I was about to shut it, the damn wereape held on to it with one of his big ol' hands.

Scowling, I let go and hurried toward my bathroom as he yelled, "Come here, woman!"

"What?" I spun around, sucking the air through my teeth. "You did *not* just say that, you overgrown caveman!"

Marcus shut the door behind him. "You're not listening to me. I need you to listen."

I pressed my hands on my hips, keeping a safe distance from him. "And why should I? You don't own me. I don't need your permission to do anything. I'm a grown-ass woman. And you certainly can't tell me what to do."

"Tessa..."

Anger wrapped around my throat. "I'm not one

of your pack, Marcus. You don't control me. I'll never let a man control me. Ever."

The chief ran his fingers through that silky, thick, glossy hair. "You're being irrational."

If he had the audacity to ask me if it was that time of the month, I was going to strangle him.

I felt some steam shooting out of my ears. "Get out before I have House throw you out."

Marcus's face went slack. "You're angry with me. Really angry."

"Congratulations. I was never good at poker. This is my face. This is what I look like when I'm pissed. But you know what? I don't have time for this, whatever *this* is. Okay? I've got things to do. Important things. Life-changing things."

Concern tightened the edges of his eyes and mouth, and he stood poised as though surprised that I was angry with him. "Like what? What things?" The huge man had the nerve to look worried. Sexy and worried. Worried and sexy. I was losing my mind.

I wanted to be the mature one here. I wanted to push aside my feelings and try to be happy for the guy. But my immaturity won. It happened a lot.

"You never even called," I ground out. "What kind of man does that? Maybe if you had picked up a damn phone and told me what was happening in your life, I wouldn't be spazzing out right now. I would never ask you to pick between me or a great job. I'm not that person. I would never get in between a person and their future. I would never mess with that. But I thought I deserved at least a freaking phone call before you decided to change your life. My life."

Marcus's jaw clenched. "I did call. Several times. None of the guys had cell phones. So I sneaked out and used an old landline down in the New York subway. I think Ruth picked up a few times, but I could barely hear her, and she couldn't hear me. The connection was terrible."

Oh shit. "You're the Nutella guy?"

The chief's brows shot up. "What?"

My heart clenched, and I felt a fire burning inside my chest. "Never mind." Heat rushed to my head. I felt like a fool now. Marcus had called at least a few times, according to Ruth. He'd tried to reach me. It was proof that he cared. So why was I still really, really angry?

"When I realized what Zeke was up to after he took my phone, I called you the moment I had some time alone," said Marcus, keeping a safe distance from me. I could tell he wasn't sure how to approach me, being a tad unstable and all. "I went there to help. I never thought the alpha would take my phone."

"You let him."

His gray eyes fixed on mine. "I did. He was also trying to get me to fight him. That's why he took my phone away. He knows about you. Knew I needed, wanted, to talk to you. I knew you'd be worried."

"That's an understatement." A chunk of my anger was suddenly replaced by the same amount of annoyance.

"Zeke used that. He wanted to get a rise out of me. He wanted us to fight. I refused. Because if I did, it would mean I was challenging him for the position as alpha."

"And you didn't?"

Marcus let out a sigh. "I didn't. But he kept pushing. He used everything to try and engage me in a fight with him, but I never did. Like I told you, I was there to help him pick, not to take his place."

"And how does that work, exactly? You'd pick an alpha for the alpha? That doesn't make sense."

Marcus rolled his wide shoulders. "It's not the usual custom. And it's the least favored way. But every alpha has the right to do what he wants to choose the next alpha. To challenge or be challenged or to simply make a choice. But when an alpha merely picks the next alpha without a fight, without a show of strength, it can lead to problems. If he chooses his next replacement, a pack member might challenge that alpha if they feel it's the wrong choice. That the new alpha isn't strong enough to lead the pack."

"So that's where you come in." I waved a finger up and down his body. "It's where all those muscles come into play. Right?"

Marcus flashed a smile, sending butterflies hitting the walls of my stomach. "That's right."

I looked away from his extremely distracting lush and shapely lips. "Are you telling me that you *didn't* take the job? You're not the new alpha?" Like a champ, I hid the emotion from my voice. But I wasn't going to lie to myself and say this was not what I'd been dying and wishing to hear all this time, because it was.

The wereape shook his head. "I already have a job. I'm the chief."

Some of the tension relaxed from my shoulders. But something still didn't make sense. "So why are they here? Why is a pack of wereapes on our front lawn? Are they offering a discount on landscaping?"

The chief laughed a deep rumble that sent shivers of delight all over my skin. "They followed me. Zeke is still trying to change my mind. The wereape's relentless."

"And will he?"

"Not a chance." His gaze fell on me, and I shifted nervously. I don't know why, but I felt like this was one of the first times we were alone together. I was both nervous and terrified at this very moment.

"Let me guess," I asked. "He still has your phone?"

"I'll get a new one."

It was my turn to laugh. "And Lucas?"

Marcus nodded. "He's the right choice. Zeke will see that, eventually. He's young, strong, and has the respect of the pack. I'm not interested in their politics. I have enough politics to deal with here."

I let out a puff of air. "I know."

"I'm sorry, Tessa." Marcus's face was strained with emotion. "If I had known I couldn't call you. If I'd known how upset you'd be by my leaving, I would have never left. I never wanted you to feel this way."

I exhaled. "I know."

"I forget that you still have lots to discover about the paranormal world," continued the chief, worry pinching his eyes. "Especially where wereapes are concerned. I should have stayed with you."

"It's fine. Really. It's over."

He crossed the room slowly, that devilish smile lingering on his sexy face. "So, what life-changing things are you talking about?"

My pulse pounded as he neared, wondering if he could hear it. Probably. "I have a way to get my magic back."

The massive wereape stopped and frowned, not the reaction I was hoping for. "And what exactly do you need to do to get it back?"

I shrugged. "I kinda have to hand Lilith over to Lucifer." I gave him the short version and watched as emotions crossed his face. A turmoil of feelings flashed in his gray eyes: urgency, rage, fear, possessiveness. His hands kept clenching into fists and unclenching. He was a man with lots of feelings locked up tight and controlled. He had to be, as chief, and it was hot.

A muscle feathered along his jaw. Next came all those muscles popping over his neck and shoulders. I could see all that protectiveness, caressing me in ways that I hadn't been caressed in for a long time, and I was totally turned on.

"You give him Lilith, and he'll return your magic?" asked the chief, his voice dangerously low and scary as hell.

"That's the plan." I planted my feet apart, ready for the fight, knowing he was about to drill into me how stupid and crazy this plan was, that I didn't need my magic, yada yada yada.

"I'm coming with you."

I raised my brows. I was not expecting that. "No. If she sees you, she'll know something's up," I told him. "That, or she'll want to sleep with you. She's a very horny goddess."

A smile played on his lips that heated my face. "Fine. I can keep to the shadows. It's my best offer, Tessa. You're not going to meet the king of hell without me. I won't let you."

He was being all commanding and controlling again, and I liked it. "Fine," I repeated, my face in what I was hoping was annoyance while my stomach was doing the achy breaky dance. "Stop looking at me like that."

"Like what?" he purred as he closed the distance between us. "You're beautiful."

Uh-oh. I knew that look. It was the I'm-going-to-ruin-your-vajayjay look.

He had many of those. A man of many talents.

I held up a hand and took a step back. "Don't. Stay away from me. I mean it." The smile and the blush on my face betrayed me.

"You're so fucking sexy," growled the wereape, moving forward. "You make me crazy. I want you. I want you right now."

I pointed at him. The fluttering butterflies in my belly turned to a full-on wasp swarm attack. "I'm warning you. Don't."

"Why not?"

A stab of desire went to my core. "Because... because I'm supposed to be mad at you, you big ogre!"

I don't know what he saw in my expression, but a

huge grin split his sexy face. "I've missed you," continued the wereape. "I can't stop thinking about how you left Central Park. How amazing your ass looked in those sweats. And how much I wanted to rip them off of you."

Ha. Lilith had been wrong about my choice of clothing. I'd been rocking those sweat pants.

My eyes moved down to the already prominent bulge in his jeans, which did wonders for my self-esteem. Nothing like a stiffy to make you feel beautiful and wanted.

The next thing I knew, his big, rough hands were on me, yanking me to him. He dropped his forehead to mine, gazing into my eyes and sending stabs of yearning into my core. His mouth found mine, and I lost myself in the passion, the desire. His lips were soft and warm, and the craving behind his kiss had my pulse hammering. Need dove to my middle and sent me alight. All those pent-up emotions from a few days ago came rushing in, elevating the desire in me until I felt like I was about to explode.

I was just... let's face it. Horny as hell.

I slid my hands under his shirt, exploring the hard muscles of his back. Just like the wereape, his skin was hot and smooth.

I pulled back. "Wait, what about Zeke and the others?" I reminded him.

"I don't care," growled the wereape as he crushed his mouth on mine again.

His tongue searched my mouth, and every thought of Lilith and Lucifer vanished from my brain. There was only this gorgeous man's desire and my pounding lady bits.

He stepped back, and my heart skidded to high gear as he yanked off his T-shirt, jeans, and his briefs in one blurred motion. Damn, those wereape clothes-ripping talents.

He stood there in his golden, smooth, hard, naked glory. His stare was blazing with some kind of animalistic carnal appetite.

"So not fair," I breathed.

I blinked, and his hands were on me again. His fingers found the zipper of my jeans and the fabric of my T-shirt, and the roughness of his fingers set my skin on fire. I blinked again, and my clothes were gone. So was my bra, along with my melted panties.

"So, *so* unfair," I said again, both amazed and really excited. "And such a turn-on." I had no idea what had happened to my clothes, and I couldn't care less.

The chief's smile was sly, and it went right to my gut, which tightened. "I've got super fingers."

I grinned lazily. "Tell me about it."

The man was smokin' hot, and he'd come back

for me. This glorious, strong beast of a man had said no to becoming an alpha and had come back to *me*.

Yay!

I wanted to run my tongue all over his body. The thought of his salty taste made me shiver.

Damn. I was so horny I was about to black out.

The next thing I knew, Marcus backed me into the wall, hard.

"Marcus!" I squealed. "You beast."

"I am," he growled, savage and feral, his animal coming over the edge, and that had my core pounding with excitement. His tongue darted out and licked my neck.

The wereape then grabbed me and tossed me over his shoulder. Yeah, total caveman. But then he gently lowered me to my bed. I welcomed his weight as he slid down over my body, my insides pulsing with greedy desire.

Oh yeah. It was multiple orgasms tonight.

I knew in a few hours things might take a horrible turn for the worse.

But right now, I let myself enjoy the moment, a few hours of bliss.

And I let Marcus take me there.

17

I strolled across the backyard. The fresh night air smelled of pine needles and earth, soothing my hot face. I wasn't hot from the multiple orgasms a few hours before, though I had been at the time. My face was heating from the stress of what I was about to do.

Moisture pooled in my armpits, and any minute now I was going to smell like a men's locker room. Why I'd forgotten to put on some deodorant again was a mystery. No. It was because I'd showered with a hot, naked chief who couldn't stop massaging me everywhere. I had to kick him out of my bathroom so I could towel dry without his big hands running up and down my wet body.

My phone had shown 11:30 p.m. when I'd left my bedroom. It was time to get my magic back.

I should be excited. Hell, I should be doing cart-wheels. But I felt ill, tight with anxiety, and my legs felt like metal rods.

"You okay?" asked Marcus. His large shoulder rubbed against mine as he walked next to me. "You got quiet as soon as we left your bedroom."

"Part of me wishes I would have stayed in bed with you," I told him, my eyes focused on the large circle of candles. Dolores, Beverly, and Ruth stood shoulder to shoulder inside the circle, their backs to us as we approached. Iris stood outside the circle, clutching Dana, her DNA album of all things hexes and curses.

"We could still turn around now and go back. No one is forcing you to do this. Say the word. I'd be happy to take you back to your room."

I spotted Ronin leaning against a large oak tree, his arms crossed over his chest. Even in the dark-ness, enough illumination remained to see the strange smile on his face.

"I bet you would," I answered as I approached the circle. "But this is my last shot at getting my magic back. I have to try. I have to do this for me."

I thought of my father and his attempt to find Derrick. I'd totally forgotten to tell him. I blamed Marcus and three of the most intense orgasms known to humankind. But I didn't have time now. I'd let him know after this was done and my magic was back.

I looked over my shoulder past the left side of Davenport House to the street beyond. "Where are all the wereapes? I'd expected to see them hiding in the trees or something. Are they gone?"

Marcus smiled. "No. Probably just checking out the town. Likely at one of the pubs."

I stepped over the candles and into the large circle, big enough to fit a good-size living room.

"Are we ready?" I asked my aunts.

The three witches broke apart as they turned toward me, giving me a full view of the altar and what was lying on top of it.

I started. A man in his late fifties, guessing by his receding hairline, the gray in his beard, and the wrinkles around his face and mouth, was strapped to the altar—naked. His manhood was soaking in the night air and probably the mosquitoes.

"Wait. What the hell is this?" I asked, flabbergasted.

Beverly smiled, her face perfect and beautiful in the candlelight. "This is Gary. He's been a very naughty boy. Haven't you, Gary? Yes, yes, he has. Cheating on his wife for the past year with his best friend's nineteen-year-old daughter."

I made a face. "Gross." I glanced at Gary again. "But why is he here?" His eyes were glazed over like he'd popped a few too many painkillers. He was definitely spelled.

"Because he's our sacrifice," said Beverly happily. "Don't worry. We won't kill him, if that's what you're thinking. We're not murderers. We just need him to bleed. Cheating bastards always bleed more."

"Right." Why did I get the feeling this wasn't the first time they'd tied a naked guy to an altar? I knew we needed blood. I just never figured it would be human blood. "Why is he naked?"

Beverly flashed me one of her perfect smiles. "Why not." She winked and turned back to Gary, who was grinning like he was on some acid trip.

My eyes found Ruth. She held a red ceramic bowl close to her chest, and a small drum hung from the belt around her waist. Lines marred her forehead, and she looked pained. Still, she wouldn't make eye contact with me.

"Okay, okay. Enough with the useless chitchat," said Dolores, shaking her head. Her long, gray braid gently bumped her back. "We don't have much time before midnight. We need to do this now." Her eyes found Marcus. "Unless you can conjure a goddess with your good looks, you shouldn't be near the circle."

"You should go," I told the wereape.

Marcus held my gaze for a beat. "I'll be right over there, in the shadows, in case you need me."

I nodded, not sure what to answer. I didn't want to have to need Marcus. If I did, things had gone terribly wrong. I watched him go in the direction of a copse, opposite where Ronin was supposedly still hiding in plain sight.

"Why the sacrificial ritual?" asked Ronin. "I mean, why not just knock your ankles together and call out her name?" He laughed. "Can't you just do a normal summoning?"

"Because Lilith is a pagan goddess," answered Beverly. "She'll respond better to the old ways."

"By strapping down some old, naked guy?" The vampire laughed harder. "Isn't that a bit of a cliché?"

"Ronin!" hissed Iris, making a show of her hands.

"What?" mouthed the half-vampire, looking rather pleased with himself.

Dolores whipped out a dagger and pointed it at Ronin. "If you don't shut your vampire mouth and leave, I'm going to cut your manhood and offer it to Lilith as a gift!"

Ronin clasped his groin. "Yes, ma'am." In a blur, the vampire put on a burst of speed and disappeared into the night. We couldn't see him anymore, but I was sure he was somewhere near, just like Marcus.

"Tessa, you stay over there," instructed Dolores, pointing to a spot right outside the circle and to the left of the altar behind Iris.

I did what I was told, trying to look calm and

focused like I was in control. At another time, I would have been irritated by her ordering me around, but right now, I didn't even have the energy to argue. Besides, I had faith in Dolores, in my aunts' abilities. It was going to work.

And in a few minutes, I was going to get my magic back.

I felt pressure against my shoulder blades, a cold push, and the hairs on the back of my neck rose with the feeling of eyes on me. I whipped my head around, searching for the originator of the feeling, but I only saw only shadow and darkness punctuated by the streetlights blinking at me.

I was losing my cool or just reacting to Ronin's and Marcus's presence, hiding in the shadows.

Iris turned and faced me. "It's going to work. You'll see. You'll be a witch again soon."

I nodded, still finding it hard to answer, like I'd superglued my lips together.

"It'll be like nothing ever happened," continued the Dark witch, clutching Dana harder like she was trying to convince herself.

"Ladies, let's begin," said Dolores, and I homed my attention back on my aunts.

Beverly took the knife from Dolores and moved next to Gary. With a quick flick of her hand, she cut the man's wrist. Dark blood oozed from the cut, and she quickly snagged a small wooden bowl from the altar and placed it under the wound. After a few seconds, she removed the bowl and smeared something over the cut, which I couldn't see in the semi-darkness. But it stopped the bleeding.

Next, Beverly moved over to Ruth and dumped the blood into the larger ceramic bowl Ruth had been holding this whole time. Ruth muttered a few words as she mixed the blood with whatever was in that bowl. Once she was done, she joined Gary at the altar. With her finger dipped into the mix like a brush, she painted a few symbols on the naked guy's face and chest. When she was finished, she placed the bowl on the altar and stepped back, taking Dolores's left side while Beverly stood on her right.

"You ready?" whispered Iris.

"Nope," I whispered back, finally finding my voice. "Not at all."

"You're doing the right thing," she added. "Just... don't overthink it. This was done to you. Remember that. You're just taking back what is rightfully yours."

"I know." I tried to take a calming breath, knowing my life was about to change, but it seemed like I couldn't find enough air.

Ruth started a steady beat from her small drum attached to her belt.

"Hail, Lilith, goddess of the shadows, lady of the night, the first witch," chanted Dolores as she raised her hands above her head, her voice tolling through the still night air like a wind chime. "On this night, we offer you this blood, this sacrifice as a gift of thanks to you."

Power surged all around and through me, and I held my breath as I felt my aunts tap into their wills and their magic. The outpouring of energy from their auras united. They chimed and resonated. It was beautiful, and I felt an ache in my chest.

I'm doing the right thing. My heart slammed against my chest. Sweat dripped down my back. I wiped my sweaty palms on my jeans, trying to see Ruth's face, but Dolores's wide shoulder was in the way.

"Let our worship be within the heart that rejoiced," continued Dolores. "For behold, all acts of love and pleasure are our rituals. Beloved goddess, we seek your guidance. We ask that you commune with us and move among us. We ask you, Lilith, to join us in the circle tonight!"

I stiffened, and my breath hissed in through my nose. The outpouring of energy from my aunts surged in shuddering waves of energy through the air. The ground at my feet sang in resonance with the impact. Gritting my teeth, a tingling sensation fluttered from my fingers to my toes.

And then, for a timeless instant, everything in the night—critters, animals, us—went utterly silent and still.

With a sudden burst of energy, two things happened. First, the blood markings on Gary glowed a brilliant red before they settled. Second, a blast of blinding light flashed before our eyes as energy rushed through the air.

I waited. And just when I thought the ritual hadn't worked, a woman with long red hair and blazing red eyes stood in the circle next to the altar.

"Well," said Lilith, and she yanked up her red leather bustier, pushing the girls higher. "This is a surprise."

18

Lilith, the goddess of night, looked resplendent and a little slutty in her red leather ensemble. Her lean figure was perfectly enclosed in a tight leather bustier and pants that no ordinary could have pulled off. She finished the look with red knee high boots. Her hair was slicked back into a low ponytail, which only accentuated her gorgeous, godly features. She radiated beauty and power.

Lilith, a puissant deity and the first witch, could snap her fingers and end my life. She was no match for witches or even demons. She was basically the mother of both.

And I was the idiot who was going to have to trick her into thinking I had a problem only she could solve. Wonderful.

Lilith took a step toward the altar, her red lips

curling up into a smile. "It's been a long time since I've been offered a human sacrifice." She dragged a long, manicured finger over Gary's chest. "I would have preferred a younger, firmer sacrifice. His flesh is somewhat... aged, but it'll do. Blood is blood."

Gary blinked up at the goddess, his eyes glazed and smiling, completely clueless.

My aunts all turned to me expectantly, not daring to utter a single word in case it all went to hell.

Right. It was my turn.

I tried to keep my mind as blank as I could, knowing but not knowing for sure if the goddess could read minds. If she knew what I was planning, I could kiss my life goodbye.

Showtime. I cleared my throat. "This is me. This is all me. Yup." My voice came out really loudly. I was practically screaming.

Lilith stared at me as though I'd just uttered some strange language she'd never heard before. "Why are you acting weird?"

Damn. I was going to screw this up. "I'm not acting. I've always been weird. Not my fault you never noticed."

The goddess narrowed her eyes at me. "No. You're acting weirder than normal. What's with you?"

I swallowed hard, trying to keep from shaking.

"Listen. I asked my aunts and my friend Iris to help me summon you. I couldn't do it without my magic."

Lilith eyed me suspiciously. "Really? And why's that? Has it something to do with that hot male of yours? You're broken up, and now you want me to take care of him for you? Is that it? Some sort of revenge killing?"

"No."

Her brows knitted together. "Why are you sweating so much? I can smell the stink on you. You're still acting really strange."

Oh shit. Could she sense that?

My aunts tensed. Dolores's dark eyes stood out on her unusual paleness. Beverly looked at me. Worry and fear pooled in her large green eyes. Ruth looked like she was about to cry. I saw Iris stiffen like she'd been cursed and turned to stone.

Damn it. I was going to screw this up. Things were not going as smoothly as I had imagined they would when I played it out in my head.

I'm doing the right thing. "Because I needed to ask you something." I tried again. "I need your help."

Lilith's eyes danced dangerously. "I don't do favors for mortals, my little demon w—ah, you're not a witch anymore."

"Exactly." I shifted my posture. "Which is why I wanted to speak with you," I said, choosing my words more carefully. "The thing is... I—we figured out how to get my magic back."

"Did you, now? Well, this ought to be good," said the goddess as she crossed her arms over her chest.

She had no idea. "It's true." Why the hell did I say that? "It's a matter of transference. Putting the magic back. That kind of thing."

Lilith's eyes widened in mock eagerness. "Sounds exciting."

She didn't believe me. "We've got Derrick." When she still looked unimpressed, I added, "the incubus who stole my magic."

Recognition flashed in her red eyes, and I saw the fury singeing behind them. "You trapped the incubus?"

I shrugged. "That was the easy part. Derrick is full of himself. He's an arrogant, power-hungry bastard, and I knew he couldn't resist us summoning him again. I knew he'd take the bait."

Lilith inclined her head. "What bait? You're all out of magic? Unless you were offering him *some-thing* else."

"No, not that. Iris," I said, gesturing to my friend, who still looked frozen. "She was the bait."

"For sex."

"Not for sex, but for her magic. Her power."

"I see." Lilith leaned over the bowl that was used

to mix Gary's blood. She dipped her finger in it and then sucked it. "Not bad. Not great."

Ew. "It worked," I continued, speaking fast as the half-truths spewed from my mouth easily. Not sure how I felt about that. "So we trapped him."

Lilith looked at me. Mild interest flashed on her face. "Here? In your house?"

"No. I didn't want to take a chance of having him hurt my aunts again. He's in the basement of a friend's house. She doesn't live there anymore. Not after the divorce. It's empty." Here I went on rambling again. "He's there now."

"And?" Lilith dipped her finger in the mix again. "Why should I care?"

I exhaled some of the nervous tension and hoped the goddess thought it was because I was about to ask her for a favor, not because I was about to betray her. "Well, the spell that transfers the magic from the incubus back into me is really complicated. It's a powerful spell. And we—my friend Iris and aunts—aren't powerful enough."

Lilith sucked on her finger, her eyes on me. "So you want me to perform this spell?"

My heart hammered against my ribs with a terrible force. "Exactly."

"I don't think I will," said the goddess, looking bored. "I have better things to do with my time. Like those two werewolves waiting for me back in my flat in London. Hung like gods, those two." She let out a breathy laugh, sticking her finger back into the bowl.

"Don't you want me to have my magic back?" My anger flared out of nowhere, but it was real, so the effect was real enough. "I helped you." I raised my arms. "And this is what happened to me. I can't do magic anymore because of you."

As one, I heard my aunts' intake of breath. Iris was still like a cement statue. I didn't think she'd even breathed yet.

Lilith's eyes narrowed with old anger. "Careful, now. I like you, but keep that up, and I will snap that pretty little neck of yours."

"You will help me," I ground out, feeling crazy to be speaking to a goddess in this way. I wondered if Marcus had approached, waiting to steal me away if things got any worse.

The goddess watched me. Her eyes burned with fury. Just when I thought I'd gone too far, her face went calm. "Fine. I'll help you this one time." She held out her hand, her index finger stained with blood. "Give me the spell."

"Iris?" I called out to my friend.

The Dark witch shook out of her trance and handed me a piece of paper, the same piece we'd used on Derrick to transfer my magic, which had turned out to be a disaster of nuclear proportions.

Lilith glanced at the paper. "Peculiar spell. I don't know it. You think this is going to work?"

"Yes," I answered, trying to put as much conviction in my voice as I could. "It'll work."

The goddess looked at me. "Where does your friend live?"

I'm doing the right thing. "Not far. Five-minute walk."

Lilith tossed the paper to the ground. "Lead the way."

Guess she had memorized it. She was a goddess after all.

"Good luck," said Iris, looking both grim and terrified.

I gave her a tight smile and flicked my gaze over to my aunts. Their faces were flustered with fear and worry. Dolores kept opening and closing her mouth like she was about to say something. Beverly's face twitched with a nervous, forced smile of encouragement. It looked painful.

Finally, Ruth's eyes met mine. We maintained eye contact for the first time since I'd told them about my plan. Her blue eyes were filled with deep regret, pain, and disappointment. I also saw a plea in there to stop what I was doing.

Crap. I spun around before my own face gave me away and headed toward the front of Davenport House. I scanned the shadows from the line of trees to my right, looking for Marcus or even Ronin, but I couldn't see anything besides trees and darkness.

"What's the hurry?" asked Lilith behind me.

"I have to pee," I said, which I kinda did.

"So, go pee," answered the goddess, annoyance in her tone.

"When we're done." I winced at my stupidity as the words came out. I wasn't supposed to be doing anything. My ears flamed as I waited to see if Lilith would say anything or sense anything, but the constant tap of her high-heeled boots never faltered.

In my mind's eye, I could see Ruth's face, the disappointment, her plea, the memory absolutely crystalline. I pushed away the image of her face, straining my mind to focus. A shiver grew inside me from guilt. Bile rose in the back of my throat. I was going to puke. If I did, I could kiss my magic away.

I'm doing the right thing.

I searched for that flare of anger and held on. The goddess had done this to me. She'd also made it clear that she'd end my life if I didn't go along with her plans to kill her husband. She was insane. And our world would be better off without her.

She wasn't my problem anymore. She'd be Lucifer's problem.

We hit Spirit Lane and turned left. The lots near Davenport House were larger, much larger than the ones closer to town, and flanked with shrubbery and woodlands, which was a good thing. Only four houses sat on Spirit Lane, and judging by the blackened windows, their owners were sleeping. I could just make out the end of the road, where Crystal Row cut across Spirit Lane, the crossroads.

A hundred more feet until I'm free.

"The house looks great," said the goddess conversationally as she walked on the sidewalk next to me, and I kept my eyes forward. "But then again, I am a master of my craft. It's lovely. The wraparound porch makes all the difference. I wonder how much a house that size goes for nowadays."

"Why? Are you planning on moving to the area?" Shame gnawed my insides like a wood saw. Lilith had given us back our home, our house. She'd done it without being asked to. She'd just... given it to us.

"Maybe."

"Wait. What?"

She was silent for a moment. "I don't have any family of my own. Even a goddess gets lonely. You're the closest thing I have to a family."

Oh, fuck me.

My foot caught on an uneven edge of the cement sidewalk, and I stumbled forward.

"What's the matter with you?" inquired Lilith. "Are you drunk?"

I nodded. "Too much wine at dinner," I lied. Yup, I was going straight to hell after this.

Lilith laughed. "Amateur. Only infants can't hold their wine."

Thirty more feet.

"Why wasn't your mother here tonight? Doesn't she live with your aunts?"

A frisson crawled over my nerves, making my heart pump faster and drying my mouth. "She and my father bought a house together. It's just over there on Moon Way. We've already passed it."

Twenty more feet.

My legs were stiff like wood planks as I huddled forward. It was a strange thing, talking to the goddess like this. It was mundane and almost friendly.

As we walked along, I swept my gaze over the street, the streetlamps casting enough illumination to see the houses set back from the road, nestled in lines of trees and shrubbery. Tree crickets chirped in the shadows, but otherwise, the street was still and quiet. I searched for a sign that Lucifer was here, or maybe some barrier or something. But I saw nothing out of the ordinary.

I'm doing the right thing. I'm doing the right thing. I'm doing the right thing!

So why do I feel like such a jerk?

Ten more feet.

Lilith pulled the end of her ponytail to her face. "I think I'm going to go blonde. What do you think?"

"Stop!" I howled, swinging out my arms like a home-plate umpire at a baseball game.

Lilith froze, but her eyes gleamed with scarlet flames. "What is the matter with you tonight?"

I shook my head. My arms still stretched out. "I can't do this. I can't do this."

"Do what?" asked the goddess, her tone hard.

"Oh, thank the cauldron," came Ruth's voice from behind us.

I turned around to see that my aunts and Iris had followed us. I'd been so absorbed with my own plans, I never even heard them. A flicker of movement to my right, and Marcus came sauntering toward us, followed by Ronin.

Lilith pressed her hands on her hips. "Spill it. What's going on?"

I knew what I was about to say was going to change my life. It could also end my life. But I couldn't do it. I couldn't live the rest of my life knowing what I'd done. Hopefully, she wouldn't kill me. It was a chance I'd have to take.

"You need to leave. Now."

The goddess watched me. "Why?"

Here we go. "Because Lucifer is out there somewhere waiting for you to reach that crossroad." I pointed to the end of the street.

Lilith's lips parted in shock. Her beautiful face twisted into a mask of anguish and fear—utter panic. I saw a glimpse of that broken woman I'd seen a few weeks ago in her New York City apartment, a vision that had torn me up inside. She had not expected that. I was not expecting that. But then she recovered quickly, her features went hard, and a fierce rage gleamed in her eyes that were fastened on me.

Yup. She was going to kill me.

My heart started ripping a clipped rhythm in my chest. Raw, sharp, primitive fear shot through my body in full force and, for a moment, swept away all thoughts and plans.

"You tricked me," said the goddess slowly. My skin pricked at the wave of wild magic, Lilith's magic. "I thought you were my friend, and you tricked me?" She leaned forward, and I saw at the same moment, Marcus coming up behind her.

Oh. Shit. Oh. Shit.

"I know. I'm a bitch," I said, talking fast. "But he promised to give me back my magic if I gave you to him. As you can see... well... I couldn't go through with it because I'm a goody-goody, right? That's what you said I was. I'm soft. I've got a big ol' conscience. Sue me."

Lilith's death stare was making my knees wobble with fear. "I should kill you for this."

I took the "should" as a good sign. "Then, make it quick because he's coming for you." My heart throbbed in my throat as I saw Marcus standing right behind Lilith. I didn't know what he thought he could do to a goddess, but I didn't want him to get hurt. I didn't want anyone to get hurt. Not my aunts. My friends. Even Lilith, apparently.

I opened my mouth to tell her to go, but between one breath and the next, she was just gone.

"Holy shit, that was intense," said Ronin, stepping from the shadows, his hands on his head. "I nearly wet myself."

I let out a breath. "I think I did."

Dolores pushed past her sisters and joined me. "But what about your magic? You'll never get it back. This was your only chance."

"I know."

Dolores frowned, her jaw clenching. "She might retaliate. She is a goddess after all, and you did trick her."

"I know that too."

"She might kill you when you least expect it," continued my tall aunt. "Kill you in your sleep. Strangulation in the shower. Aneurysm on the toilet."

"Great."

"I knew you couldn't do it," said Ruth, beaming at me. "I just knew it. I knew you couldn't do that to our Lilith."

Our Lilith? That was new. "Really? I didn't. Not

until a few moments ago."

"I'm sorry, Tessa," said Iris, slipping Dana into her large bag. "I know how important this was to you. And now…"

"And now I'll get used to being nonmagical," I answered. The feeling of being sick came back up again. Maybe my father would get lucky and find Derrick.

"Oh, shoot," said Beverly. "I forgot all about Gary." She laughed. "Did you see what he did?"

"No," I answered.

"He had a hard-on for Lilith, stupid bastard. I better untie him and send him home to his wife. Naked," she added with a mischievous grin, her hips swaying as she made her way back up Spirit Lane.

Together, we all headed back to Davenport House in a sort of mutual contented silence. Breathing and listening to the sounds around me, I felt a warm, hard hand press against my lower back, and I turned to find glorious gray eyes looking down at me.

"You okay?" asked Marcus, his hard body brushing up against mine just as we crossed over Davenport's front yard. "You're shaking."

"I am?" I hadn't even noticed that. Must be the after-effects of the adrenaline. Or the shock that I'd just done what I did. Because I'd basically just screwed myself.

"Man, I can't believe what you did," said the half-vampire, grinning at me. "You're crazy. You know that?"

"So I've been told." Now that Marcus had mentioned the shaking, I didn't think I could stop.

"I thought the chief here was about to tackle the goddess and put her in a wrestling hold," said Ronin. "Sorry, dude, but she would have killed you."

"Well, thank the cauldron that didn't happen." I pressed harder into Marcus, taking in his scent. Now that the show was over, I was hoping to get on with another naked, multiple-orgasmic show. I totally deserved it.

"Who's that man?" Ruth pointed at something behind me.

"Man?" Beverly spun around faster than I could have imagined and was on her way back. "Is he handsome? Single?"

My orgasmic thoughts vanished. I turned slowly, and my knees buckled.

A tall man stood just beyond our property line. His blond hair was shaved at the sides and pulled back into a long braid. Even in the darkness, I could see the anger flashing in his blue eyes with the storm of what was to come.

Damn. It didn't look like I was going to get lucky tonight.

I took a breath and said, "Lucifer."

19

Oops. I'd forgotten about the king of hell. How does one forget about the king of hell? The most dangerous and sinister celestial being? Apparently, it was something I could do.

"Are you sure?" asked Ruth, peering at Lucifer like he might be one of her rare mushrooms. "He looks friendly."

"Oh, I'm sure it's him, and he's not friendly," I told her, knowing I would never forget a man, god, whatever, like that. Once you got a look at him, it was imprinted on your retinas for life.

An elbow bumped into me. "I never thought the king of hell would be so sexy," purred Beverly, her eyes rolling over every inch of the god, like she was trying to imagine him naked. "Look at that body.

The things I would do to him are illegal in some countries."

"Can you stop thinking with your vagina for once?" Dolores joined us. "This is not some boy toy you picked up at the local bar on your way home. This is a deity. A celestial being who arranged to have Tessa's magic taken from her. Or have you forgotten?"

Beverly rolled her eyes. "What? I'm just saying that maybe we're wrong about him. Maybe he's here for a social call." She pushed up her breasts, adjusting her bra while still eyeing the king of hell like he was the catch of the season.

"I doubt it." Nope. He was here for me. And he didn't look happy to see me. He looked pissed.

Lucifer glared at Beverly, and whatever she saw on his face seemed to sober her up as she slowly took a step back behind me.

The hairs along my arms rose as a shiver ran through my body in fear at the savagery in Lucifer's eyes and the promise of violence.

"He's got some serious muscle," said Ronin. "I dig it. He's built like a god."

"That's because he is a god," I told him.

"Tessa." Iris was next to me. "He looks really angry."

My pulse throbbed in my throat. "Tell me about it." I also knew this was on me. If I'd given him Lilith, he'd have a smile, not the *I'm going to kill you and your family and friends* face.

"If I had known you were going to change your mind about Lilith," continued Iris, tension in her voice, "I would have come up with some sort of protection spell. Maybe even call up a few demons for protection. I could have been prepared if I'd known what you were planning."

My eyes were on Lucifer. He just stood there, unmoving, watching me and listening. "I didn't know until I did it." Which was the absolute truth.

"What are we going to do?" hissed Beverly, glancing around with a wild look in her eyes. "He's going to kill us! I can't die. I'm too beautiful."

"Look. I think he's smiling," said Ruth, still unwilling to admit that he was a foe and not a friend.

"That's a snarl, you idiot. Can't you tell the difference?" snapped Dolores.

Ruth made a face. "It's dark. It *looks* like he's smiling."

"We could give him Gary, and hope for the best," said Dolores, her fingers twitching at her sides like she was about to get into a magic brawl. "He did come here for someone. Let's give him a someone."

"Yes. Yes. Great idea," said Beverly, pointing at the altar across the yard behind her. "Let's do that."

"It's the wrong someone," I said. "He'd never go for that. Not when he's been looking for his special someone." A mortal man was nothing to the king of hell. He'd come here for his queen, not a lowlife cheater. And he wouldn't leave until there was pain, blood, and death.

Marcus placed himself before me like a human shield, sensing my unease. I found myself pressing back into him, soaking in his heat, the scent of something musky and male reaching me. If I wasn't so scared out of my mind at this very moment, I would have thought it incredibly romantic and hot. He was eyeing the god, sizing him up as a potential adversary. As ferocious predators, I knew wereapes had a sixth sense, instincts that enabled them to spot weaknesses in the enemy. That would work on another demon or creature, but I doubted it worked on gods.

He turned his head, and our eyes met. His jaw clenched, and it looked like he was about to beast out into his alter ego, King Kong.

"The house," said Dolores, panic making her voice high. "We make a quick break for the house. It's the best protection we have." She started to walk back.

"It won't make a difference," I told them, looking at Ruth, who was still goggling Lucifer with more curiosity than fear. "You know how many times Lilith's been there. The wards are useless." Though Davenport was protected from demon invasions except for my father, it had nothing on gods and goddesses.

"You have a better idea? If you do, I'm all ears," accused Dolores, looking livid that I'd insulted her magical abilities, the fear of the god's wrath forgotten. Her eyes flashed, and I could see a vein throbbing in her forehead.

"At the moment, I've got nothing." I stepped around Marcus's body shield, though my own body quivered with terror. "There must be a reason why he wanted me to lure Lilith away from here," I guessed, my voice low, but I doubted it really mattered. "There's a reason. There has to be. I just can't figure it out. It's not just because he needed a crossroads for whatever he was planning. He needed her away from the property." But why?

At that precise moment Lucifer decided to move. The king of hell stepped onto our property and walked toward us at a leisurely pace, his blue eyes pinned on me. Ruth was right. He was smiling, but not in a good way.

Ohhhhh, crap.

I caught movement next to me, and in a blur, Marcus stood there, jacketless and shirtless as he yanked off his jeans and kicked away his boots. Before I could stop him, fur erupted from his body as his animal took over. His features swelled in his skin, heaving and extending his body to impossible proportions. Suddenly a massive silverback gorilla stood next to me. His roar thundered, shaking my bones and rattling my nerves. He shook himself before standing on all fours, his front hands resting on his knuckles.

I couldn't help but stare at this glorious yet terrifying beast. The muscles on his chest flexed as he stood on all fours, his top half resting on his knuckles.

His beast form was resistant to some magic, and he'd surprised me with Derrick's magic too. Maybe he'd surprise us all against Lucifer's.

"Now what?" Beverly's voice came from behind me. "What do we do?"

"Run," I said, my eyes on Lucifer. "He came here for me. You guys should leave."

"You have no magic, Tessa," said Dolores. "What are you going to do? Tell him to leave and hope he listens?"

"I don't know, okay?" I snapped, the urge to flee crossed my mind, but I pushed it down. "But you weren't supposed to be involved. This is all on me. I can't expect you to stay." *And be killed.* "Take Lilith's cue. She left."

I wasn't prepared to die, but what were the odds of fighting a god and surviving? Not great, especially when I had no magical mojo whatsoever to help. I didn't want to die tonight, but I didn't want Marcus,

Iris, Ronin, or any of my aunts to die either. I knew Marcus would never leave, but I was surprised my aunts and my friends all stayed put. They were just as stubborn as me.

The only one who'd left to save her own skin, knowing we'd die, was Lilith.

Makes you wonder why I didn't hand her over. Doesn't it?

Lucifer stopped when he was about twelve feet away. A cold pulse of power that seemed alien yet familiar sizzled in the air around us, carrying the scent of sulfur—the stink of demon. Or rather, the stink of the demon king.

Now with Marcus next to me, it was clear Lucifer was taller and thicker than my wereape. Lucifer was a massive, muscular creature.

I forced my facial muscles into a smile. "Hey, Luce. Nice night for a stroll into town. The pubs are excellent if you're looking for a drink. You look like a Guinness guy." My motto was always, when in fear, go for dumb.

"I thought we had an agreement, Tessa," said Lucifer. His voice was emotionless, but his eyes still held that cold anger. "You lied to me."

I raised a finger. "Technically, I never actually said yes."

"You never refused either."

"True. But as deals go, I had the right to change my mind." I just made that up.

Lucifer's face hardened. "You have no rights where my wife's concerned."

"As a woman, I have the right to step up when another woman is in danger. Women rule, buddy." I prayed Lilith was far, far away. Somewhere safe and away from the Viking-looking-god, abusive creep.

Lucifer shook his head. "I asked you to do one thing. One simple thing, and you defied me. It was an easy task."

"Easy?" I cocked a brow. "Have you met your wife?" I cast my gaze behind and around the king of hell. "Looks like you didn't bring Derrick with you. You were never going to give me back my magic. Were you?" He'd lied. Didn't know why I was ticked about that.

Lucifer's eyes glowed, flickers of amusement and malice sharing space in them. "I don't need the incubus to transfer back your magic." He raised his right hand, and from his palm rose a white-and-black flame.

A horrible pang went through my chest as I stared at what I knew was my magic. Demon and witch magic intertwined in a perfect combination. The other thing I knew was that I'd never wield it again.

He watched my face for a moment. His smile

turned pleasant and mendacious. "So you see... I had held my end of the bargain. In a matter of speaking," he said, and the flame above his palm vanished.

I narrowed my eyes at him. His words felt false. I'd been played. "You're a real asshole."

Lucifer gave a mock laugh. "You mortals are such sensitive creatures. You live in a very strange world. I've always hated it. The smells. The weakness. The mortality. I cannot understand why my wife chooses to live here among this." With a disgusted look on his face, he raised his hands, palms out, like he was insinuating that the Davenport grounds were the bowels of our planet.

"Maybe because her douche of a husband doesn't like it here."

"Wwach iit," warned Marcus in a whisper, his hard body pressed against mine.

"Too late for that," I whispered back. Too late for a lot of things.

Lucifer tsked, staring at me like a petulant child. "You should have given me my wife. It was such a simple thing. You had her... and you simply let her go."

I thought I'd felt creepy deity eyes on me before. Looked like Luce was a stalker too.

I felt foolish and a need to be brash. "You're not used to being told no. I get it. But unfortunately for you, I grew a conscience. I like Lilith." I was shocked as the words came out, but they were true. "I just couldn't hand over someone I like knowing you were going to kill her."

Lucifer's eyebrows twitched. It was the only flicker of emotion I saw. He clasped his hands in front of him, his face all business again. "I could have given you your magic back. Instead, you chose to defy me and die. Strange creatures, you mortals."

"I didn't plan on the dying part," I told him, hearing the nervous shifting of my aunts and Iris behind me. "But, yes, we are strange creatures."

"Even though you befriended my wife, I can't let you live," he threatened, and my face went cold. "Because of what you are."

"Told ya," came Ronin's voice, and part of me wanted to turn around and smack him.

Lucifer smiled, and it scared the crap out of me. "You're too..."

"Smart?" I prompted.

"Rare, dangerous," answered the king of hell. "An anomaly, really. It's why you shall die tonight."

A deep growl ripped out of Marcus's throat, and I reached out and squeezed his shoulder, telling him to stay put for now. We all knew what would happen in a few moments.

I caught a glimpse of frustration tightening in

Lucifer's eyes and felt the tension in him, the overwhelming need for his wife he was trying to hide.

I swallowed as a question burned into my brain. "Before you kill me, I have a question." Still, not planning on the dying part, but I was a curious creature.

Lucifer eyed me with the same kind of interest Ruth was watching him with. "Ask your question."

Huh? That was a surprise. "Why couldn't you take Lilith here, on this property? I just don't get why I had to bring her to the corner of Spirit Lane and Crystal Row."

Lucifer smiled. It was disgustingly sexy. "Mortals are greedy, stupid creatures. Above all else, you serve yourselves. I underestimated you."

"You're welcome." I grinned, though I was disappointed he wasn't going to give me the answer. I wanted to tell him he was a greedy sonofabitch, too, but under the *we're all going to die soon*, I decided to keep that to myself.

The god's smile condensed, like he was overly confident he would eventually win, and Marcus angled his body so that half of it was in front of me, shielding me. "But I will find my wife," said the god. "Even without your help, I will have her again. She can't escape me for much longer."

"She will," I countered.

"You and this precious little town are all going to die."

Balling my hands into fists, I lowered myself into a crouch. I wasn't much with one-on-one combat skills, as Allison could attest, but I wasn't going to go down without a fight.

Murmurs of spells and curses reached me, and I knew my aunts and Iris were getting ready for a hell of a showdown. A familiar wave of energy rolled in the air, the scent a mix of pine needles, wet earth, and leaves with a wildflower meadow—White witches. I also felt a trace of cold, recognizable energy pulsing with a hint of sulfur—Iris's Dark magic.

The witches were ready and waiting.

Adrenaline soared into me, making me all hot and twitchy. I waited, watching the king of hell and anticipating one of his fingers to flick or snap or whatever he did when he was ready to kill us poor mortals. But the guy hadn't moved, and by the calm and collected expression on his face, he didn't look like he was planning on moving either.

I frowned, not liking that Lucifer hadn't even twitched an eyebrow, let alone flicked a hand or something. "What are you waiting for? I thought you wanted to kill me."

"I don't like to get my hands dirty with mortal

blood," said the god, glancing at his hands. "Which is why I won't."

My lips parted. "So, you're not going to kill us?" I heard Ronin's loud exhale.

Lucifer's blue eyes bore into mine. "I'm not. But they will."

From the shadows outside of the light came a series of deep hisses and growls. My skin erupted in goose bumps as the things that made the hissing sounds stepped out.

Great hounds, the size of ponies with dark fur, gleaming white teeth, and red, flaming eyes, too many to count, walked out. Picture Dobermans on steroids, and you'd be right. More hounds stepped out of the darkness, pacing in bloodthirsty joy. Hell-hounds. I'd read about them. I just never thought they were real.

Next, a group of men simply appeared as though formed from the darkness itself. Forty strong and clad in silver armor and masked helmets decorated with wings and sigils, their swords gleamed in the moonlight. It was something right out of a *Lord of the Rings* movie.

It was an army. Lucifer's army.

Well, sweet merciful crap.

20

This was a perfectly acceptable moment to panic. And so I did. I panicked the hell out of myself.

First came the denial, the *this can't be real* moment. Next came the tremors, followed by the intense pounding of my heart that would surely crack a rib.

How could my aunts and my friends fight an army like this? An army from hell? We might hold off for a few minutes, but soon they'd kill us all.

And it was all my damn fault. If I had given him Lilith, none of this would be happening.

Nice going, Tessa.

But then, I was pretty certain Lucifer would have killed me anyway since I still posed a threat to him.

Maybe not tonight or next week, but the day would have come.

He might have my magic with him, but now that I was staring at him in the face, he was full of anger, pride, and lust for power. Lucifer was a being of violence, deceit, and a thirst for dominion.

Ronin had been right. Lucifer wouldn't have let me live. So, I'd have lost either way.

Marcus, the gorilla, grabbed me and yanked me closer to him, cutting off my random mind babbling.

"Wee ffiiiht," growled the gorilla.

"There're too many," I said, wishing I had some magic to do something. Fighting without magic sucked. Fighting with untrained, useless upper limbs was even worse.

I felt so incompetent, and I hated feeling this way. I was a doer. Sitting on the sidelines wasn't my style. But what the hell was I supposed to do?

When I flicked my eyes back to where I'd last seen Lucifer, he was gone.

The hounds and the rest of the army spread out until they made a half circle around us. The scent of sulfur and wet dog wafted in the night air so strong it made my eyes water. My heart was pounding so hard I felt it on my scalp.

Behind me, voices rose in the air with spells and incantations, strong and confident. My aunts were badass witches, fearless, with incredible battle magic skills. I'd seen them fight. They could be brutal, but we were seriously outnumbered. We might last for a while, put on a good fight and even kill a few, but we wouldn't make it in the end.

My insides gave a tug. It would be a bloodbath. And it wouldn't be Lucifer's army. We would not survive this.

But then something unexpected happened.

Loud growls burst from somewhere behind me. When I turned around, fearing the worst, shapes I recognized exploded from the shadows. Shapes similar to the massive silverback gorilla still holding on to me.

Zeke's pack.

A hundred strong, fierce and bowel-watering feral gorillas came rushing forward and put themselves between us and Lucifer's army and hellhounds. I didn't recognize Zeke in the pack, but I spotted a tuft of red fur, which I knew was Lucas. But then white fur appeared among a sea of grays and blacks. A white-and-gray massive gorilla walked forward on his knuckles. He was huge. I knew without a doubt that I was looking at Zeke.

My knees wobbled as gratitude rushed through my body. The relief I saw on my aunts' faces echoed my own as the big gorilla pack formed a protective wall.

"They never left? This whole time?" I stared at Marcus.

The silverback gorilla shrugged. "Wee ffiiiht," he repeated. The gorilla pounded his fists on the ground, agreeing to the terms and acknowledging that he was indeed going to fight.

I fisted my hands and raised them. "Okay. But I'm warning you. I might accidentally punch myself out."

The next thing I knew, I was floating in the air. My ass hit something solid as I landed on the gorilla's back, straddling him like I would a horse. His thick, coarse, springy hair rubbed against my hands as I grabbed a fistful.

"Okay. This is better." I squeezed my thighs against his massive rib cage. My heart skipped a few beats. Even though we were about to fight beasts from actual hell, I couldn't help the grin that spread over my face. Fear and excitement were intoxicating feelings.

Okay, even though we were facing mortal peril, this was cool. And now, I had a ride.

"Nice." Ronin flashed me a smile. Then he cracked his neck and rolled his shoulders. "Too bad you've lost your magic for this fight. It's okay. I'll kill enough for the two of us," said the half-vampire, his eyes dilated as they flashed to black. He raised his hands as talons sprouted from his fingertips and hooked thumbs at himself. "I'm feeling especially violent tonight."

I didn't have time to comment as a mass of giant hounds came rushing at us, spilling through the night like the evil spawns from hell they were, as though the darkness itself had vomited them. The smell that oozed from the beasts was violently rotten, like a combination of puke and feces.

The white-and-gray gorilla opened his mouth full of teeth and roared. The gorilla pack burst into motion, moving with the speed and precision of predators as they met the hounds head-on. The ground shook like we were experiencing an earthquake—the tremor of the pack's rage.

"Aann onn," said Marcus the gorilla.

A mix of fear and excitement arrested me again. Leaning my body forward, I wrapped my arms around his neck and pressed my knees tightly against his muscular rib cage.

"Come and get me, mutts!" yelled Ronin, a manic smile on his face as he vaulted forward and threw himself at the nearest hellhound, slashing his talons like daggers across the creature's face and chest.

Dolores's voice rose above the snarls and the shouts. With my heart in my throat, I saw yellow flames spewing from her outstretched hands. Her fire hit one of the hellhounds, flooding it, but the beast kept moving, barely feeling the effects of the flames as it threw itself at a wereape. They both went down, and I lost them from view.

One thing was certain. The hellhounds were resilient. But so were the wereapes.

I looked over my shoulder. The armored men, demons, still hadn't moved. They were waiting. And I didn't like it.

Shouts and cries rang out, shrieks that could have been human and bellows and roars that couldn't have—a wild storm of music, of teeth rattling, overwhelming and charged with adrenaline. Sounds of efficient, brutal violence mixed with the howling of pain and breaking of bones. The air smelled of blood, animal, and sulfur.

A flash of dark fur caught my attention to my right, and I twisted around. A large hellhound came galloping at us like the ugliest pony that ever was.

Instinctively, I let go of Marcus's neck and raised my hands, a power word on my lips, ready to blow that ugly puppy into nothingness. I tapped into my will... and then stopped. I closed my mouth like a fool, feeling a great emptiness where there'd once been a well of magic.

I remembered I had no magic.

I flailed to the side as the gorilla pounded his fists on the ground. Terrified, I managed to scramble myself back up and throw my body forward, grabbing hold of his thick neck and possibly swallowing a few hairs in the process.

The wereape shifted his weight, and with a powerful thrust of his back legs, he shot forward and rushed to meet the hellhound as I bounced up and down, hanging on for dear life. Why was this a good idea again?

The hound opened its maw full of teeth, going for Marcus's jugular and probably my head in the process.

Marcus's gorilla fist shot out in a blur, landing a vicious blow on the hellhound's temple. I heard a horrible crack as the creature's head snapped back. The hellhound staggered to its knees. Marcus was on it in a second. He climbed over it with me still hanging on strenuously and feeling like a hiker about to fall off a cliff. With his fists, he smashed the creature's head, over and over again until it wasn't recognizable anymore and looked like Ruth's raspberry jelly.

I swallowed back the bile from my throat. That was pretty gross.

"Uuu gooood?" asked the gorilla, angling his head toward me. His gray eyes flashed with cold fury.

"Never better. We should do this more often. Like date night."

The gorilla flashed me a mouth filled with teeth,

in his version of a smile that would have scared the crap out of an ordinary person. Good thing I wasn't ordinary. I might be nonmagical, but I still lived in the paranormal world where killer gorillas were our boyfriends.

I could tell Marcus was enjoying the fighting and the killing—all those primal, protective instincts on overdrive. He was built for this. All those muscles and unmatched strength were to protect those he loved and his town. And he was good at it. Was it weird that it turned me on?

Yeah, he was obviously an excellent choice for an alpha. But he was Hollow Cove's alpha.

Roars sounded around us. Looking up, I got a glimpse of the whirling masses that were the gorillas Lucas and Zeke, fighting side by side. Zeke slammed his body against two hounds before picking them up and crushing them together. Their skulls snapped like smashed eggs. Zeke let out a roar like that of a mighty engine—to kill the threat. He was impressive to watch. He didn't look like he was ready to retire. But I didn't have time for that.

"Aann onn," said Marcus.

And we were off again.

Muscles flexed and slid under me as Marcus the gorilla vaulted forward in a burst of speed across the grounds. Wind lashed at my face, my hair tossing into my eyes. It was hard not to smile, not to feel empowered riding above such a magnificent beast. There was also the holding-him-between-my-thighs part.

Yeah, I was smiling, grinning like a fool. I was quite possibly mad.

I let out a shriek as the gorilla leaped over the garden shed in one bound, and for a second, I nearly lost my grip and tumbled off his back. Not that falling would hurt that much. I was more worried about my ego. Projectile Ex-Witch was not a nick-name I looked forward to. But I latched on, my grip on his throat tighter but not so tight as to choke him.

All around us was a whirling mass of hellhounds and gorillas. Blurs of teeth, talons, muscle, fur, and death.

Marcus let out a terrifying roar, letting the hounds know he was coming for them. It was almost like he *wanted* them to know. Yeah, he totally did.

I should have been holding a sign over my head that said *Free Punches Here*.

A hellhound with black fur and red eyes came at us from the right side with its jaw open. Marcus didn't stop. Hell, he didn't even slow down but put on speed. He knocked the demon with his right arm in a languid effort. The hound flew back and crum-pled to the ground. I could see the bones from its spine standing out sharply from its gaunt, emaciated back.

"Seee dat?" said the gorilla proudly, his muscles bulging beneath me. "Imm gud. But bedder aat sseex."

"You're crazy." I laughed, my face flushing. I really shouldn't be laughing. We really shouldn't be talking about sex either.

His shoulders bounced as deep laughter erupted from his throat. Which only made me laugh more. We were a match made in heaven. We were both mad.

"Marcus!" I shouted.

Two more hellhounds barreled our way. Like a brutal rhinoceros, the gorilla plowed through the demons, scattering them like pins in front of a bowling ball.

I lifted my head and scanned the area until I spotted Ronin, slicing the neck of a hellhound and using his talons as though they were blades, like a gruesome version of Edward Scissorhands. Just as the demon collapsed, another threw itself at the half-vampire. Ronin spun around and hooked two talons right in its jugular. And just as that one fell, another came.

A red gorilla, Lucas, smashed his fist against the base of a hound's skull and drove it right through soft flesh and muscle, causing black blood to ooze. Then he yanked out his hand, taking with it part of the demon's spine. I'd seen Marcus do that before and supposed it was a wereape thing.

The attack was bloody, brutal, primal, and violent. It was an annihilation. It was a kill-all-demons-before-they-do-us-in kind of killing.

Thunder tore the air apart as a bolt of white lightning struck a hellhound, throwing it in the air and hurling it violently on the ground. Beverly's face was twisted in a mix of fury and concentration while she hit the creature again as another shockwave of thunder boomed. The hellhound twitched and never moved another muscle.

If we hadn't woken the neighbors yet, this surely would.

Iris was next to Beverly, tossing what looked like hex bags at an approaching hellhound. One exploded on contact into a cloud of red dust. The impact sent the demon to the ground.

Dolores and Ruth stood shoulder to shoulder. Dolores held her palms out to Ruth, and yellow flames danced above her palms. Ruth sprinkled something over her sister's palms. The flames rose twice their size and changed from yellow to dark green flames. Then Dolores turned, and green fire shot from her outstretched hands at an unsuspecting hound.

The hound disappeared under the tall green

flames. The beast staggered and then exploded into ash.

Nice trick.

I looked around quickly, feeling a change in the air. It smelled less sulfury.

Then the sudden silence hit me. I wiped the hair from my eyes, spat out some of the gorilla's hair from my mouth, and looked around.

We stood in a sea of corpses and blood. Everywhere I looked, bodies of those hellhounds lay crumpled and crushed, beheaded, burned, and very dead. I spotted a few wereapes with bleeding gashes across their torsos, legs, and arms, but I didn't see any of them lying among the dead.

Dolores, Beverly, and Ruth were red-faced and winded but unharmed, from what I could see. Iris knelt beside a fallen hound, pulling out what I could see were some hairs.

And Ronin, well, Ronin had one foot planted on a dead hound's body, resting his hand on his knee in a Captain Morgan pose.

We'd all made it. All of us. And we'd defeated the hellhounds.

"We did it," I said, impressed and ecstatic that my family and friends were still all alive.

And that's when Lucifer's soldiers swooped in.

21

I propped myself up and watched in horror as the forty-strong armored demons advanced on us like a king's guard straight out of a medieval movie. The light of the moon glittered on their armor and swords, rushing forward like a lethal, bejeweled tide.

One of the armored demons cut down a gorilla and then turned to another, his free hand spinning through a series of gestures. Cold power surged around that gesture, and one of the gorillas simply stopped moving. The crackling in the air around them grew. The gorilla still didn't move, as though it was spelled.

"Shit. The armored guys have magic," I breathed.

And then, with a great swipe of his sword, he sliced off the gorilla's head.

"Well, that's not good," I muttered.

"Uuuck," cried Marcus. His body trembled in rage, making me feel like I was sitting on a massage chair.

I understood now why Lucifer had sent the hounds first—to ensure we were tired and weak and to make us believe we'd won just before he sent in the big guns. Clearly these armored dudes were the real threat.

The armored soldiers raised their swords in unison, and suddenly red flames surrounded their blades.

"Uuuck," cried Marcus again.

"Fuck is right," I said to the gorilla's wide back. "They have fire swords."

Around me, I heard the gorillas crouch down, growls bubbling in their throats as they attacked with a full-frontal charge. They let out full-throated howls, eerie and savage.

"Come and get it, tin men!" Ronin shouted in his version of a battle cry. He'd lost some of his smile. With his face set tight, he took a step back. His talons worked to slice flesh and even bone, but they were useless against steel.

A few of the armored soldiers broke away, moving steadily toward my aunts and Iris. The soldiers made swift hand gestures accompanied by bursts of magic pressure pulsing in the air around us with whatever magic they were going to cast.

"Get back, you devils!" Dolores cried, raising her arms above her head like she was about to make an offering, as the air buzzed with elemental energy.

Beverly, Ruth, and Iris were standing together with Dolores, all moving their hands expertly as their lips formed what could only be a protective spell to ward off whatever magic the armored soldiers were about to throw at them.

Together, the line of armored soldiers made fists with their free hands, and I felt the hair on the back of my neck rise in time with the change in air pressure. Red energy, the same color as their eyes, coiled around their palms.

And then, as one, they flicked their hands at my family.

Clasping their hands together until they made a circle, my aunts and Iris shouted a spell I couldn't make out, and a shivering dome of blue energy expanded over them just as a blast of red magic hit.

The shield shook under the pressure, and I held my breath for a horrible moment when I thought their shield would fall. But it held.

"Thank the cauldron," I whispered. But I knew it couldn't hold on much longer, not under this threat.

The sounds of fists hitting metal and flesh rose in

the sudden roar of battle as the two groups clashed. The armored demons struck hard and swift as a burst of wind with their supernatural speed, and I gawked in horror at the fallen bodies of a few gorillas in their wake.

A surge of red magic hit a gorilla in the chest. He faltered for a moment, and I hissed through my teeth. He shook his head and then pulled back his lips and roared, flinging himself at the armored demon that had attacked him. In a flash of fur and muscles, the gorilla grabbed the demon and lifted him as though he weighed nothing at all—and brought him down on his knee. With a horrible crack, the demon's body split in half, like the gorilla had just snapped a French baguette.

"Ahhh!" I shouted as Marcus sped forward without warning, sending me to bend backward in a bad version of a yoga camel pose. My body angled back like I was hit by a g-force.

With ab muscles I didn't know I possessed, I managed to fling myself over his back, wrapping my arms around his neck once again.

"A little warning next time!" I cried into the fur in his neck, my adrenaline soaring. "You almost lost me."

But Marcus never answered.

My body bounced as the silverback gorilla

charged at something with the speed and strength of a freight train. I raised my head a little as I heard the cry and the sound of tearing flesh.

A white gorilla fought two armored soldiers. A long red gash marred his arm as he punched and kicked the demons, his movements tired and slow. But even then, I saw what he was doing. He was keeping the demons from using their magic. Smart.

He rolled to the side and landed a massive, bone-shattering kick on one of the demon's legs. The armored demon fell.

Just then another armored sword bit into him, just below his ribs, thrusting up and back. The sword tore through him and out through his back, emerging like a bloody blade of grass.

"Nooooo!" shouted Marcus, putting on a burst of speed.

I couldn't take my eyes off Zeke, the blood a stark contrast against his white and pale-gray fur. He faltered, his mouth opened in a gasp.

The demon twisted his blade with a sickening pop and yanked it back out.

Zeke fell to his knees. His head bounced as he stared wide-eyed at the tear in his chest. And then he collapsed.

Marcus's roar was straight out of your worst nightmare. I'd never heard anything so ear-piercing with heart-wrenching terror at the same time. It was scary as hell.

The armored soldier's head whipped around toward us. But it was already too late.

Marcus hit the demon with the strength of a bus hitting a cement wall at fifty miles an hour.

We went sailing forward. Me. Marcus. Said demon.

I barely felt the landing. I was too busy trying to stay on the gorilla's back.

My body jerked like I was riding a bronc bare-back at a rodeo as Marcus pummeled the demon's head with his fists, breaking into a rabid frenzy of blows.

I felt the fury of the storm beneath me as Marcus ripped the limbs off the soldier. I guessed his armor didn't protect him from sudden amputation. With a final tug, the demon's head was pulled from his neck, and Marcus tossed it away.

And then he was moving again.

He launched himself at a group of armored soldiers, like an EFC fighter, kicking, punching, and tearing with a blur of fists hitting metal, among roars, teeth gnashing, and dark fur flying. Metal tore. Bones snapped. Each crushing punch sent bile rising to my throat.

I flinched as the tip of a blade whooshed over my head. Shit. That was close.

Marcus's rage vibrated through him. I felt it in the tightening of his muscles and the shifting of his skin. I felt the bloodlust. In his wrath, he'd forgotten I was on his back. All I could do was hang on for dear life as he swung himself at another group of armored soldiers.

Marcus tore at Lucifer's subjects with voracious rapidity, his powerful body a killing machine on steroids.

My thighs and arms burned in pain as I strained to stay on the gorilla's back. I wasn't known for my upper body strength. Sweat poured down my back and forehead as I clung to the beast.

I'm going to fall. I'm going to fall.

"Marcus! I'm slipping. Can't hold on!"

Marcus was lost in his rage and couldn't hear me.

The gorilla threw himself at another group of armored demons. A sword sliced his arm, causing blood to ooze from the cut, but Marcus barely took notice as he exploded into motion.

He swatted a demon in front of him like it was an annoying wasp and took another's head between his massive hands, crushing its helmet like a beer can. I heard a pop and the sound of bones crushing before the demon went limp in his hands.

A brute force hit Marcus on the side, just as I felt a burn in my body like I'd been electrocuted. I lost my grip and went sailing over the gorilla like a crash-test dummy without a seat belt.

I flew off Marcus's back and landed hard on the ground. Thank the cauldron for the soft cushioning of the grass and my extra fat. Otherwise, I'd have some serious broken hip bones and coccyx.

But it still hurt, especially when I hadn't been able to plan my landing with a fancy roll or anything.

Mouth open—because apparently, that's what you did when you were falling—I inhaled some grass, a bit of dirt, and possibly a pebble or two as I rolled to a stop.

I felt the breath leave my lungs, from hitting my chest on the ground. Gasping, I gagged at the choking smell of rot, sulfur, and burnt hair.

My head pounding like I'd been hit with a sledgehammer, I blinked and rolled over to my side. My head swam for a moment, and blackness clouded my vision. Blinking the black spots from my eyes, I pushed myself to my knees while taking in some air and turned to see Marcus still as a Greek statue and unmoving, just like I'd seen the other gorilla stiffen under the armored demon's spell. His gray eyes were the only things moving. They pinned me, and all I saw was complete and utter fear and desperation, not for him but for me.

I frowned, thinking that he thought I'd hurt myself in the fall. I did, but I'd live.

And just as I went to push myself up, I blinked at the sharp edge of a gleaming silver sword. The helmeted soldier's red flaming eyes looked at me through the visor of his helmet.

And then he brought down his sword.

22

Over the past year, I'd had several life-flash-before-my-eyes moments. Still, I'd never get used to them.

I stiffened like a fool, even peed a little, as I stared at the advancing, sharp blade of the sword.

Yup. I was going to die.

And when the blade was a millimeter from my neck, the moment when I felt the ice-cold blade touch my skin, it exploded into a cloud of ash. So did the armored demon.

I coughed at the disgusting ash I'd swallowed because apparently, I also opened my mouth before my moments of supposed death. I spat what could only be described as the taste of cat litter. Disgusting. Wiping the ashes and the tears from my eyes, I tried to make sense of what I was looking at.

"Lilith?" I must have hit my head in my fall. Surely I was hallucinating. The goddess could not be right next to me.

"No. The tooth fairy," she snapped, her long red hair loose and floating around her like she was underwater. "Get up. Or do you plan on sitting on your ass all night?"

Okay, not hallucinating. The left side of my head throbbed, so I did bump it in my fall. "You're actually here? Right here? At this very moment? But... why are you here? I thought you left?"

The goddess glared at me. Her eyes sparkled with barely contained wrath. "If you don't get up now, you die."

Okey dokey. I jumped to my feet, wobbled, and stuck out my arms to steady myself. I was still in shock at seeing the one person, goddess, I'd never expected to see in a bazillion years. I wrinkled my nose at the stench of burnt hair.

Lilith stared at me a beat too long. "What did you do to your hair and eyebrows?"

"What?" I reached up and winced as I felt a large bald spot on the entire left side of my scalp. I slid my hand over my hairless brow bone where my eyebrows used to be and shrugged. "Too much Head and Shoulders?"

"It looks terrible," said the goddess, like my vanity was supposed to be more important to me than my life at the moment. "Bald is not a good look on you. I, for one, can pull it off. Well, because I'm a goddess, and my beauty is immeasurable."

Speaking of my life. "You just saved my life." Again, the goddess was pulling her tricks, saving my life when I'd betrayed her and had nearly handed her over to the one god she'd been running from all this time.

"I know." Lilith's red eyes blazed with fury. She didn't really look happy about the fact, like for some reason she had to do it. "I can't let you die," she said.

I narrowed my eyes, my head feeling like it was filled with water. "Why not? It's not like you didn't threaten my life before. Many times, if I remember correctly. Why is this different?"

"We're connected through your blood," said the goddess, and again my mouth fell open.

"Huh? Can you speak slower? My hearing is still trying to make its way to my temporal lobe. I can see your lips moving, but nothing that's coming out makes sense."

"It's not complicated. When you released me from my cage, you used your blood. We're connected."

Yeah. I didn't really get that, but I didn't have time to argue with her, and my head still felt muddled.

But right now, I had more pressing matters to

attend to than this good Samaritan version of the goddess of hell.

Marcus.

Whatever spell had burned off a section of my hair and eyebrows had also hit him.

I ran toward the silverback gorilla, well, more like a waddle. By a miracle, he still had his head connected to his neck. He blinked at me as I neared, anger and that fear still present in them. I pressed my hands over his chest, my fingers tingling in fear, but he was still warm, still hard. But as stiff as a cement block.

"Oh shit. I need a spell or a counter-curse. Damnit. Can you undo this?" I asked Lilith as she joined me. "He's super hard!" Yeah, not exactly what I'd meant to say, but you get my drift.

A smile appeared on the goddess's face as she looked down at the gorilla's groin.

"You know what I mean." My heart lodged in my throat. "Can you uncurse him or whatever? Please. He can't stay like this. He'll be dead in seconds."

She rolled her eyes dramatically like I was an idiot for asking and snapped her fingers.

I felt a sudden slap of air pressure against my skin. A cool wind wafted around me, bringing with it the scent of spices.

"Eett duwwn!" Marcus threw his body over Lilith and me, crushing us both to the ground as I caught a glimpse of something silver rush over our heads.

I felt Lilith's hot breath brush against my face as she turned to me under Marcus's hard, warm body. "You sure you don't want to lend me your male? Just one night. The things he could do to me... the things I could do to him..."

"Urgh!" I kicked out my legs until Marcus got the message and hauled his massive body away from us.

The silverback gorilla ducked and spun around, grabbing the armored demon from behind and ripping off his head, helmet and all.

"Seriously. Just one night," said the goddess, staring at Marcus the gorilla like she wanted to jump his bones at this very moment. "He's splendid. I'd take him just like that. As a beast. For your information, they're much *bigger* when they're in their beast form."

If she hadn't just saved my life, I would have punched her.

Instead, I pointed to the battle. "Can you do something about your husband's army?" I growled through gritted teeth, staring at the armored demons cutting through more gorillas. My pulse skyrocketed when I saw a group of five demons hurling their red magic at my aunts' and Iris's shield. The shield wavered, and for a moment, I thought it was going to fall.

It didn't. Not yet.

The silverback gorilla put his body between Lilith and me and whatever idiot armored demon wandered our way.

"Lilith?" I cried. "Please do something if you can. We're being slaughtered."

Lilith's face flashed with disappointment. "No need to shout. But I would like to point out that they're here because of your scheming, lying ass."

"Seriously? You're doing this now?" My heart sank when I couldn't see Ronin anywhere. Where was that damn half-vampire? If he was dead, I'd kick his ass in the afterlife.

"I am." The goddess pressed her hands on her hips. "You brought this on yourself. You lied to me. You tricked me. Maybe you deserve to die. Maybe I should let them kill all of you."

"Really?" I fumed. "If I remember correctly, I saved your lame ass from that cage. This is not just me. You're involved in this too."

The goddess gave a shrug. "I thought we were friends."

"Oh. My. God! You're killing me." In a flash of brown hair, I spotted Ronin encircled by a group of demons near the garden shed. My moment of relief was replaced by sheer panic as I noticed their flaming swords pointed at his throat. Most of his face was lost to shadows, but I could just make out the terror on it. I'd never seen him look so scared.

Shit.

Lilith stared at her perfectly manicured fingers, looking bored. "Aren't we friends? I thought we were friends. Friends don't betray one another. Friends tell each other the truth."

My blood pressure was reaching a dangerously high level. "Yes. Yes, we're friends! I made a mistake. I'm sorry. Friends also know when it's time to forgive. Like right now. Please. Help us!" I said, waving my hands around like an idiot.

Lilith beamed, looking perfectly radiant, like she'd just stepped out of some posh New York City salon. "See." She reached up and squeezed my cheek. "That wasn't so hard. Was it?"

Incredulously, I watched as the goddess turned around, took three steps forward, and then splayed her arms to her sides as words spilled from her lips that I didn't understand. Could have been demon. Could have been gibberish.

A wind blew, carrying the scent of spices, the smell I now associated with Lilith's magic. Slowly, she raised her arms. I heard a sudden crash of thunder and saw a flash of light followed by a wash of heat.

Then, like a domino effect, every armored demon's body exploded into a cloud of dust and ash until all that was left were piles of gray ash and the scent of rotten eggs.

I stood staring for a few beats, making sure she hadn't missed an armored bastard. My gaze flicked to Ronin, who was sifting through a pile of ash like he was looking for a souvenir or something. His strained face twisted into a smile as he caught me staring.

"We got 'em, Tess. We fucking got 'em."

"We did."

The pressure in the air dropped, and I looked over to see my aunts' and Iris's shield gone, their faces happy and relieved.

Ruth pointed to a mound of ash that Dolores was about to smear with her shoe. "Don't. It's good compost for my garden."

Not sure I'd want to eat the veggies that came out of that garden, but whatever.

Among the ashes lay the bodies of six gorillas, including Zeke's white one. The remaining gorillas, all ninety-four of them, bent a knee to the ground, their heads bowed in sorrow and respect.

The air shifted next to me, and Marcus rushed over to Zeke's body just as I saw Ruth kneeling next to him, applying pressure to his wounds.

"He's alive," I muttered, suddenly aware of the aches and pains of my own body. It was going to hurt like a bitch tomorrow. And this time, I would take some of Ruth's healing tonic. I'd take a freaking gallon of it.

"Only four dead," announced the goddess, her tone businesslike and formal. "The others are seriously injured but alive."

"How do you know?"

Lilith arched a brow at me.

"Right." I exhaled, my body trembling as the effects of my adrenaline wore off. "Thank you for coming back. You didn't have to, but you did. You saved us. You saved me. I still don't get why you did that."

"Well, if I move here and you're all dead, it would be a little boring," said the goddess. "What's the point in living out here if it's a ghost town? I like to keep my entertainment close."

I noticed that she was avoiding my eyes—something I'd come to understand she did when she was uncomfortable.

I grinned. "You really like me. Don't you? I mean, you think of me as your family. Like a sister? Admit it."

Lilith rolled her eyes again, but I saw a clear twinkle in them. "You know, you're going to have a lot of work to do on your lawn. There're holes in the grass everywhere. You could break an ankle."

"Don't change the subject. You think I'm family."

"Don't be ridiculous. Mortals are not my friends.

I used to feed on them. You're nothing but animals. The superior beings eat the weaker ones."

Yeah, that was gross, but I smiled anyway. "Fine, but to clarify, you totally like me."

The goddess let out a puff of exasperated air. "Don't annoy me with your stupid mortal—"

Lilith's red eyes flashed with wild fear, her mouth opened in a silent "o."

I spun around.

It happened so fast.

Lucifer appeared behind us. His face was set in fury, his eyes glowing with some kind of hell mojo. He was pissed.

Without warning, he flicked his wrist and hurled a ball of darkness at Lilith.

"No!"

And like an idiot, I threw myself in the way and got the full intensity of Lucifer's spell.

23

I was the champion when it came to doing stupid things in my life, but this took the number-one spot.

A hard burst of energy hit me, sending me soaring across the grounds. I landed sprawled on my butt with my legs in the air. Not exactly pretty. My head smashed against the ground a moment later, complete with a burst of black spots in my vision and very real pain. My palms curled into claws as I panted through the pain and tasted blood in my mouth.

That's when the convulsions started.

I coiled into a ball as cold, acidic energy spread through my bloodstream, burning me from the inside. My head felt like it was splitting in two, and my vision blurred as the pain swelled. The scent of burnt flesh filled my nose. Was that my flesh? Was I really burning from the inside? Possibly.

I struggled to keep my breathing even as something cold and unfamiliar seeped inside me. My head snapped back as this new energy pooled into me. My body cramped, and my fear spiked as power cascaded over and inside my body like liquid light. I felt the simple touch of someone else's mind. Lucifer's.

His magic pounded and beat inside me. I sucked in a breath at the sudden outpour of magic creeping up my hands and arms. The power grew, strong and steady, seeping into me with a sort of hungry eagerness and replacing my pain and fear with nothing but power and ferocity. It was very dangerous and seductive.

My muscles quit seizing, and I sucked in a ragged breath. I took another breath and then another. My body relaxed, leaving only my pounding head and the taste of something metallic in my mouth.

I felt a tingling like thousands of ants crawling over my body and sighed in relief as the pain in my head subsided. I took a slow breath. God, that felt good.

Was I *breathing*? How was I still breathing? I'd been hit by Lucifer's mojo and survived? How was that possible?

I looked up to see Lilith standing over me, her eyes round and her red hair falling around a face set in utter shock. That made two of us.

"You're alive?" She rolled her eyes over me as though she was expecting to see some smoke or some missing parts. "How are you not dead?"

Good question. I opened my mouth to answer, but someone beat me to it.

"Tessa!"

Warm, hard hands were rubbing my arms up and down as I turned and blinked into Marcus's handsome face.

"How could you do something so stupid?"

"When do I not?" I answered. My throat burned and was a little dry. He was back in his human form, all golden, muscled, sweaty, and naked. Just the way I liked him.

He pulled me to my feet, looking me over just like Lilith had done. "But you're okay. You're fine. You're okay," he added, more to himself than to me.

I took a breath. "Looks like it." I'd never heard of someone being struck by a god such as Lucifer and surviving. Hell, I'd never even heard of Lucifer striking anyone or anything. But if he did, I was pretty damn sure that was the end of them. So, why did I survive?

"Oh, my cauldron! Tessa!" said Dolores as she rushed over, followed by Ruth, Beverly, and Iris.

With her hip, my tall aunt shoved a naked Marcus out of the way. She held my chin in her hands, staring at my face and eyes. She held up her hand. "How many fingers?"

"Three," I answered. "I can see fine. Nothing is wrong with my eyes."

In a blur of movement to my right, Ronin was there. "Tess. You're bald on one side," he laughed. "You've got no eyebrows, and now you're smoking. Literally smoking hot."

"Good to know."

Ruth stepped closer and was gently touching my scalp with her fingers. "I have an ointment that can fix that in a jiffy. Smells like poop but works wonders."

"Can't wait."

Iris was staring at me with a strange smile on her face. I knew that smile. It was part fascination and part envy. She was the only witch alive who'd trade places with me just to feel what it was like to be hit by one of Lucifer's spells. She was nuts, just like me. That's why we got along so well.

"We should get her inside," said Beverly.

"Yes. Yes," said Dolores, tugging my arm.

I pulled out of her grip. "It's all very interesting and fascinating that I'm standing here, though smoking, but we're kinda forgetting something important." I turned my head and spotted the king of hell.

Lucifer was watching our exchange with a puzzled expression. His face wasn't twisted in fury, and his eyes were clear blue, not gleaming with that murderous death stare. He looked... curious.

But Lilith's face went all kinds of crazy.

"You bastard! You tried to kill me!" Lilith marched over to Lucifer, her hair and clothes all lifting in the air with some invisible magic. I'd seen her mad before, but this time she looked like she was about to rip his head off with her bare hands.

Lucifer flicked his eyes to his wife. "No. That's not what this is."

"Wasn't it enough that you kept me your prisoner for over a thousand years? Now you want to end my life!"

Lucifer shook his head. "I didn't try to kill you. Listen to me. I just—"

"Liar!" raged Lilith. And then they both switched into some strange language I'd never heard before, speaking really quickly, shouting really, with lots of hand gestures. It was like we were witnessing a married couple having a fight in another country.

The only good thing about this was that Lucifer had lost interest in me.

"We should go while they're arguing," said Marcus, his voice low and reading my mind. His hands still rubbed my arms up and down, sending delicious little tingles inside me.

"He's right. Come on. Let's go," urged Dolores, and as usual, she took charge as the one leading us back to the house.

I started forward, but something in Lilith's tone made me stop and turn.

They were still throwing their hands in the air in a heated argument, but something was off. I saw it in Lilith's face. She looked... she looked scared.

When Lucifer grabbed Lilith's wrist forcefully, I kinda lost it.

Something inside me snapped.

Instinctively, I gathered my energy—from my anger, my fear, my aching head and burnt scalp, and even a bit from my hurt ego regarding my missing eyebrows. I raised my right hand, and a lance of black energy hurled out of my palm and soared across the grounds.

I didn't realize what was happening or what I'd done until it was too freaking late.

I watched as everything seemed to shift in slow motion. My eyes followed my lance of black energy as it flew straight and hit Lucifer right in the chest. It was a perfect shot. Apparently, I had much better aim when I wasn't focused.

Wwwwwwwhooops.

The king of hell stumbled back, his mouth open

and looking even more surprised than I did. He rubbed his hands over his expensive silk shirt, like he was looking for holes or something. His expression went through different stages—surprise, curiosity, and then full-on rage.

Double whoops.

"Okay, I think that's bad," I whispered, and I was hit with a sudden knowing feeling, like I was missing something important here.

Hang the fuck on!

"Wait a minute." I stared at my hand. "Holy shit. I've got my demon mojo back. How is this possible?" There was no mistaking it. I felt the cold, familiar pulsing inside me, flowing through my veins like it had never left.

I felt my power, the confidence all rushing back into me. All of it. My stolen magic came back to me, filling me up like a bottle with an almost-painful tingle as I held on to what was mine.

I'm back, baby.

"Tessa," warned Marcus, and I felt his body smack into mine as he pushed me behind him.

I looked over to Lucifer and lost my smile. Anger crept over his face. He clenched his jaw, making the veins at his temples stand out.

Maybe I wasn't going to survive this after all.

My aunts were staring openly at me in both fear and shock. The only one who looked impressed and happy was Iris, and maybe a bit envious that I'd hit the king of hell with my mojo.

"Tess, we need to split," hissed Ronin, appearing on my other side. "Like, right the hell now."

My heart pounded as I started to move away, Marcus still using his big body as a shield. My eyes moved from Lilith to Lucifer.

Lilith brushed a long strand of red hair back from her face. Her eyes were hard as she stared at her husband. "You deserved that."

Lucifer's head snapped in her direction.

And then something extraordinary happened again.

Lucifer, the supreme overlord of the Netherworld—started to laugh.

It started as a quiet sort of laugh you did at a restaurant, but then it exploded into the hard, loud laugh, the one where you had tears coming out of your eyes followed by stomach cramps.

"Okay, who else thinks this is weird?" I halted, staring at Lucifer as he laughed and continued to laugh hard until I started to get annoyed.

"What the hell did you do to him?" asked Ronin.

I shook my head. "How the hell should I know." I really didn't. And I'm not sure I liked this version of him either. It was creepy.

All I did know was that whatever spell or magic

Lucifer had thrown at Lilith had somehow returned my magic.

And then, to top off the creepiness and awkwardness of the situation, Lilith started to laugh too.

"You should have seen your face," she howled, pointing at her husband. "It was all..." She made a face, attempting to imitate his expression, which was really kind of scary. "And then you got all tense. I thought you were going to cry."

Lucifer burst out laughing again. "A mortal witch just shot me. She shot me. *Me*." And then he was overcome in a fit of hard laughs that had him bending forward.

I was really seriously annoyed at their laughter, but he'd just called me a witch, so I'd forgive him for that.

"I'm really confused right now," said Ronin.

"Better that they're laughing than trying to kill us," informed Dolores. She exhaled loudly. "I believe this fight is over."

"I should go look after Zeke," said Ruth. "He's going to need some stitches for the deeper wounds." I watched her bound across the grounds to where the alpha gorilla was now sitting in his human form.

"What happened to the bodies?" Most of the wereapes were all back to their human forms, naked, some sitting and some watching the exchange of

Lucifer and Lilith with strange expressions on their faces.

Beverly's eyes widened at the sight. A slow smile spread across her lovely face. "I think I'll go help Ruth." And then she was off, running toward the mass of naked men like she was competing in the women's hundred-meter dash.

"They moved the bodies away from view, out of respect," answered Marcus. "They'll be taken back to New York City tomorrow."

"I'm sorry. They didn't need to die."

Marcus took my hand. "It's not your fault. They chose to fight. They didn't have to, but they did."

"Still doesn't make me feel any better."

Marcus cupped my face and kissed me.

"Okay. Maybe *that* did a little."

The chief flashed me a smoldering smile. "I'll be right back."

"You can't leave after a kiss like that. It's not fair to my lips."

"I have to find my clothes," answered the chief as he bounded away. I stood staring at his very fine ass.

"Why do you need clothes?" I called back, my eyes still on that very fine butt of his.

Strange. He never really cared about his clothes, which were probably ripped to shreds. It's what usually happened when he beasted out.

"That's weird. Right?" said Ronin.

I turned to the question in his voice. "Oh. My. God!"

Lilith and Lucifer had apparently taken off their clothes in the space of me turning around for a few seconds and were in a very sensual kind of embrace.

And they were floating.

Ronin whistled. "Looking good, gods, looking good."

"Wow, I can't believe this," expressed Iris, her face darkening two shades. "Are they... are they just going to do it right here, in front of everyone?"

I shrugged. "They're gods." I thought that was answer enough. Strange how all of us seemed unable to take our eyes off the sexing deities.

Ronin nudged me. "Quick. Give me your phone. I lost mine."

"What? Why?" I couldn't pull my eyes away from the gods' naked bodies as they hovered in the air. Two feet, three feet, five feet.

"I want to take some pictures... maybe a video," answered the half-vampire. "What? I've never seen celestial porn."

At that point, Lucifer spun Lilith around, fondled her very large breasts, and then bent her over. He grabbed her hips and—

"Gotta go, people." I laughed, eyes wide, and spun around. I could never *unsee* that.

Iris grabbed a grinning Ronin and pulled him

away forcefully from the ongoing porn show, and we all headed back toward the house.

Ronin was right. Things couldn't have gone weirder tonight. I had the feeling Lucifer wasn't interested in killing me anymore. He wasn't interested in anything to do with me. I took that as a win.

One thing was for sure, my feud with the gods was over.

Or so I hoped.

24

I sat on a stool next to the kitchen island, too pumped with adrenaline and the intoxicating feeling of having my magic back to care about how tired I was, what parts of my body hurt, or what I looked like.

"Stop fidgeting," ordered Ruth, a smile on her cute face. Wearing a pair of pink kitchen gloves, she held a jar of green ointment and a flat wooden stick. "You don't want me to put on too much of my Hair-Grow ointment. Otherwise, it'll grow all over your face, and you'll look like a sasquatch."

"Marcus will hate it," meowed Hildo, lying on the island. "Or maybe he'll *love* it."

I smiled like an idiot, even though her ointment smelled and looked like something that crawled around in the town sewer. "I've got my magic, Ruth. I'm back. I'm a witch. I can be a Merlin again." The notion that I could be a licensed Merlin again had me on a high, like I'd downed ten espressos in one go. Even if I wanted to, I couldn't stop fidgeting. It was like my skin wanted to leave my body and do some cartwheels in the kitchen.

Ruth giggled. "I know." Her large blue eyes pinned mine. "Funny how things manage to fix themselves," she said, and I remembered our conversation a few weeks back when she'd told me precisely the same thing. Hmm. Was Ruth a psychic?

A cool sensation spread over my scalp as Ruth applied another layer of her Hair-Grow. I felt a tingling on my scalp, like a slight burning sensation, similar to when you dye your hair. It started to itch.

I raised my hand.

"Don't," warned Ruth, and I froze, my hand still in the air. "Unless you want some hairy fingers."

"Ah. That explains the kitchen gloves." I lowered my hand.

"Hey, Ruth." Ronin leered behind my short aunt. "You think you can save me some?"

Ruth eyed Ronin. "Sure. But why? Your hair looks fine."

Ronin gave a smug smile. "Thanks, darling. But it's for my chest." He lowered his T-shirt collar, exposing his smooth, hairless, muscular pecs. "Iris digs the more virile type. You know, for role-playing in the bedroom."

"Ronin," hissed Iris, sitting next to me. Pink spots had appeared on both cheeks.

"I'm thinking woodsman with a plaid shirt, even an ax," continued the half-vampire. "Rented a cabin up north. Keeping things exciting in our sex life is a real responsibility. Something I take very seriously. And I'm exceptionally creative with a sharp attention to detail."

"Oh, God, Ronin, stop." Iris hid her face with her hands. "Why do you always have to be so open about our sex life? It's supposed to be private. You know... between the two of us."

"He's a vampire," said Dolores, not looking up from the note she was writing. "It's in his nature to brag about his sexual endeavors."

I cocked a brow and looked at Iris. "I want to know more about this cabin in the woods."

"Urgh." Iris leaned on the kitchen island and buried her head in her arms.

Another cold sensation assaulted me as Ruth smeared some of her ointment on my eyebrows, or where my eyebrows should be since, apparently, they'd been singed off. I took her word for it since I hadn't looked in the mirror yet.

Once she was done, she leaned back. "There. Done. You should start feeling some tingling, and it might sting a bit. That means it's working. Don't touch your face."

I lowered my hand again. Crap. I hadn't even realized I'd lifted it. "How long will it take for my hair to grow back?" If it took a week or so, I'd have to cut my hair, and I really didn't want to. Maybe I'd start wearing hats.

"Fifteen minutes."

"Oh? Wow." My Aunt Ruth was truly gifted in potions and magical ointments. I was thrilled she wasn't upset with me anymore. She was making actual eye contact again.

I grabbed my tiny aunt and gave her a hug, enjoying how red her face got. "You're amazing, Ruth," I told the top of her head and then released her.

"And hot," said Ronin, adding another layer of red to my aunt's face.

"Oh, you two." Ruth stared at me, her face scrunching like she was trying to remember something. "Oh. And you need to rinse it all off after fifteen minutes, and then you can wash your hair as you normally do."

"What happens if she doesn't wash it off?" asked Ronin, though I wanted to know as well.

Ruth shrugged and said, "Then you'll wake up in the morning looking like Cousin Itt, from *The Addams Family*."

"Nice," laughed Ronin. "Iris might dig that too."

"I'll make sure to wash it all off," I answered, now a little bit freaked out.

Ruth picked up Hildo and wrapped him around her shoulders like a scarf. The cat familiar purred loudly, clearly pleased at being used as a cat shawl. Still smiling, Ruth made her way out of the kitchen and disappeared into the potions room.

Iris straightened. "Where's Marcus? I thought he was with you?"

"Outside. Looking for his clothes, I think. He's probably with Zeke and the others."

The Dark witch leaned closer to me, eyeing my scalp. "Wow. I can see some of your hair sticking out of the ointment already."

"Really?" I reached up to touch my head but stopped. Having hairy fingers would definitely dampen my sex life. Maybe I should find some kitchen gloves before I got myself into trouble.

My father came strolling into the kitchen, holding a glass of golden liquid that looked a lot like gin. "Well, I believe Lucifer and Lilith are gone. We can all relax."

Calling my father was the first thing I did as soon as I'd entered the house. He needed to know what had happened, and I wanted him to stop whatever investigations he had going for finding the incubus Derrick.

"Where's Mom?" I grabbed my coffee and took a sip.

"Sleeping," answered my father. "She's been painting the new house all day. She's exhausted. I didn't want to wake her."

I knew she'd be angry that I didn't tell her about my magic. But it was only one day. Waking her up wouldn't make a huge difference. My magic would still be there tomorrow.

"Did you ever find Derrick?"

"I did," answered my father. He took a sip of his gin. "He's dead."

I spat the coffee from my mouth, showering the kitchen island. "I'm sorry. What?"

My father took another mouthful of his drink, joining us around the kitchen counter. "It explains why I couldn't find him. But he's most definitely dead."

"Good," muttered Iris and flipped a page from Dana on the kitchen island.

I made a face, resisting the urge to scratch my scalp. "You think Lucifer offed him?"

My father rested his glass on the island, careful not to lean where I'd spat my coffee. "That's my thinking, yes. Get rid of the evidence and all that. Can't say that I'm sorry to see him go. Dreary fellow."

"Me neither. He was a bastard. But he was still Lucifer's guy."

"Netherworld politics are complicated. We might never know the real reason he was taken out. But I suspect he knew too much about Lucifer's plans."

"Right. Or the fact that Lilith and Lucifer were suddenly having hot sex out in the yard," I told him with a laugh. "It's been a strange yet eventful night."

"Indeed," agreed my father.

"Oh, hi, Obiryn," said Ruth stepping back into the kitchen. With Hildo still draped around her shoulders, she had an ash bucket in one hand with a small shovel and broom in the other.

"Where are you going?" I asked my aunt.

"Going to pick some of the demon ashes for my garden." She beamed like she was going blueberry picking in the middle of the night. "See you later!" she called and disappeared out the kitchen's back door. I watched her go. A ball of light appeared just over her head, a witch light. At least she was prepared.

The door swung open again, and Beverly waltzed into the kitchen looking luminescent and fresh, not at all as though we'd just battled a bunch of demons a few hours ago. I think it had something to do with the naked men in our backyard.

"Isn't this marvelous?" She beamed and made her way to the kitchen. She piled a few clean rags in her hands. "All these muscular, gorgeous, available men."

Told ya.

"What's so marvelous about that?" growled Dolores, not looking up from her letter.

Beverly tugged a strand of blonde hair behind her ear. "I've got a date for each night this week with all different men." She smiled devilishly. "You can't tame this lioness, not when there's so, so much prey to be had."

"You sound like you want to eat them," muttered Dolores.

A wicked little smile played over Beverly's full mouth. "Who said I didn't?"

Ronin lifted his beer to Beverly. "You go, girl."

Beverly's eyes lit. "Oh, I'm going. I'm going hard."

Not sure how I was supposed to answer that, I just gave her a tight-lipped nod.

I watched as my Aunt Beverly filled a bowl with water, checked her reflection in the toaster, and then disappeared through the kitchen's back door.

I raised my hand to scratch my scalp again. "Damn it." I stuffed my hands under my butt to keep them from moving.

I looked over at Dolores, curious. "Who are you writing to at two in the morning?"

"To that old crone Greta," answered Dolores, looking pleased. She put her pen down and pulled off her reading glasses. "She needs to know that your magic has returned. Can't wait to see that look of surprise on her smug, wrinkled face when you show her. Ha! It'll be like Christmas."

I wrinkled my face. "Please don't tell me she has to come back and test me? Not again."

Dolores blinked.

"Well?" I prompted.

A smile twitched on her lips. "You told me not to tell you."

I let out an exasperated sigh. "Okay fine. I've got my magic back. She can test me all she wants. I'll only need a few days of rest, and I'll be at my old self again." It made sense that she had to test me to make sure I was a dud, and now she had to test me again to reinstate me as a Merlin.

"You better get your beauty sleep," said Dolores. "Because they'll be here tomorrow morning, bright and early."

"Of course they will." I sighed and checked my phone. I had about four minutes left before I had to wash out the Hair-Grow ointment. I stood up from the stool. "Well, I better get some sleep."

"Yeah, we're going too," announced Iris, standing and slipping Dana into her bag. "I'll be back tomorrow morning. I don't want to miss those tests."

"Thanks." I turned to my father. "I'll see you tomorrow night or earlier, depending on how Mother reacts."

My father smiled. "Better get more sleep."

With that, I left the kitchen and made my way down the hall. Just when I was about to go up the staircase, the front door opened, and a half-dressed Marcus emerged.

"Couldn't find your shirt?" I asked, admiring the golden muscles on his hard chest, my fingers itching to touch it. My tongue wanted to lick that little drip of sweat I spotted on his right pectoral.

"No," he said, flashing one of his million-dollar smiles. "I didn't think you'd mind."

"Not one bit," I purred, my gaze traveling down to his jeans and wanting to rip them off. An orgasmic tournament with Marcus was just what I needed right now.

He angled his head, frowning. "What's that on your face and your hair?"

My mouth opened in mortification and a bit of panic. What the hell did I look like?

And then I remembered I didn't care. "Ruth's hair-growing ointment. I have to wash it off." I started up the stairs and looked over my shoulder. "You coming?" I realized then how that sounded, making my face flush.

A tiny growl erupted from his throat. "You bet I am."

Heart pounding, I marched up the steps, aware that Marcus was right behind me. "Are you staring at my ass?"

"It's a very fine ass," said the chief, making my skin erupt in delicious goose bumps.

The staircase couldn't be any longer. My hormones raged as we hit the landing to the attic and stepped into my bedroom.

Just as I closed the door, he grabbed my shoulders and spun me around to face him. I let out a little cry of surprise, which was cut short by the crush of his lips on mine.

Oh, yeah. It was happening.

His kiss was hard and possessive, and I melted into it, enjoying the feel and taste of him. He tasted like spices and something wild and fierce, and I couldn't get enough. My arms slid around his neck as I pulled him to me. His growl sent heat through me, awakening all my senses. I pressed tighter against him, my hands slipping down his neck and over the cords of hard muscle on his back.

His hands slid up my shirt, caressing my back, and expertly unfastened my bra. Then they slipped to the front and grabbed my breasts. His fingers brushed my nipples, teasing and making them ache while sending shivers through me.

"I'm going to make you scream tonight," growled the chief, pulling his lips from mine to catch his breath. "Many, many times."

Yay me!

"We need a place of our own," I breathed,

knowing that even Davenport House's walls couldn't conceal the amount of screaming that was about to come out of my throat in a few minutes. "Our own place. A new place where we can start putting real roots down." I wanted to move in with him, just not over his office where his employees would see my comings and goings. We needed something new.

The muscles on his neck and chest bulged. He looked feral like he was about to eat me alive.

Double yay me!

"We will," he said, his voice ragged with emotion, and I realized we'd both agreed to this next step in our relationship. "We can start looking tomorrow. Tonight, we're doing this here."

"Yes, Chief." Chief me, please.

He kissed me again with a hungry groan, and then he grabbed my ass and pinned me against his very hard bulge in his jeans. His scent and the heat from his body were making me dizzy.

My body clenched under his touch. I didn't want to let go. Hell, I wanted to jump his bones right at this moment, my lady regions pounding for a little action.

But I had goo in my hair, and I stank like a men's locker. Some things just had to be done with a bit more class and hygiene.

I pulled away. "I'm disgusting. I need a shower. I'm not letting you touch me anymore until I've scrubbed the demon ash and all other scum from my skin."

Marcus yanked me back, a sinful gleam in his eye. "I don't care. I like you all sweaty and dirty. It turns me on. Must be my animal side," he added with a grin.

I pushed him away playfully, getting seriously turned on by the hardness of his manhood. "I have to wash that gunk out of my hair too. We're both disgusting."

Marcus growled, his expression lecherous. "You're making me crazy. I don't think I can wait that long."

If I had any doubts about how I made him feel or any insecurities about my cellulite, flabby arms, or my wine gut, they vanished at the lust he had for me.

With his gray eyes holding mine, I saw a blur, and he then was pant-less, standing in his naked glory with a very hard penis.

"One day, you'll have to teach me how to do that," I told him, knowing that my clothes were so dirty, I'd have to carefully peel them off if I didn't want any skin to strip away at the same time. "But don't worry." I stared at his long, hard manhood. "I'm going to destroy little Marcus."

The wereape laughed, his eyes sexy. "He's not that little."

"No, he isn't." I smiled. "You go ahead and take your shower. I'll be right there."

Marcus folded his jeans and placed them on the chair next to my desk. Then he stepped into the bathroom. I heard the sound of the shower as I moved to my master closet and in front of the tall mirror.

"Ruth was right," I said. "My hair grew back." The left side was nearly the same length as my right. I just needed to give it a couple more minutes, and I'd be as good as new.

"At least I have eyebrows."

Thrilled to have my hair and eyebrows back, I carefully peeled off my dirty, ash-stained clothes.

"You coming?" came Marcus's voice from the shower.

"In a minute," I shouted back.

As I rushed to the bathroom, I hit my hip on the chair next to my desk because I lacked motor control, and Marcus's jeans fell with a flop.

"Urgh." I bent down to yank them up, and something small and square fell from one of the pockets.

A box. A small black box.

I froze, my heart thumping. Why would Marcus be carrying what looked like a jewelry box? That's why he'd hunted for his jeans. He'd had the box with him.

I looked over to the bathroom. The door was

slightly ajar, so I couldn't see Marcus, but I could hear the water splashing.

What does a witch do when a pretty black box falls from her boyfriend's jeans?

She grabs the box and opens it, that's what.

I leaned over and snatched the box, my fingers trembling slightly. Holding my breath, I snapped it open.

A ring sat on a white cushion. I picked it up and held it closer. It was white gold with small diamonds circling around it like an eternity ring. It wasn't a gaudy ring, with a diamond the size of a pea, one that you had to blink away the glare when it hit the light. It was simple. It was beautiful. It was perfect.

I caught a glimpse of an inscription on the inside. Angling it in the light, it read: *MINE.*

"Oh boy! Oh boy! Oh boy!" Yeah. I sounded like a happy Labrador retriever.

MINE.

I'd never belonged to anyone before, not really.

MINE.

Holy crap on a cracker.

My first thought was that Marcus was going to propose. The second?

Allison was going to hate this.

25

I stared at the ceiling. Dawn was a golden promise across the horizon, and I had yet to sleep a wink. I'd been staring at the ceiling for about an hour, listening to Marcus's low, even breathing. His handsome face was smooth and peaceful, his breathing low and rhythmic. I was so tempted to brush my fingers along his brow or rake them through his luscious black locks, but that would surely wake him up. The man didn't even snore. He was perfect.

And I was to be his.

Which was the main reason I couldn't sleep and kept waking up, dreaming of giant rings rolling down the hill, me running away, them trying to crush me.

Rings were everywhere. And, if I stared at a spot on the ceiling long enough, I could see a ring. If I closed my eyes—again, rings were painted on the inside of my eyelids.

The rising sun was a ring. The shapes in the clouds were rings. Rings. Rings. Rings.

I was a mental case. And I couldn't stop smiling, a large, goofy grin that nearly touched my ears.

Marcus hadn't shown me the ring yet, but it was coming. He had it with him, so he meant to do it soon. Why else would he bring it with him?

I'd thought he was going to do it last night after I'd stuffed the box back in the pocket of his jeans. We'd done some orgasmic gymnastics in the shower, me even more enthusiastic about our lovemaking since I knew his secret. But after we took the shower scene to the bed and lay there for about an hour, it didn't look like he was going to do it.

I'd left it at that. I didn't want to be that woman, the one who ruined his presentation because she's just so damn excited.

But I was excited. I couldn't help it.

"You okay?" Marcus had asked as he lay on his side next to me a few hours ago, running a rough hand down and up my arm. "You're all fidgety. Nervous about tomorrow?"

No. "Yes. A bit. More like I'm anxious to show Greta and Silas that I'm back." Which was partly true. I was eager to see Silas's face when I kicked his ass.

Marcus dropped a kiss on my shoulder and then my neck. "You'll do fine." He rolled onto his back and folded an arm under his head. "I don't know why they were in such a hurry to take away your Merlin license. If they had waited, they wouldn't have to come here in the first place."

I shrugged. "I don't make the rules. I just have to try and abide by them. Even if I think they're stupid."

The chief smiled. "Think of it as the last time. You won't have to do this ever again."

I turned my head on my pillow so I could see his face. "Unless Lucifer decides to take my magic away again." It was still a possibility because of my unique blood. It was something I'd have to live with.

"You think he'll do that? I had the impression the guy had resolved his issues with his wife." He laughed. "It seemed they were getting along just fine."

"They did. I hope you're right. But you know, I'm not going to think about it anymore. As far as I'm concerned, it's done. I need to move on and live my life... think of my future... our future."

Hint. Hint.

The chief stared at the ceiling, his expression unreadable. "I'm glad you have your powers back. I know how much they mean to you. But even if you didn't, it wouldn't change how I feel about you."

Oh boy! Oh boy! Here it comes.

Marcus turned to look at me, his gray eyes dreamy. "We should celebrate. I'll take you out to dinner to celebrate. There's a new restaurant in Cape Elizabeth I'd like to try. The reviews are good."

And then my happy balloon deflated.

Trying not to sound disappointed, I forced a smile on my face. "Sounds great." We were quiet for a while, me thinking of rings and Marcus thinking of God knew what.

"When is Zeke going home?" I asked after I couldn't handle the silence anymore.

"Tomorrow. They need to take the bodies back and prepare the funeral arrangements."

"But not all of them. I think Beverly has a few hot dates with some of the pack."

The chief laughed. "Yeah. A few guys are sticking around for a while."

My blood hummed in my ears. "Is Zeke upset that you refused? I mean, he came all this way to try and tempt you. He's gotta be a little disappointed."

Marcus stared at the ceiling for a while before answering. "He knows I'll never accept," answered the chief. "He knows now. Recognized it. Lucas really stepped up. He fought like a champ. He proved to the pack that he was truly the right choice as alpha. The pack is behind him, all of them. Even Zeke."

"Good," I said, smiling.

Marcus turned and lowered himself on top of me. "I'm not going anywhere."

"You better not," I said, right before his lips found mine.

After another round of the horizontal tango— but who's really counting—we'd fallen asleep. Well, he had while I was being tortured by dreams of rings, and kept waking up.

When I couldn't stare at the ceiling anymore, I swung my legs off the bed and tiptoed to the bathroom. Once I'd done my business, I got dressed and went in search of breakfast.

I was ravenous. And I needed a full stomach, energy to kick Silas's ass.

Feeling like I was on cloud nine, or rather cloud *MINE* (see what I did there), I closed my bedroom door behind me and rushed down the stairs.

The scent of butter and something sweet like vanilla filled my nose, mixed with the aroma of brewing coffee as I entered the kitchen. Making my way, I could see Ruth at the stove, smiling as she whisked a batch of what looked like French toast. Hildo, her familiar, dipped his paw in the batter as usual. Dolores and Beverly were seated at the kitchen table, Dolores reading her morning paper while Beverly went through her small black book of eligible men she kept tabs on.

They both looked up as I approached, and I made a beeline for the coffee machine. I needed caffeine like I needed air right now. Not that I thought it was smart to add caffeine to an already jumpy body, but I needed it.

I filled my cup, took a long, deep drink, and smacked my lips. "Yum. This is really good coffee," I said, turning around and resting my butt on the edge of the counter. "How is everyone doing? You guys look good. It's going to be a nice hot day today, I think."

Dolores peered at me from above the rim of her reading glasses. "You're in a good mood."

"It's all that sex she had with Marcus last night," interjected Beverly, a mischievous smile on her beautiful, perfect face. She looked at me and winked. "This house has thin walls, darling. I mean, *really* thin walls."

I opened and closed my mouth. I was in a good mood but not good enough to have a conversation about my sex life with my aunts.

Beverly flipped a page from her book. "I'd be all smiles, too, if I'd gotten four orgasms last night," taunted my aunt, her face fresh and her makeup flawless as usual.

I cringed. Could they hear us in the shower too? It was time to find a place of our own, like yesterday.

Ruth turned around from the stove. Her gaze was bewildered. "Four orgasms? Is that even possible?"

Dolores choked on her coffee.

Yup. Kill me now.

Beverly giggled. "Of course it's possible, silly." She smiled proudly and said, "My record is seven orgasms in one sexual encounter." Her eyes met mine. "You still have a ways to go if you think you can beat that."

"Uh... Ummm..." What the hell was I supposed to say to that? It was barely eight in the morning, and we were talking about orgasms.

But I was saved from having *that* conversation as Ruth placed a plate piled with two French toast pieces on the kitchen island.

"Here you go, Tessa," she said, all cheery and smiles. "The maple syrup is right there." She pointed to the can of maple syrup with a large red maple leaf on the label. "My friend Sophie sends me a batch every year. She's a witch just across the border in Quebec. Bon appétit."

"Thank you."

"There's lots more. You need your strength for the tests this morning," said Ruth as she turned back to the stove.

I cleared my throat as I took my seat. "And we're sure they'll be here? This fast?"

"Of course we're sure," snapped Dolores, having recovered from her coughing fit.

I waited for more, but I guessed that was all the answer I was going to get. After I poured a generous serving of maple syrup, I dug into my French toast and took a bite. Yum.

"Soooo good," I said with my mouth full. "Thanks, Ruth."

"Oh, you're welcome, dear," said Ruth over her shoulder. She turned her head, a question on her face. "Do you think Marcus will want some too? I've got lots."

I swallowed. "I'm not sure. He's still sleeping."

"I'd be, too, after all that work last night," said Beverly as she flipped another page from her black book.

Dolores stared at her sister. "I thought you were already booked for this week? Don't you have dates with some of the wereape men?"

"I do." Beverly looked up from her book, looking pleased with herself. "But a girl can never have too many dates."

"Sure she can," said Dolores. "They're called working girls."

Ruth giggled like this was any normal morning in the Davenport household. Guess it was.

I took another bite of my French toast. "So, who're you going on your first date with?" I'd never been that interested in my aunt's dating scene, but seven different men on seven different days? That deserved to be talked about. Hell, she probably deserved a medal.

Beverly looked up from her book and flashed a dazzling smile. "Zeke is taking me to lunch."

I set my fork down. "Zeke? Are you sure?" She gave me an *are you kidding me look*, like how dare I ask her if she was sure about a gentleman. "Okay. You're sure. I just thought he was on his way back to New York. That's what Marcus told me."

"He changed his plans for me," said my aunt. "I'm known as the woman who gets what she wants from a man. I'm blessed with gorgeous looks and body and the ability to persuade the opposite sex."

"More like manipulate the opposite sex," snorted Dolores. "The way you wave your vagina around? Of course you get what you want."

Beverly's cheeks flushed, but she was smiling. "I don't *wave* my vagina around, Dolores. I present it."

It was my turn to choke, and I coughed, but thankfully I was able to keep all my French toast in my mouth.

Beverly laughed. Even Dolores started laughing. This conversation was just getting better and better. I was thankful Marcus was still sleeping. He didn't need to be subjected to this.

Ruth leaned over my shoulder, eyeing my plate.

"I make shapes out of my French toast too," she whispered, like we were sharing a secret.

"Huh?" I looked down. "Oh. I carved a ring." I'd carved out a ring out of my last French toast, and I'd never even noticed. I needed help.

"What's that?" asked Dolores, raising her head and trying to see my plate.

I sliced my French toast in half with my fork. "Nothing. Just messing with my food." I had to get my head on straight and stop thinking about rings so I could focus on what I was about to face this morning. My career as a Merlin depended on it.

The doorbell rang.

Dolores whipped her gaze in my direction. I could see the wheels spinning in her head.

I smiled and cracked my fingers. "Game on, ladies."

26

The sun burned the top of my scalp as I stood in the backyard facing a smiling Silas and a patio that looked more like a jury panel, judging from the frowns and critical brows.

The tattooed witch stood with a smug edge to his stance. So irritating. And strangely satisfying.

"Are you smiling because you missed me?" I asked him.

Silas's goatee stretched along with his smile. "I'm smiling because I'm going to beat you again. I'm smiling because I'm going to enjoy inflicting pain on you."

"Oh, really?"

"You're just an attention-seeking loser. This time, you're going to stay down."

"Come again?"

He stared at me for a moment. "You can't have your magic back. Yeah, witches can lose their gifts with age. Just like looks, the magic goes with the years. They surpassed their well of magic. It's dried out. But it never comes back. Once a witch loses their magic, it's lost forever."

I hooked a thumb at myself. "Not this witch."

Silas snorted. "You're not a witch. You're a dud. And today, I'm going to prove it again."

I wanted to strangle him with his ponytail. "We'll see."

I flicked my gaze over to the patio to the old woman in a light-blue silk gown. She sat in her chair proudly, like it was a throne. Her short white hair swayed in the morning breeze, and she didn't look one bit tired. She didn't look like someone who'd just traveled about four hundred and fifty miles in a short time.

It was highly unlikely anyone could make a trip this quickly from New York City unless they had a private jet or something better... or unless they'd used a magical means of transport.

"You must have really fast brooms to be here this quick," I told Silas.

Silas snorted a breath through his nose. "Wouldn't you like to know."

"I would, actually." I waited for a reply, but he

never opened his mouth. Oh well. That would have been interesting.

Still, I had a feeling Greta used ley lines like me, which would explain the reason why I was never suspended from using them in the witch trials because she used them as well. And Silas, being the frustrated, envious witch he was, didn't want me knowing.

Dolores sat in a chair to Greta's left. My aunt's chair rested a foot farther out than Greta's, and I knew Dolores had done that on purpose. Kinda like a dog marking its territory. This was her way of showing Greta who was in charge here.

Beverly was next to her and kept looking over her shoulder like she was expecting someone. The said someone was Zeke. The man, wereape, had been seriously injured last night, or so I thought. Either he healed really fast, or he just didn't want to miss a date with my beautiful Aunt Beverly.

Ruth looked more nervous than me. She sat on her hands, rocking back and forth and looking a little pale. Hildo wasn't on her lap. Knowing him, he was probably stuffing his face with all the leftover French toast.

Standing behind them and leaning on Davenport's back wall with his arms crossed was Marcus. He'd appeared down the stairs just as the doorbell rang about a half hour ago.

"I'm going home to change. Be right back," he'd said as he kissed the top of my head and disappeared through the kitchen's back door, leaving me alone to greet Greta and Silas.

Now he was standing on the back porch dressed in fresh clothes with a concerned frown on his face. I looked at the pockets of his jeans. I couldn't see a bulge. Wait. I could make out *a* bulge, just not the sharp bulge of a small box in one of his pockets. I felt like a pervert, staring at my man's junk. Did he have the ring with him? Did he leave it in his apartment? If he did, what did that mean? Did he change his mind?

I was a mess. A jittery, unfocused mess.

Yet, Marcus was all focused on Silas with murder in his eyes, like he wanted to punch a hole through Silas's chest. There was history there. The witch had imprisoned Marcus and beaten him, all the while having put a magical amulet around the wereape so he couldn't heal and would be in constant, excruciating pain.

I hated that bastard. It seemed Marcus hated him too.

I caught Silas watching me. His evil smile conveyed that he sensed my unease and felt how unfocused I was. Shit. This was not how I had fantasized about this moment. I'd fantasized about it a lot. I needed to clear my head.

"You're going to fail," sneered the witch, mistaking my jitters for the tests.

Ignoring him, I spotted Iris and Ronin walking beside the house, coming to join my aunts and everyone at the back patio.

It gave me an idea.

Heart pumping, I rushed over to Iris and got right into her face. "I need you to do me a favor."

Iris blinked. "Sure. Anything. What do you need?"

I shifted my weight. "Hit me."

Ronin snorted. "This is like one of the dreams I've had. You and Iris—OW!" The half-vampire rubbed the spot where Iris punched him.

The Dark witch flicked her gaze back at me. "You're not making any sense. You want me to *hit* you?"

I nodded. "I can't focus. I keep thinking about the ring and Marcus—"

"Wait. What ring? There's a ring?" said Iris, her eyes wide like they were about to pop out of their sockets.

"Yes. No. The point is, I have to focus if I want to pass these tests, and my mind's not in it. That's why I need you to slap me across the face as hard as you can. Do it. Do it now. Because if you don't, I'm going to fail, and I won't get my Merlin license. Is that what you want? You want me to—"

Iris's hand came out of nowhere. Her palm hit my left cheek hard, and my head whipped to the side, nearly giving me whiplash.

"OW!" I pressed my hand on my throbbing cheek.

"Too hard? Sorry." Iris looked a little terrified at what she'd just done, but I could see the corners of her mouth twisting up, like a part of her had really enjoyed slapping me in the face.

"No. It's good. It worked. Thanks."

Iris beamed. "Any time."

Ronin shook his head. "Women. Complicated creatures. I really don't get you."

With my cheek still throbbing, I rushed back to my spot where Silas waited. Strangely, he wasn't looking at me. He was looking at the patio with a frown on his face.

"Who's the redhead?" he asked.

I followed his gaze. Shit. Lilith was here. Apparently, she thought it okay to take a chair and sit next to Beverly. I didn't know all the rules and regulations when it came to witches and the courts, but I didn't think being friends with a goddess would look good on my record. If Greta or Silas found out who she was, it might not turn out well for me. Not well at all.

"Our cousin," I answered, keeping my voice even. "She's taken, so you can forget it," I said quickly, thinking this type of declaration would sound real enough. "You're not her type."

Silas made a face like he wasn't interested, so I knew he'd believed my lie.

Marcus was staring at me like I'd lost my mind. Maybe I had, just a little bit. Call me crazy, but the slap had worked. I was focused. All I could focus on was the throbbing of my cheek and the tests. It was on, baby.

I did a few jogs on the spot, planted my feet, and rubbed my hands together. "We doing this or what?"

Silas watched me for a beat and then turned to Greta, seemingly waiting for her approval.

Her dark eyes met mine, she held them, and then she gave a single nod.

Okay then.

"Where's your bag of tricks?" I asked, just realizing Silas didn't have a bag with him like he did the last time.

The tats on Silas's face and neck glowed red. "I'm it."

The next thing I knew, the witch pulled off his shirt, just as Beverly gave a clap and some excited "oohs" and "ahhs."

His toned bare chest was completely covered in tattoos. The runes and sigils covered his arms and shoulders up to his neck. I knew his ink was his magic. I'd seen him use them before. He'd had the tats inscribed in him for power.

So, he was going to use his magic on me. I could play this game.

"Bring it," I told him and motioned with my hand.

When I looked over at Marcus, the chief had moved away from the wall and was standing near the edge of the patio. The tilt of his head and the tension in his posture showed that he was furious. His eyes gleamed with animalistic fury, the kind where he was seconds away from beasting out and tearing into Silas if he so much as hurt a hair on my body. That was all kinds of hot.

Back to Silas.

The tats on his face and neck continued to glow. A tattooed rune on Silas's left pectoral muscle shone red. I felt a sudden vibration in the air, pulling my skin tight. He snapped his fingers, and red flames hovered above his palms. He splayed his hands to his side, a cliché gesture for the arrogant magical practitioner. Show-off.

I could show off too.

I was a witch. A Shadow witch with my own bag of tricks.

Adrenaline surged, mixed with an intoxicating high of magic.

Silas thrust his hands forward. Two shoots of angry red fire came at me like dual flamethrowers.

Bastard. Not sure that was legal. The witch wanted to roast me.

I didn't move. When his fire was about five inches from my face, I pulled on a ley line, jumped in, and my body was yanked away in a blink of an eye.

I heard Silas's intake of frustrated breath and tried hard not to laugh. No, I laughed. I laughed hard.

I didn't go too far, just twisted and boomeranged the ley line back to bring me right behind the tattooed witch.

He straightened, his head moving from side to side, looking for me.

And then, for shits and giggles, I kicked him in the ass.

Silas pitched forward onto the ground, his arms and legs flailing like he was performing a nosedive. He didn't stay down long. I blinked, and he was up on his feet with murder in his eyes. All the tats on his body glowed red.

"You look like a Christmas ornament," I told him.

He flung his hands at me again.

But I was ready for him.

"Inflitus!" I thundered, unleashing my will and

all those repressed emotions from having my magic stripped from me as I thrust my hands at the witch.

A kinetic force hit him, throwing him end over end thirty feet back.

I ran over, my magic still coursing through me, to make sure he stayed down. But then, with a grunt, the bastard pushed himself up, bending from the waist, clearly in pain.

"Bitch," he seethed. "You're dead."

"That's enough, Silas," came Greta's commanding voice.

I looked at the male witch and flashed him a smile. "Be a good dog and listen to your master."

Silas's eyes glimmered with hate. "You're nothing. I'm going to rip you apart."

"I doubt it. Your power's no match for mine. You're a small-timer. You've got too much dick in your personality and not enough in your pants."

Silas's snarl was vicious, like a wild coyote about to go for my jugular. "You fucking whore."

The air sizzled with energy. My heart sped up, sensing the magic he was going to pull on me. I'd humiliated him. I got that. But he had tried to roast me like a Thanksgiving turkey.

"Enough," ordered Greta. It was just one word, but it worked.

The tats on Silas's body all faded to black. Without even another word or glance, he walked away. I watched him go until he walked past the house and disappeared somewhere down the street.

"Tessa Davenport," called Greta, and I found myself walking back to the patio. "I've seen all I need to see," continued the old witch, who was standing now. "It's obvious. You have reacquired your magic. I'm curious as to how that is even possible. In all my years, I've never heard of a witch regaining her magic once lost. Care to explain?"

Oh crap.

My aunts all stiffened. Ruth looked like she was about to puke.

I swallowed hard. "Let's just say the incubus who took it died, and then my magic was returned." It was sort of true. "Good enough?"

The old witch watched me, and I could tell she didn't believe me. Then she turned and stared at Lilith, who was bouncing a leg on her knee, looking bored.

I felt like someone had thrown a bucket of ice water down my back. If she found out about Lilith...

"Congratulations, Tessa," said Greta, turning her focus back to me. "Your Merlin license will be reinstated. I'll have the necessary paperwork to sign sent to you." Her eyes sparkled with something I couldn't see, but I did see the tiny smile on her face. The old woman didn't smile often. I could count the times she'd smiled at me. Two—counting this one.

With a final glance at each of my aunts, the old witch stepped off the patio.

"I'll walk with you," said Dolores as she joined the older witch, and the two began a conversation.

"You did great," said Marcus as he appeared next to me, a hand pressed on my lower back as he pulled me to him. He crushed his lips on mine. Yum. I kissed him back. It was quick, but it filled my senses and had my hormones raging. It also brought back the thought of the ring. I used the moment to run my hands over his thighs and did a quick frontal swipe that ended with an ass rub. Nothing was there. He didn't bring the ring with him.

Marcus let out a tiny growl, mistaking my body search for a hint that I needed some sex.

I pulled back and smiled at his handsome face, seeing the desire in his gray eyes. "Thanks. I thought it might have been a bit overkill with the kick."

"Kicking him in the ass was the best part," said Ronin as he and Iris joined us. "You couldn't see his face, but we could. It went all kinds of red. I thought he was gonna cry like a baby."

"I'm glad you did it." Iris gave me a tight-lipped smile. "He totally deserved it. And worse. He's a nasty piece of work."

I opened my mouth to answer just as Lilith joined our group.

"Are the games finished?" she asked, and at my nod, she added, "How disappointing. I thought I was going to witness a witch duel. A real witch duel with curses and blood and death. But you just... kicked him in the ass," she sneered, looking all godly and beautiful.

I laughed. "I did. I really did." I frowned as the goddess decided to run a hand over Marcus's left bicep. I cleared my throat. "Lilith, since you're here, I have a question to ask," I told her. I couldn't put these questions out of my mind until I got a real answer.

"Make it quick," said the goddess, still rubbing her hand over Marcus's arm. "I have a sex date with my husband."

My lips parted. "So... you guys are, like, back together? You're a thing now? All is forgiven?"

Lilith shrugged. "Married couples fight. It's not unusual. But the sex... the sex is incredible."

"But he locked you in a cage? For a *very* long time. Did you forget about that?"

Irritation flashed on the goddess's face. "Careful now, my little demon witch. We might be friends, but there is a limit."

Yeah, pissing off a goddess wasn't smart, but at least she stopped touching my man. "Fine. Do you know why your husband wanted me to take you away from Davenport House? He asked that I bring you specifically to the corner of Spirit Lane and Crystal Row. Why?"

Lilith shrugged a shoulder. "Because I poured some of my magic into rebuilding your house, I'd given myself protection. The house's magic and the earth's magic around it would have acted as a safeguard against Lucifer's magic."

Interesting. "Does that have anything to do with how I got my powers back when he tried to kill me—you—with his magic?"

"Yes. But it wasn't a killing spell," explained the goddess. "It was a *possession* spell. Lucifer tried to ensnare me with the spell. But when he used it, well, it had the opposite effect. Because of my magic already infused in this place, his spell acted as a release instead of a possession spell. So when you were hit, your powers were transferred back. End of story."

I grinned. "Interesting. But my story is just beginning." Because my man had a box with a ring, and now he didn't. What the hell did that mean?

That's when things got weird. Weirder than normal, that is.

The ground shook, and a noise crashed down, making me recoil, like the sound of grinding rocks. The impact reverberated below my legs as though the earth itself was about to split open.

"Uh... what's happening?" I whipped my head

around, looking for the source of the noise, and met Marcus's wide eyes. He grabbed my waist and pulled me close.

We felt another impact, and the ground trembled closer now. It was coming from about a hundred feet from us. A thunderous rumble echoed up through our feet.

"Earthquake!" shouted Ruth and pressed her hands over her head like that was supposed to protect her.

I didn't think it was an earthquake.

I glanced at Lilith. "Is this you? Are you doing something?"

Lilith looked slightly annoyed at my questions. "No. I'm not doing anything right now, apart from staring at you."

"Then?" I left my question hanging in the air.

Energy hummed around us, and then, a large crack split the ground like the earth herself had opened her mouth. And from the hole in the earth rose a shape, a big, white shape. We saw a sudden blast of light, and when the light diminished, I blinked. And my jaw dropped.

A tiny cottage, no, a farmhouse with a black metal roof, white wood siding, and a glorious wraparound porch supported by thick, round columns stood at the spot where the ground had torn apart a moment ago but was now even.

It was... it was a replica of Davenport House. The exact same, only much smaller.

"Holy shit," I breathed. "House just had a baby."

It sounded ridiculous, but I was staring at it.

"Babies? I love babies," said a happy Ruth, her eyes wide with awe as a smile blossomed over her face.

Beverly was standing with her mouth open, staring at the new tiny house like she couldn't believe what she was seeing. "I had no idea House had that level of magic."

"Me neither," I told her.

"But why? Why would Davenport House do this?" Dolores came rushing toward us. "Why would it create a smaller version of itself right in the middle of the backyard?"

Ruth giggled. "I think it's cute. Maybe House was lonely and needed a friend."

"Houses don't get lonely," snapped Dolores. "They get renovated. Spruced up. Painted. They don't birth out tiny house babies."

"This one did." And I knew why. I knew it in my gut.

I untangled myself from Marcus and stepped forward, feeling like I was in a dream. My eyes rolled over the beautiful tiny farmhouse with a row of Anabelle hydrangeas snuggled around the front porch. *My* farmhouse.

"It's for me. For Marcus and me," I said, knowing it to be true. Because House had heard me in my master closet, he did this for me.

Emotions welled, and I blinked away the tears. It was perfect. I'd be living in Davenport House without actually *living* in Davenport House. I'd finally have my privacy with my man.

I turned to the wereape and said, "Welcome home."

Don't miss the next book in The Witches of Hollow Cove series!

BOOKS BY KIM RICHARDSON

THE WITCHES OF HOLLOW COVE
Shadow Witch

Midnight Spells

Charmed Nights

Magical Mojo

Practical Hexes

Wicked Ways

Witching Whispers

Mystic Madness

Rebel Magic

Cosmic Jinx

Brewing Crazy

WITCHES OF NEW YORK
The Starlight Witch

Game of Witches

Tales of a Witch

THE DARK FILES
Spells & Ashes

ABOUT THE AUTHOR

Kim Richardson is a *USA Today* bestselling and award-winning author of urban fantasy, fantasy, and young adult books. She lives in the eastern part of Canada with her husband, two dogs, and a very old cat. Kim's books are available in print editions, and translations are available in over seven languages.

To learn more about the author, please visit:
www.kimrichardsonbookstore.com

Made in the USA
Monee, IL
02 November 2024

69171469R00196